F
HAR

Hardwick
The Shakespeare girl

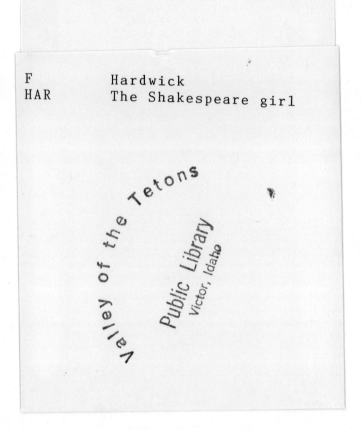

The Shakespeare Girl

THE
SHAKESPEARE
GIRL

A novel by
MOLLIE HARDWICK

St. Martin's Press
New York

Library of Congress Cataloging in Publication Data

Hardwick, Mollie.
   The Shakespeare girl.

   I. Title.
PR6058.A6732S5   1983   823'.914   83-9744
ISBN 0-312-71425-4

First published in Great Britain in 1983 by Methuen London
Ltd.

First U.S. Edition

10 9 8 7 6 5 4 3 2 1

CONTENTS

The Shakespeare Girl

CHAPTER ONE
O brave new world!

Miranda and Editha sauntered down the drive towards the gates of Fairlawn School. They were not in any particular hurry, and in any case it would not have done to be seen running on school premises, even though the summer holiday had officially begun.

'Well, that's that,' said Miranda, sighing. 'How I hate Speech Day. All the same thing, whoever they get to give the prizes – cultivate your finer natures, girls, prepare to be the noble women of the future, our Empire's pride and joy. And the same people going up on the platform, every year. Never you, never me.'

'True,' replied Editha. 'Me too stupid and you too clever.'

'I'm not!'

'You are. You're positively brilliant at history when it's the bits you like.'

'I know. I could recite all Charles the Second's mistresses in my sleep,' said Miranda proudly. 'If only there weren't so many rotten wars and treaties and things. I mean, who cares, really cares, about the War of the Austrian Succession?'

'Or the Hundred Years War?'

'Or the War of Jenkins' Ear?' They giggled. There had been a notable examination paper in which Miranda had felt herself to have done really well, until it was pointed out to her in front of the whole class that she had inextricably mixed up the American Civil War and the War of Independence. It was the same with English: Miranda could stand up and recite whole chunks of *The Eve of St Agnes* (thrilling) while remaining incapable of remembering two consecutive lines of *The Excursion* (boring). Undisciplined, said her form-mistress in end-of-term reports, flippant and given over to idle daydreaming. As this was also the opinion of Miranda's grandmother there seemed to be little doubt about the truth of it. Miranda regretfully concluded that they were right.

The two girls reached the gates and, as they always did, turned to look at the red-brick mass of Fairlawn, ornamented with every caprice of its Victorian architect's fancy – turrets, arabesques, trefoils and garlands, pinnacles like rabbits' ears and gargoyles in the shape of little devils. Once it had been the home of a wealthy Birmingham manufacturer, now removed with his family to some less built-up area. As a house Fairlawn was no longer fashionable. The end of the first decade of the twentieth century was in sight. Builders of houses were turning to the simpler dwellings advocated by such leaders of thought as H. G. Wells and George Bernard Shaw: fewer stairs, less toil for the servants, more bathrooms. And so Fairlawn, with its endless stairs, lofty moulded ceilings, miles of corridor and cavernous fireplaces, had become a school for young ladies.

Miranda gazed at it with affection and regret. It was the place where she was happy. The mistresses were on the whole a decent lot, ranging from comical old spinsters of forty or so like their form-mistress Miss Duke, whose shaggy hair and lowering way of looking at you with her head down had prompted Editha to label her The Mammoth, to youngish teachers not long down from university, the objects of juvenile passion, recipients of flowery sonnets smuggled on to their desks, fought-over partners at the yearly dance. Miranda herself was just getting over a romantic obsession with Miss Cora Marshal, a young classics mistress with ivory skin, dark eyes, and a crystal pendant on a chain always worn round her neck. Others had teased Miranda that it was a lover's gift, worn instead of a ring, thereby causing her torments of jealousy. Even more painful had been Miranda's devotion to Sibyl, Captain of Games, tall, wand-like and ashen-fair, who had captured her impressionable heart with a dashing performance of Ivan Petruski Skivar, the Muscovite hero of one of the Sixth Form's entertainments, in knee-high boots, breeches and a scarlet cavalry cloak.

Editha had shared some of Miranda's crazes, had laughed at others, was always there to share things with, whether jokes, adorations or secrets. She giggled a good deal, and had recently been sent out of the room for snorting over *Three Men in a*

8

Boat, which she was surreptitiously reading inside her Latin textbook. They were such good friends, yet so contrasted, Editha a small round comfortable person still layered deep in puppy-fat, pink-cheeked, with very white prominent teeth which gave her the look of a juvenile Marie Lloyd, Miranda taller, slender almost to thinness, a maid-in-waiting for something unknown. She was not yet pretty, at sixteen, but she would be, when the pointed face filled out a little; now her soft vulnerable mouth seemed large in proportion, and her wistful round eyes of dark hazel larger still, under cloudy brown hair she was allowed to wear in a fringe, not scraped back as everyone else's was that year, to disguise her high forehead.

She hated her school clothes, even today, when the long fitted navy-blue jacket covered the white dress which was statutory wear for Speech Day, instead of the usual blouse and skirt. She detested the way the dress finished at knee-length, instead of sweeping gracefully to the floor like a lady's. When one's legs were too thin, and looking even thinner in black wool stockings, it was humiliating to have to put them on show. She longed, as did Editha and every other girl of their age, to be eighteen with hair up and skirts down. She thought the entire population of Birmingham must be talking about the awful spots which disfigured her skin, despite nightly scrubbings with rainwater collected in a tub, and frequent applications of borax and oatmeal bags. She was quite sure she was hideous.

'Poor old school,' she said. 'Do you think it will miss us?'
'Shouldn't think so. Probably be glad to see the back of us. I known *I* shan't miss *it*.' Editha would be away for almost all the six weeks of holiday, first at an hotel in Bournemouth with her family, then on a Devon farm where there were ponies to ride and cousins who had their own camp-site in the grounds.

And Miranda would be going nowhere. Her grandparents were not in the habit of taking holidays. Grandmother might preside over a stall at her chapel's summer sale, or attend a series of afternoon lectures by some visiting lay preacher or missionary, while Grandfather shut himself up in the spare bedroom with his stamp collection. He worked in an insurance office, which, he said, provided him with quite enough travel in the course of investigating claims. At least, that is what he had said when Miranda had once asked him why they never went for holidays like other people. He spoke less than anyone Miranda knew, so little that he might as well have been dumb, conveying his wishes in monosyllabic grunts; she wondered how he managed to ask enough questions when he went to investigate scenes of burglary, fire or storm damage.

Grandmother talked a good deal. She had many complaints of the imperfection of things and people; Miranda often heard her in the kitchen, muttering to pots and pans and foodstuffs. There was a permanent frown-line between her grey brows, and the corners of her mouth were drawn down with discontent. It was impossible to feel very cheerful in her company, which was why Miranda almost ran to school in the mornings from the suburban house a mile or so away from Fairlawn.

She was lucky to be there, at the best high school for girls in the district, with every opportunity to learn not only lessons but all the social skills a lady might need. It was the often-expressed belief of the Headmistress that 'an accomplished lady is not only an ornament in society, but she serves to contribute in a large measure to the happiness of her own home'. And, of course, there were such nice friends to be made. Miranda had made several; but they had dropped off, one by one, as their invitations to her were not returned. Mothers who gave expensive parties were displeased when their daughters were not asked back to the guests' homes. Grandmother would not have Miranda's friends in the house. Strangers, she said, worried her. Editha had gone there once, after school, without invitation, and had been almost frozen out of the kitchen by the icy blast of Grandmother's disapproval.

The thing she disapproved of most, more than guests, was any form of dramatic entertainment. Not only the biograph and the theatre proper (and Miranda had never been inside either) but even the school plays to which parents were invited. Miranda, who loved dressing-up and saying lines, cried very much the first time she was absolutely forbidden to take part in one.

'But why, Grandmother, why?'

'Because I say so.'

'But *why*?'

'You don't know where it may lead,' had been the grim answer. Miranda and Editha discussed deeply just where it might lead, coming up with the conclusion that the answer must be to Worse than Death, a fate of which they had only the sketchiest notion. Editha said that was rubbish, and pressed her friend to try again. The result was a note from Grandmother to her form-mistress, requesting that on no account should her granddaughter be permitted to take part in stage performances, to which she herself had religious objections.

But she had given the note to Miranda to deliver by hand, and Miranda, backed up by Editha, had not delivered it. The school dramatic society that term had as its star a long-legged handsome creature in the Sixth, who always played the heroes; the temptation to appear on the same stage with her was too strong to resist. So began Miranda's web of lies and evasions, difficult to keep up but well worth it. The idol might change, but was always replaced by another in Miranda's romantic heart. There were no men in her life, other than Grandfather and the old porter who carried coals to the classrooms. She had never even seen a photograph of her father. If she thought about men at all, it was as beings far inferior to these fair-faced delicate-limbed darlings, the Sybils and Peggys and Millicents who were all gallantry and poetry and virtue, with no taint of fleshly coarseness.

When Miranda herself entered the Sixth she would attend the three statutory lectures on Life given by the school doctor, a craggy-faced Scotswoman whose powerful Aberdeen accent, together with the euphemisms she employed, effectively prevented the girls from learning anything that would be remotely useful to them in their dealings with the opposite sex. But the school had done its duty; its pupils' eyes were opened, as far as was decent.

At the end of the road the two girls parted.

'See you next term,' said Editha. 'Enjoy the hols.'

'You too.' They did not kiss, for kissing was soppy. Slowly, not really wishing to get there, Miranda walked home.

Grandmother was in the kitchen, preparing tea. She never came to Speech Day or any other school event. Her small upright figure moved to and fro between the table and the

11

fireplace. A coal fire boiled the kettle, a built-in oven at the side roasted meat and baked bread. Grandmother would not hear of gas cooking-stoves, though they had been in use for fifty years. She was clad, as usual, in a slate-grey dress with a darker stripe in the material, which smelt strongly of petrol for days after it had been cleaned. The high-boned neckband pushed the wrinkles of her lower chin upwards, her gold-rimmed spectacles were lodged half-way down her nose, secured from falling off by hooks behind her exposed ears. Her grey hair was parted in the middle and scraped back into a bun secured by metal hair-pins.

'Go and take that frock off,' she said, without turning to look at Miranda, 'change your shoes and put your pinafore on.' Miranda would like to have protested; the hated, all-enveloping pinafore was the badge of small childhood, something for which she was far too old, but protesting would do no good. 'Here's my report,' she said, laying the envelope on the table. When she came downstairs it had been read.

'You've not improved much, have you.'

'Haven't I?'

'Not according to this. Dreamy, slipshod, could do better work if you concentrated. Too little attention paid to accuracy. I don't think this is what we pay all that money for. I don't think it's good enough.'

Miranda flushed painfully. 'I do my best, Grandmother. I got quite decent marks in English and History.'

'Twenty guineas a year. That's what we pay. Twenty guineas. For you to idle about. I suppose you think you're staying at that school for ever.'

'No, I . . .'

'I've a good mind to take you away before next term. I said so to your grandfather only last night. Wasting good money.'

'Oh, no, Grandmother! Please, please don't. I'll try to work harder, really. Miss Dukes is quite pleased with me, only she likes to keep one up to standard. Don't take me away, I do beg you!'

Something distantly related to a smile touched Mrs Heriot's lips. There were not many pleasures in life beyond jam and hot drinking-chocolate, but causing anxiety and distress to her resented, disliked granddaughter was one of them.

'Well, it would save a lot,' she said. 'You could do all the errands for me, and a lot of the work. Feckless you may be, but those who have to learn will learn.'

Miranda stared, shocked. To spend the rest of her life sweeping carpets, emptying slops, watching her hands turn red and wrinkled on washing-days, black-leading the grates, clearing out the ashes and carrying them to the dustbin, grit blowing in her eyes and filling her hair: she did all these things in the holidays, though not in term-time, because her grandmother had some kind of compunction about letting housework-roughened hands be seen at school. The Heriots' house was the only one in Chamberlain Road to employ no servant, Mrs Heriot having no tolerance for strangers under feet, chattering nonsense and drinking tea. A gloomy silent woman called Alice came in once a week to do the scrubbing, but otherwise the lady of the house did the work, with all the satisfaction that can be gained from punishing inanimate objects. Miranda herself was treated as a servant would have been, receiving shelter and food – no money, of course – without affection, kindness or understanding. There had never been any love, any petting; she could not remember either of her grandparents kissing her, or a touch from her grandmother that was not harsh and impatient. When she had been little her clothes had been dragged over her head as though she had had no more feeling than a post, the bristles of hairbrushes forced through her hair, her face washed with careless roughness so that soap got in her eyes. Now perhaps Alice would be dispensed with.

'Not much use educating me, if that's what I'm going to do for ever,' Miranda said, choking on the beginnings of tears.

'It's what people do with education that matters, and it seems to me yours is being wasted. Yes, I think you'd better leave, and your grandfather thinks so too.'

Then Miranda burst out crying and was ordered up to bed with no tea.

But the threat had only been a threat; it would not have done for the neighbours to have seen a young lady permanently employed as a skivvy. And so the blessing of another school-year was won, the dreary holidays lived out, golden September bringing reunions and the old, happy routines of classes and breaks, the joyful start of rehearsals, the secret enjoyment of them under pretence of extra coaching.

And yet, now that she had moved into her seventeenth year under the sign of Libra, Miranda was changing. There seemed nobody left to adore now that she was herself a Sixth-former. Younger girls, mooning over their divinities, appeared just a little silly. For the first time she noticed how much Editha giggled, and what a prosaic mind she had. Somewhere, outside school, outside Chamberlain Road, she knew there was something mysterious and marvellous waiting; something which had as yet neither face nor name, yet cast before it not a shadow, but a luminescence, as an angel might.

Her body was changing, too. She had grown a little, and filled out into rounded slenderness. Her flat little bust had quite suddenly become a charming twin-pointed bosom, which decorum insisted should be quickly suppressed by her first corset, a strangely-shaped contraption of cotton and whalebone, curving outwards at the front to give the impression that the wearer's breasts were somewhere just above her waist, and presenting the general outline of a pouter pigeon. Miranda felt that there was something not quite pretty about the look, but it was the fashionable one, and must be worn.

The hated spots had faded and vanished, one by one. At last she could see herself in the mirror without wincing. Suddenly she was not satisfied with the life of school, and even less so with existence at home. Fires banked up inside her must one day break into flame.

The day came in late spring, the time of blossom and birdsong, when even industrial Birmingham wore a cheerful air, and the suburban streets were almost beautiful. Miranda's form-mistress was new, a bright no-nonsense Girton graduate who thought her young pupils should not be restricted by sticking to book-learning. At the beginning of an English lesson she clapped her hands for silence – once only – her sharp eyes raked the classroom and a reverent hust fell.

'Girls, this morning we begin reading *Twelfth Night*. By examination-time I expect we shall all have had enough of it – I know *I* shall. Now what do you say to our going to see the play, and having it fresh in our minds, so that we know just what it's all about? There's a local gentleman, Mr Barry Jackson, who's founded a company called the Pilgrim Players. They used to perform at his father's home, and now he's taken St Chad's Hall for public performances. There isn't a lot of seating space, but I could manage as many of you as would like to come from the Sixth, and anybody from the Upper Fifth who'd like to join us. Only two shillings each – and a matinee, so nobody would have to go home after dark.

'I'll begin taking names tomorrow, so you'll be able to ask your parents' permission tonight. Now then: books open. You know what parts you're to read, from the blackboard. Gladys, the Duke's opening speech, please.'

Gladys rose at her desk.

'If music be the food of love, play on,
Give me excess of it . . .'

'I shall do it!' Miranda said to Editha. 'This time I shall ask her, and I'll *make* her let me go. I'm not half as frightened of her as I used to be, you know, and she must see it's time I got out and saw Life.'

Editha raised sandy eyebrows. Her opinion of her friend's grandmother was a low one. Used to being taken to panto-mimes and plays since she was old enough to enjoy them, she felt that the old lady must be not only mad but some kind of ogress.

Miranda screwed up her courage to ask her grandmother immediately after tea. The reply was made with a cold stare.

'I wonder you bother to ask. You know my views, and your grandfather's.'

'But it isn't a proper *theatre*, with real actors. Miss Teasdale says they're all amateurs, very respectable ladies and gentle-men. Mr John Drinkwater, the author, is one of them. There's nothing you could object to.'

'How do you know what I object to?'

'I don't, I don't. It all seems so silly. Miss Teasdale will be with us – what can possibly happen to me? Is it the play you don't like? because we're doing it in school now, so I shall know all about it – I do know, anyway, and the plot's quite . . . quite . . .' Miranda struggled for a word, her eyes pleading with the old woman who would not look at her, only down at her knitting.

'It's educational, don't you see? It will give me a better chance of passing my exams. You want me to pass, don't you? And everybody's going, nearly the whole form. Grandmother, I'm seventeen, nearly old enough to put my hair up. You can't pretend I'm a child for ever.'

'You are a child, a stupid child, and my responsibility. I never asked for it, oh no. It was not my wish or my doing, to have a thankless child like you on my hands, a devil's child with no health in her. But I've borne it for years, and please God I shall bear it to the end without complaining. As to this wicked playhouse, I've said my say, and there's an end of it.' The length of grey wool lay over Mrs Heriot's sharp knees, drab and dull and never-ending; like the warp and woof of Miranda's life. Suddenly she rose and ran upstairs. The spare room was quiet, but she knew that her grandfather was inside. She knocked once and went in without waiting for an answer. He turned from the table where his stamps were spread out, little patches of colour, dead things of paper waiting to be buried in the album with the brown embossed covers, Whitfield King's catalogue and *The Stamp Collectors' Fortnightly* on a smaller table. Albert Heriot's skin was pale, papery and dry, as though so much contact with stamps had contaminated him. His scanty hair was white, though he was younger than his wife. Miranda could hardly remember having seen him smile, and he did not do so now as she invaded his privacy.

'Grandfather, please help me! I don't often ask for things.' She poured out the story, incoherent by now, knowing that the more impassioned she was the less he would like her for it. At last he said, 'It has nothing to do with me, Miranda.'

'But it has! Grandmother says you both feel the same way about – about the theatre and things. Can't you even tell me why?'

But he turned his back on her, saying over his shoulder, 'You'd better ask your grandmother. I'm very busy just now.'

Editha said next day, 'I think it's a rotten shame. If I were you I'd go, anyway, even if you tell them you've been somewhere else, like you do with the school plays.'

'Oh, it's all very well for you. Nothing would happen to you at home if you – oh, I don't know – if you went to London and shouted rude things outside Buckingham Palace.'

'And what do you think's going to happen to you?'

'Grandmother might beat me – she used to, often enough. Except that I'm bigger than she is now, and a lot stronger, so I suppose she might lose if it came to a struggle. I can see the headlines, can't you – "Schoolgirl murders aged grandmother on kitchen hearthrug". No, it's no good, Edie, I'll have to let it go, this time anyway.'

Editha looked mutinous. 'It's not at all fair – in fact it's downright fiendishly unjust. Here you are, old enough to be married, and you can't go to an educational performance in a church hall. You don't think your grandmother's dotty, do you?'

'I hope not – if she is, then I've a good chance of turning out the same. Oh, let's forget it.'

But Editha, loyal and a fighter, did not forget it. The visit to *Twelfth Night* passed, July came, and examinations with it; and Miranda, from a self-punishing stubbornness, did badly in her English paper. She had not seen the play as the others had, and therefore couldn't be expected to know anything about it. Her end-of-term report was reproachful. 'Miranda does not show the keenness I have come to expect of her. Perhaps a quiet talk at home would help.'

The quiet talk was not on the lines Miss Teasdale had envisaged, but Miranda listened impassively, hugging to herself a secret she was not going to let out.

It was Editha who thought of it. She said, alight with mischief, 'We aren't going away for another week yet.'

'How sad,' replied Miranda with sarcasm. 'Some people aren't lucky enough to be going away at all.'

'That's just it, if you'd only listen. Mummy says I can go to Stratford for a matinée performance. Why don't you come, too?'

'Stratford! But –'

'But what?'

'I've never been there. Grandmother wouldn't let me go – I know, without even asking her.'

'Then don't tell her, idiot. Say we've been asked to a tennis party – she lets you go to those. If you don't take a chance

17

you'll never be able to stand up for yourself at all. Come on, be a sport. I give you five minutes to think about it.'

Miranda thought, as they walked down the long dull road. At the corner where their ways parted she stopped and faced Editha resolutely.

'All right. I'll come. Only if it's a wet day the whole thing will have to be off, of course.'

'It won't be. They admire courage up there.' Editha gestured towards the cloudless blue sky. 'It'll be a perfectly splendid day and we'll have a perfectly splendid time, just you wait and see.'

The day *was* splendid. Miranda left home in her cream tennis-frock and striped blazer, white plimsolls and sailor-hat, carrying her racquet in its case. It was a most unsuitable costume for a train journey, but she cared nothing for that, on such a summer day, and with such a prospect before her. Editha was waiting outside the station.

'There you are. Well done! Let's put that racquet in the left-luggage – we've got oceans of time. I say, aren't you thrilled? Didn't I say it wouldn't rain? I've found out which platform the train goes from. We've got time for sandwiches and lemonade. Isn't it a ripping day? I said it would be.'

Somehow they were on the train, rattling through dingy south-eastern suburbs, Miranda conscious of having embarked on a most dangerous adventure, and rather wishing herself somewhere else. The small ugly houses with their back yards began to fall behind; then came fields and trees, villages, little churches, farmhouses of deep pink brick, cows and shorn sheep resting in warm sunshine in the gentle landscapes of Warwickshire.

The journey was short. The train was sliding round a bend, bringing into sight a sign-board declaring that this was STRATFORD-UPON-AVON. Editha flourished their tickets. Then they were outside the station, breathing air which was not that of Birmingham, nor like any other air Miranda had ever breathed.

They walked up the long station approach, past the open cattle-market, into a street of ordinary houses and shops, neither new nor old, that were not at all what Miranda expected. Yet very soon the old began to appear, small, crooked, half-timbered. Miranda wanted to stop and look

18

at them, but Editha rushed her along. 'We'll be late – do come on.'

'It's all right for you, you've been here before,' Miranda protested, as she was hurried down Bridge Street to where the waters of the Avon reflected blue sky and white clouds, round a corner – and there was the theatre.

Miranda had never seen a theatre. She hardly knew what she had expected; possibly something of a wickedly Babylonian aspect, decorated with carvings of naked satyrs, such was the impression of wickedness she had received from her grandmother. What she saw was a bright red-brick building, its main part circular, as though the architect had faithfully striven to rebuild Shakespeare's own Globe, topped with a pointed blue hat studded with gabled windows. Adjoining it was a square tower, which would have reminded a Londoner strongly of the Byzantine campanile of the new Westminster Cathedral, but for the little blue Gothic turrets surmounting it, apparently borrowed from some minor Rhine castle. It was undoubtedly quaint, and even more undoubtedly respectable.

Editha pointed to a moving snake of people. 'Look, they're going in. Come on!' Miranda panted after her, like Alice after the White Rabbit, seeing out of the corner of her eye the cottages of Waterside, boats and swans on the river, great willow-trees. Then they were inside the Theatre, rushing up the stairs, then inside, being shown to their seats by a severe-faced lady in black, and all Miranda's dim notions of vice and squalor were melting like shadows before the light of dawn.

The orchestra, far below them, broke into the National Anthem, and everybody stood up. Then the brass section blew a martial flourish, and the great tasselled curtain, glowing at its foot with mysterious light, went up.

Of all that eager reverent audience, one person was transported in that moment out of her past, out of the dull dream that had been her life, into a world of magic, poetry, beauty and romance; as though an angel had smilingly shown her into Heaven without giving her the trouble of dying first.

CHAPTER TWO
Look here upon this picture . . .

Of the moment when she awoke and came into her inheritance Miranda would always remember every detail. *King Henry the Fourth, Part One, Act One, Scene One: A Room in the Palace.* In a noble chamber of immense height, heavily beamed, hung with rich tapestries, there sat beneath a regal canopy, the crowned leopards of England behind him, the dejected figure of an ailing king, purple-robed, majestically slow of voice.

So shaken as we are, so wan with care,
Find we a time for frighted peace to pant,
And breathe short-winded accents of new broils
To be commenc'd in strands afar remote.

A gloomy nobleman with the name of a county broke the news of victories which caused the king to appear even more cast down. King and court departed, the throne was borne away by silent attendants; enter two men, a young one and an old, the young man in doublet and hose with a gold chain round his neck, bright blond hair and a merry eye, the old man vast, a mountain of padding in shabby brown garments, his head bald but for a few tufts of grey, his pointed beard bristling. Wheezily he asked his companion the time of day, to be answered roundly. At which the old fat man nodded, an arm round the other's shoulders.

Indeed, you come near me now, Hal; for we that take purses
go by the moon and the seven stars, and not by Phoebus – he,
"that wandering knight so fair."

Some dialogue between the old Falstaff and the young Prince Hal, in whose jesting there seemed a sour note; then entered a slender youth, clad all in mulberry, who perched himself on a table and swung his long legs. Wide jagged sleeves

20

like wings set off his slimness, dark hair fringed on the brow fell to his shoulders, as he chatted lightly with the two of them about a highway robbery the next night in which they all three should take part, though it seemed from his later talk with Hal that the jest would be turned against the fat man. Miranda gazed and gazed at him and the boy-aping girls she had once adored melted into unreality and vanished for ever.

Left alone, Prince Hal (who was handsome enough in his way) stepped forward and took the hearers into his confidence, telling them that like the sun, he allowed his brightness to be hidden so that when he pleased to be himself, being wanted he might more be wondered at. Then came the king again, a tall gaunt man with a noble face and a visionary's eyes, whose speech was a sonorous drawl, strange, yet compelling to the ear. Miranda peered at her programme: *King Henry IV, F. R. Benson*. She forgot him when the youngest of the lords stepped forward impetuously and began to harangue him in a rough northern accent, for this was Harry, the Hotspur of the North, bold of eye and broad of shoulder, with the lion statant of the Percies on the breast of his leather doublet. She would never forget, all her life, his looks and his words as he jestingly cast off his wife who clung to him as he called for his horse to bear him to the magician Glendower. She would remember the Welsh song Lady Mortimer sang, while Hotspur lay and mocked, his head in Lady Percy's lap, though she had never heard it before and understood no word of the language. She came across it, many years later, in an old songbook – it was called *Caradoc*.

Intent on Hotspur, she still paid respectful attention to the king, his reproaches to his son and the prince's remorse, for F. R. Benson, whoever he might be, had a magic as powerful as Glendower's own. As for the fat man who talked and behaved so outrageously, it was impossible not to laugh at him even though Miranda understood his jests no more than she had understood the Welsh. As the heavy curtain swished down, she let out her breath, unaware that she had been all but holding it. Editha looked at her curiously as the lights went up.

'What's the matter? Don't you like it?'

Miranda blinked. 'Yes. Yes, of course.'

'You look funny, sort of pale. Do you want some fresh air?

We could go and have some tea.'

Miranda shook her head. She wanted only the air of the theatre, which held things strange and alluring. To move from her seat would be to risk the play re-starting without her. 'You go, if you like,' she said.

Editha went, a shade disappointed. She had planned the expedition to liberate her friend, introduce her to the world of entertainment, and cheer her up generally. And here was Miranda looking as if she had had a shock, unready to chatter or enthuse. It was almost like being by oneself, not much fun at all, and a very history-lesson sort of play. But there was always tea, and a bun if one was lucky. Edith galloped over the little bridge and down the Moorish staircase, forcing her dumpy presence between more leisured playgoers.

Miranda studied her programme. The names of the cast meant nothing to her. Hotspur's name in real life was Godfrey Arnold, Falstaff was Charles Law, the shrill-tongued Hostess Mrs F. R. Benson. It seemed impossible that these people existed outside the frame of the proscenium, anywhere but among heavy mediaeval furniture and leafy cardboard glades. She closed the programme and gazed round the theatre, small, intimate, curved gently like arms enclosing the stage. It had been here all her life, and she had been kept from it, lied to, cheated. She laid her cheek against the gallery rail, cool and smooth, half-listening to the remarks of the women in the row behind.

'. . . not like the London theatre at all. When they've got a long wait they go out and jump into boats and row on the river. You can see them in their costumes if you nip round to a back window.'

'Go on!'

'That's right. Crowns an' swords an' all.'

There were small figures moving in the orchestra-pit, a few enthusiastic musicians come back early. The audience seats were filling up. Editha arrived, plumping herself down, wiping doughnut-sugar from around her mouth. The orchestra was tuning up, the house-lights dimmed; a spirited march struck up, and the curtain rose on the rebel camp near Shrewsbury, blue tents scattered with silver moons and half-moons, Hotspur in silver armour and a golden surcoat, and Miranda

22

lost herself in a world that now seemed more real than reality. Nobles orated, Falstaff showed himself to be a cowardly braggart (Miranda did not altogether like him), another interval came and went during which Editha chattered and Miranda answered vaguely; the last scene of all was set, a plain near Shrewsbury, men fighting against a stormy sky; Hotspur met with Prince Hal, hero against hero, two stars keeping their motion in one sphere, until Hotspur was slain, crying 'O, Harry, thou has robb'd me of my youth!' and was dragged dead from the field by Falstaff. After that nothing was left to do but end the battle, with the king down centre stage proclaiming benevolently that

Rebellion in this land shall lose his sway,
Meeting the check of such another day,
And since this business so fair is done,
Let us not leave till all our own be won.

The house lights went up and the audience rose smartly to its feet as the National Anthem was played. Miranda followed Editha slowly down the stairs, lingering on the final flight to gaze at the stained glass windows illustrating the Seven Ages of Man, unconscious of the people round her.

Editha was waiting impatiently outside.

'Do come on! There won't be time for tea if you don't hurry.'

The air outside the theatre was warm with summer, rich with the scent of trees and water and new-mown grass. It had not altered since Miranda had last seen it, yet she saw it with different eyes, clothed in the play's magic. When they sat down in the crowded tea-room she realised that she was healthily, wolfishly hungry. As they consumed toast, scones, jam, cream and cakes Editha, her mouth full, asked questions.

'Did you like it? You were so quiet I thought you weren't well.'

'Yes, oh yes. I liked it. It was wonderful.'

'I don't know about wonderful – I thought it was a bit dull, all that talking and fighting. You ought to have seen *Romeo* last year – that was divinely romantic, though F.R. was a bit old.'

'Who?'

'Mr Benson. Everybody calls him F.R.'

'Oh, the king.'

'Well, of course he was the king, he always plays the lead parts. Never mind him, what did you feel, going to the theatre at last? Did you understand why your grandmother wouldn't let you go?'

Miranda selected a cake that was a wedge of iced pastry filled with cream. 'I haven't the slightest, foggiest idea. I thought . . . I don't know what I thought it would be like. People dancing with nothing on, perhaps. She can't have seen a play, ever.'

'What a mystery it all is. I wonder if you'll ever find out.'

Miranda found it very hard to tear herself away from Stratford. First they had to go back to the theatre and look at it again. The playbill outside announced that the evening performance would be *Henry the Fourth Part Two*. She eyed it longingly, to be pulled away by Editha.

'No, you can't stay to see it. We've missed one train, we've simply got to get the next one or even Mummy will be asking questions. Let's go this way, it's quicker.'

But it was not, only even more alluring than the way they had come from the station. The gentle rising curve of Southern Lane, rose-red cottages on one side, the willowed river-bank on the other, led them to where Shakespeare's church stood, gravely beautiful at the end of its avenue of limes, looking towards Old Town, where Editha pointed out the house in which Shakespeare's daughter had lived with her doctor husband, and the home of Miss Marie Corelli, the celebrated authoress. Everywhere the eye rested was a living finger beckoning the visitor to stay. Miranda envied passionately people entering their homes, riding past in traps or chaises, old folk sitting at the doors of the alms-houses. 'I should like to be as old as that,' she said, 'and never have to leave Stratford again.'

Editha said, 'You must be potty.' She gave a shriek as the hour of six chimed out from the square tower of the golden-grey Gild Chapel. 'Oh, mercy heavens! We'll never do it. Come on, run!'

They ran, along High Street and Wood Street, past the White Swan. The station was in sight, there was only the long approach before them. They were half-way down it when a train hooted and began to move away from the station. Editha stopped short.

'That's it,' she said flatly. 'We shan't be back before eight now. You'd better come home with me – it may soften the blow a bit if there's two of us. Mummy won't be as furious with me in front of you.'

Miranda's spirits dropped as the next train made its slow way to Birmingham. The radiance of the day was fading. She had wanted to travel back in peace, living it all over again, summoning up images, gently intoxicated with enchantment, and now it was spoiled. Her white shoes and cream tennis-frock were streaked with railway grime, she was cold; she wished she had not eaten so much tea and then had to run so hard.

At Editha's home the front door was opened by a maid.

'You're to go straight to the drawing-room, Miss Editha, the mistress says. My, she hasn't half got it in for you!'

Mrs Finch, Editha's mother, was a small-boned, handsome woman, elegant in a way her daughter might never achieve. Her face was pink with annoyance at having to be called away from dinner, and with the stress of having had to endure the company of the person who sat upright and unmoving on a straight-backed chair in a corner of her drawing-room. Miranda's heart plummeted as she saw her grandmother, who gave her an expressionless stare.

'I'd like to know what time you call this, Editha, and where you've been,' Mrs Finch said, tapping one satin-shoed foot. It would all have been so much easier if that dreadful old woman had not been glaring there like the legend on the wall at Belshazzar's Feast, one of the very few details she recalled from the Old Testament which had been liberally quoted to her during the last half-hour. To be embarrassed in one's own house was really too bad.

'You know quite well, Mummy,' Editha said calmly, with her usual flair for taking the drama out of a situation. 'You said we could go to Stratford for a matinée.'

'I'd hardly call this matinée-coming-out time.'

'Well, no, it isn't, but there was so much to see, with Miranda never having been before, that we missed the train – two trains. I'm sorry, Mummy.'

25

'I see. But I do think you might have telephoned. Station-masters are quite good about that sort of thing.'

A voice from the corner said, 'I've not had an explanation.'

Your ball, dear, said the mother's eyes to the daughter's.

'What of, Mrs Heriot?' Editha asked innocently.

'You took my grandchild to a playhouse.'

'Yes, I did. I thought it was time she went.'

'Time she was corrupted?'

'Time she started living like an ordinary person,' returned Editha. 'There's nothing wrong about the theatre – certainly not about Shakespeare. I don't think you can ever have been to a Shakespeare play, you know, or you wouldn't feel so strongly about it. It's very educational, all the history and costume and . . . isn't it, Miranda? If you really knew, you wouldn't mind at all, Mrs Heriot. You can see my programme if you like –'

The spare figure rose to its feet and moved to the door, with a backward jerk of the head towards Miranda, who looked helplessly at the others.

'You must go with your grandmother, dear,' said Mrs Finch, and Editha threw her friend a look in which sympathy and apology were equally blended. Without a word, the old woman left the room and the house, Miranda trailing miserably behind. Like that they walked back to the tall terraced house in Chamberlain Road, blind-eyed behind its dusty laurels. Miranda had expected to go into the kitchen as usual, but her grandmother led the way upstairs, to her bedroom, where they stood confronting each other.

'Take your garments off,' Mrs Heriot said.

'What?' Miranda looked down at her crumpled blazer and the soiled frock that had been so immaculate that morning, and began to undo buttons.

'Your nether garments. You know what I mean.'

'My . . . I don't understand, Grandmother.'

'Your drawers. Take them off.' She snapped her fingers impatiently, then picked up something which had been lying on the bed and flourished it. It was a large bone-backed hairbrush with bristles. 'I intend to thrash the wickedness out of you. Take them off and lie face down on that bed.'

Miranda lived a long moment of shock and terror, the terror

26

she had felt in her childhood when Grandmother had got out the brush. Then, to her surprise and joy, it passed, giving way to pure anger at the desecration of her beautiful day, fiery anger that filled her as though she stood in a pillar of flame. It blazed and died, leaving her full of strength. She was looking down at her grandmother, not up, as she had done when a timid child. For the first time she saw the tyrant who had ruled her life as merely a small scraggy woman with a face of sour discontent, now touched with a shadow of doubt.

'Put that down, Grandmother,' Miranda said. 'I'm too old for such things now.'

'We'll see about that!'

'No, we won't.' She snatched the brush and flung it into a corner. 'There! Now sit down and we'll have a talk. Don't you think it's time?'

She saw, with a curious detachment, her grandmother back slowly away and sink into a chair, without looking behind her, and she knew she had won. She perched herself on the bed, keeping her eyes fixed on the cold faded ones in their nets of wrinkles.

'I should like to know why you've stopped me going to the theatre all my life. I know now that it's something good and beautiful, not what you led me to expect. Don't think you'll get anywhere by being angry with me, because you won't. Just tell me.'

'Why should I, you impertinent hussy? I'll call your grandfather and he can deal with you.'

'Do,' said Miranda pleasantly. 'You'll find he's too busy, and in any case he always leaves things to you.' An intoxicating sense of power filled her, as though she wore the armour of the knights at Shrewsbury Field, and had her hand on the hilt of an invisible sword. 'Come on now, you must tell me. Can't you see I'm grown up, and I won't put up with nonsense any longer?'

Doubt and uncertainty hovered on the old woman's face as they stared at each other. She said abruptly, 'The family Bible will be yours one day.'

'Oh, good. But that doesn't tell me anything.'

'Perhaps it would.'

'Well, I don't want to wait for it. Suppose *you* tell me.'

27

Silently her grandmother rose and went out of the room, leaving the door open. Miranda followed. They were at the door of the bedroom her grandparents shared, a gloomy stuffy room whose furnishings had not changed during her lifetime. The bed-head had always frightened her as a child by the impression it gave of being three wooden tombstones in a row, and the huge triple mahogany wardrobe so obviously contained upright skeletons, like the press in the Dickens story, that as a child Miranda had never dared even to approach it. Even now she felt a twinge of the old dread as her grandmother opened one wing of it. Inside there were shelves, the top ones shallow, the lower ones deep. A strong smell of moth-balls floated out from them. From one Mrs Heriot lifted a metal box, black-enamelled, which she placed in the middle of the dressing-table that was uncluttered by any feminine trinkets, scents or cosmetics, not counting the large forbidding comb which belonged to the bone hairbrush. Then from a top drawer she took a key, threaded on a piece of faded pink tape, unlocked the box and threw back the lid.

Papers filled the interior. As they were lifted out and piled up dust rose above them, and the dried corpse of a moth fluttered down. Some of Miranda's new self-confidence threatened to topple as she waited for whatever awful secret lay at the bottom of the box. The knowledge of something she would have to live with for the rest of her years – murder, perhaps? The grim room seemed to speak of death, as though a body had been laid out there and forgotten. At last, still in silence, Mrs Heriot handed something over to Miranda.

A photograph. Old, faded to sepia, with the embossed address of a local photographer on its mount. The head and shoulders of a girl, wearing the high-boned collar of twenty years ago, dark hair piled up above a classically high forehead and a wistfully pretty face. Miranda stared at it.

'My mother?'

'Yes.'

'Why haven't I seen it before?'

Silence.

'Why have you never talked about her? All I know is that she died when I was born – she *is* dead, isn't she?'

'Yes.'

28

'I thought perhaps it was because you were too . . .' she had been going to say 'grief-stricken', but it sounded ridiculous in her mind applied to the stony-faced old woman. 'I thought you preferred not to remind yourself of – of whatever happened. And my father – did he really die at almost the same time?'

'A year later. Somebody sent us a newspaper clipping. I don't know why they bothered.'

'Perhaps they thought you'd be interested.' said Miranda sarcastically. 'And now do you mind telling me what all this mystery is?' She put the photograph on the far side of her, as if to protect it with her body. For answer, Mrs Heriot handed over another photograph. It bore no photographer's name, and was clearly a snapshot, yellowed by time, like the other picture. It showed two young men, the railing of a promenade and a glimpse of sands behind them. Both were in pierrot costume, long white jackets, baggy trousers and sugar-loaf hats, all decorated with black pompoms. The standing figure nearest the camera held a guitar, which he seemed to be strumming; the other, turning away to look at him, an object which might have been a tambourine or cymbal. The face of the guitarist was alight with laughter, a boy's face, the features hard to make out in the bright sunshine of that long-ago day, but the charm unmistakable.

Miranda looked up from it. 'Who are they?'

'She ran away, with *that*. We'd taken her to Llandudno for a holiday, the summer she left school. She was always dragging us to see the pierrots in that booth they had on the sands. We didn't know she went there by herself when she told us she was going for a walk. Just a fortnight it took, from the time she first saw them. The morning we were leaving she wasn't in her bedroom – there was just a letter, a stupid, mad letter. Then we heard from her with a London address where we could reach her, because she was always travelling about with that mountebank. We never wrote, of course.'

'*What*?'

'He came here after she died, to ask us to take the baby. Your grandfather talked to him, I wouldn't see him. The next thing we knew he was dead himself – caught cold on the chest touring about in all weathers with that troupe of actors. Somebody sent us a few things of his and hers – I burned them all, except that.' She jerked her head towards the pierrot's photograph.

Miranda was shivering, from shock and an overwhelming revulsion.

'Why?' she asked. 'Why?'

'Why what?'

'Why did you hate him so much? It was silly of her to run away, of course, but you could have forgiven them – couldn't you?'

'She was tainted. Play-actors are the spawn of the devil. They shall go into the everlasting fire. See this!' She made a dart towards a carved box that stood on a table by itself. It held a book, quarto-size, thick, seeming to be of immense age. Mrs Heriot opened it at the end, where several pages covered with handwriting appeared to have been stuck in. Miranda guessed it to be the family Bible she had heard of that night for the first time. She followed the thin forefinger down the last page that held entries.

Born, October 25, 1893. Miranda, child of Grace Heriot and Frank Forbes. '*As is the mother, so is her daughter.*'

Died, January 30, 1895. Grace Heriot, concubine of Frank Forbes. '*Their worm dieth not, and the fire is not quenched.*'

'You see?' the old woman's voice was triumphant. 'That's what comes of sin and play-going. You take heed, miss, or you'll go the same way – you've proved that this day, to my satisfaction.'

'You're mad,' Miranda said flatly. A hand shot out and hit her across the side of her face, hard enough to have broken the cheekbone.

'Mad, am I? We'll see about that. Go to your room and stay there.'

Miranda went, without the spirit to argue, the fight gone out of her. A sick dislike for her grandmother possessed her. For hours she lay on her bed, still dressed in the crumpled tennis-frock, staring at the uncurtained window holding a square of dark sky. She was full of grief, a grief too heavy to find relief in tears, for the two who had died without knowing her, the result of their love, victims of some savage superstition she failed to understand. Actors, the spawn of the devil? The play she had seen went through her mind, picture after picture, the beautiful Chronicle people, the glitter and colour and music, Mr Benson's noble craggy face and the brave verse. Surely none of it could have come but from God. But perhaps not the God of Grandmother's chapel, a stern tyrant with no taste for enjoying Himself.

At last she lit a candle and looked at the photograph she had picked up and brought with her, the only relic of a home and family long since destroyed. Her father's young face looked out at her, smiling into the sun.

'It's so unfair,' Miranda said to him aloud. 'You weren't even an actor, poor thing. Only a pierrot.' And at that the barriers broke, and she wept, long and bitterly.

When she appeared at breakfast next morning her face was so swollen and disfigured with crying that Mrs Heriot glanced uncertainly at her before slamming down a plate of porridge on the table. Miranda pushed it away.

'What's the matter with the food?'

'I don't want it.'

'You must. You've not eaten for hours.'

Albert Heriot peered over the top of his *Birmingham Post*. He heard a note of impending trouble in the voices of his womenfolk, and of all things Albert disliked trouble, or, indeed, disturbance of any kind to the supremely dull surface of his life. The night before his wife had given him a brief account of Miranda's disgraceful behaviour and her disclosures. He knew from her tone that she was more troubled by it than she would admit, and he hoped worse would not follow. He neither understood nor shared her fierce principles, only accepted them because she laid down the law in the house, as she had done since they were first married. They had met at a chapel social, and something in her had recognised that Albert was as near to being a nonentity as a human being could be: someone to impose her will on, because she had no other outlet for the confused, angry spirit within her. The child Grace had made no difference. Grace's young life had been as sternly ruled as Miranda's, so that all the love pent up in her had rushed out to meet a boy's smile and the sweet, silly, sentimental ballads he sang by the Irish Sea. It was as well Grace had gone when she did, Albert had thought, though putting on a mild show of outrage. She would never have had any sort of life, and there would inevitably have been trouble.

Now there was going to be trouble with Miranda. He prepared to take off his glasses, fold his paper, and slip silently from the room when it broke. But his grand-daughter only said coldly, 'I'll cut myself some bread.'

(And from that time, as long as she lived in the house, she would eat nothing that her grandmother's hands had prepared or even touched.) But to Albert's relief nobody made a scene over breakfast. Towards the end of that cheerless meal his wife said, not looking directly at Miranda, 'You won't be going back to school, you know.'

'No.' It was neither question nor agreement.

'Your grandfather and I have been talking. You'll be going to a secretarial college in a week or two, to learn typewriting and shorthand.'

'Oh?'

'Then your grandfather's going to look round for a job for you. You could earn about a hundred pounds a year as a secretary, you know.' A faint hint of propitiation, a sideways glance to see whether the swollen, bruised face was turned towards her? But it was not. The damage which had been done the night before could not be undone, the unimaginable had happened; she had laid down the law according to her gods, and it had been challenged, the slave had rebelled. But surely, with firmness, it would be possible to slip back the chains. Hard work in a good steady humdrum atmosphere would put the girl in her place and take the rubbish out of her head.

Miranda endured four months' training at an excellent secretarial school, typing in rhythm to a tinny gramophone, learning the complex language of Pitman's shorthand, failing to learn the principles of book-keeping. The certificates she was awarded at the end of the course won her a typist's job in an insurance office, not her grandfather's; an office where she was neither welcomed nor accepted. Her voice was too hoity-toity, with never a trace of Brummagen, her appearance, even with her hair up, too youthful (and too pretty, the older typists thought). From one of her bosses she received her first kiss, a sloppily disgusting affair which sent her rushing for the Jeyes' Soap to wash out her mouth. From another she received so much work that the day's length was not enough, so that it spilled out into the evening, yet no more money was offered for the extra time. The pound a week that was her wages she gave to her grandmother, taking back, by that lady's extraordinary generosity, five shillings to spend on herself. She walked to work, lunched on penny rolls and cheese, gave a halfpenny to the pool money for tea, and saved the rest.

On a spring evening, with an exciting wind blustering along Birmingham streets and a young moon peering through scudding clouds, Miranda ran away.

CHAPTER THREE
These our Actors

Frank and Constance Benson were finishing their breakfast. Which is to say, Constance had enjoyed a hearty meal including four rounds of toast, while her husband still toyed with a limp slice on which the marmalade had coagulated, a book propped up in front of him against the heavy silver coffee-pot. His lips moved, but to Constance's relief he no longer declaimed at the top of his powerful voice when in their room. Here in the Shakespeare Hotel (the Wagstaff, as the company called it), their home when they were in Stratford, he was loved and indulged, but Constance felt compunction about their neighbours in the adjoining rooms of the rambling Tudor house. Nowadays, with the Shakespeare Festival an annual theatrical event lasting from April to August, visitors from London frequently stayed for as much as a week; Stratford's tourist industry had begun. And one never knew – the next room might contain a critic, whose notices would be influenced by being roused from his morning sleep too early. Constance was highly sensitive to the feelings of critics: she had been their target too often to ignore them.

She looked across the table at Frank (whom nobody, not even she, called Frank, only F.R. or F.R.B. or Mr Benson, Sir, or Pa.) Founder of the Festival, dedicated servant of Shakespeare, uneven actor veering between greatness and caricature; he had never been handsome, only magnificent, as he still was, in his early fifties, with the face of a soldier-saint, long and craggy, the Roman nose slightly drooping now, the grey eyes fixed on distance, seeming to pierce through the person he was addressing, to their discomfort. Constance had been his loyal partner for a quarter of a century, his opposite number on the stage as well as in life. She had cured him of some of his unworldly habits, such as having windows open day and night, whatever the weather, with no fires, drinking quart upon quart of cold milk, and never taking wine or tobacco, but consuming cold apple tart, nothing else, for supper every night, after the play. Constance was still smiling over a letter she had just received from an ex-member of the company, remembering how, after a gruelling day of rehearsals for *Macbeth*, without a break or a bite to eat, Frank as the Thane had said the line 'They have tied me to a stake, I cannot fly', and from the starving actor had come a heartfelt cry, 'I wish to God they'd tie me to one!' Constance cherished such stories for her intended book. Frank, when they were read to him, would smile vaguely, as an archangel might at the tale of some mildly amusing human frailty.

Frank raised his head from the book, a small, manageable edition of the *Works* which he kept for meal times.

'Do you think we might just consider *Troilus*?'

Constance threw out the cold remains in his coffee-cup and refilled it. 'You mean, might *you* consider Troilus?'

A shadow crossed his face. He had given up Romeo and Orlando, and Prince Hal, but reluctantly. 'Well, perhaps not. But there are some strong parts – Agamemnon . . .'

She reached across the table, took the book, and read at the point her finger touched.

'*Renew, renew! The fierce Polydamus*
Hath beat down Menon: bastard Margarelon
Hath Doreus prisoner,
And stands colossus-wise, . . .'

'Really, F.R., it's not tremendous. All those awful names!'

F.R. looked ceilingward, as though the reproachful shade of the Bard might be hovering there. 'We could always cut . . .'

'No.'

'Well, Achilles, then – a hero-figure, surely.' He murmured, savouringly:

'*Come, tie his body to my horse's tail,*
Across the field I will the Trojan trail.'

'No. It's Hector they like, not Achilles. Anyway, there's nobody for me but Cassandra, and she's nothing to do but wail and get raped – off stage.'

F.R. threw her a pained look. His Irish Constance had a fiery spirit and a mischievous delight in the kind of realism that shocked clergymen; her bawdy virago of a Doll Tearsheet had caused her to be preached at from the pulpit, and attracted such good business that F.R. had fitted out the production with new costumes on the strength of it. Stirring his coffee round and round mechanically, without the slightest intention of drinking it, he pondered on the possibility of the company eventually performing the whole Shakespeare Cycle. There were problems, of course, mainly of censorship. Miss Beale, headmistress of Cheltenham Ladies' College, had insisted on words like 'God' and 'Hell' being replaced with others less shocking to girlish ears. There had been a school performance of *Dream* in which a headmistress had insisted on Bottom being replaced by 'Bothwell' throughout. *Measure* was difficult, *Titus* almost impossible (though full of good stuff) and the bed-work in *All's Well* would have to be tactfully handled. He turned the pages of the book, and with a worn-down pencil from the pocket of his sports blazer began to rough in paraphrases.

A knock at the door. 'A young lady to see you, sir,' said the maid.

Constance muttered something which would have raised Miss Beale's eyebrows. 'Mr Benson usually sees applicants at the theatre, not here.'

Whisperings were heard, off. The maid reappeared. 'If you please, she said Mr Benson told her the hotel.'

F.R. called out something which may not have been 'Bid her approach', in so many words, but had the same majestic ring. Round the edge of the sturdy oak door, bearing the room's name, *Rosalind*, slid a young person whom Constance, after a swift raking glance, decided to be more promising than some. She was not over-fond of her own sex, preferring to be the only Venus of the skies, but this child had at least a hopeful look, allowing for nerves and for the quite awful coat, skirt and boots, only suitable to a shop-girl bound for a Methodist meeting-house. Almost as tall as Constance herself, her figure was slight without being bony (useful for pages, sprites, and Princes in the Tower), her face a delicate oval, high-browed (some brains, then), her complexion free from unsightly

36

schoolgirl spots and blackheads which make-up only rendered worse, and large eyes that were, like Constance's own, neither green nor brown, but something between.

F.R. dragged his eyes from a censorable passage of *All's Well*. 'Miss Er . . .?' he enquired, as might St Peter, bending down from a cloud to ascertain the name of one of ten million souls passing through the pearly gates.

'Heriot. Miranda Heriot.' The words came out in a gasp but the voice was pleasing and free from the dreadful accent of Birmingham, with which so many would-be recruits spoke. As the name seemed to cause no change in the mild gaze bent on her, Miranda struggled on. 'I wrote to you, Mr Benson, and you were kind enough to answer and say I might come to see you.'

'Was I? Well, well, perhaps so.'

Constance got up and produced an office folder from a drawer. 'It's probably in here with the audition letters.' She riffled through it, producing a sheet with an engraved heading. Her strong eyebrows met her curly fringe.

'"Bromsgrove Household and General Insurance Company?"'

Miranda blushed. 'That was just an accommodation address. The place where I work – worked.' She noticed with alarm that F.R.'s eyes were already straying back to his book.

'What was the matter with your home address?' Constance asked. She had had to deal with angry parents before, come to reclaim their errant children from a life upon the wicked stage.

'My grandmother wouldn't have approved of my writing, so I had to use the firm's address.' What a morning of elation it had been, when the postboy had thrown on her desk that envelope addressed in a sprawling schoolboyish hand, and she had had to open it under the suspicious eye of Mr Harker, a senior member of the firm with a knack of being present whenever a member of his staff was doing anything in the least questionable. Now her fate rested on her own letter to Mr Benson, being scrutinised by this awe-inspiring lady with the brilliant eyes and long, clever mouth, who was not quite beautiful at this hour of the morning in a pink bed-wrapper, but could easily become so in a stage setting, Miranda thought.

'So,' said Constance, folding the letter, 'you came to

Stratford for the first time last summer, saw our *Henry Four I*, and decided you wanted to make the theatre your life.'

'Not the theatre exactly – your theatre. I want to be here, in Stratford.'

F.R. looked up, seeming to see her for the first time, though his visionary's gaze appeared to go right through her and the outside wall and over the ancient pink roofs between the hotel and the river. 'You have heard the Song?' he asked keenly, his slightly harsh voice lowered to a thrilling stage-whisper, as though enquiring of Galahad whether he had seen the Holy Grail.

'Song . . . sir?'

'The Song of Shakespeare.'

Miranda said nothing for a long moment. She did not know in the least what this strange man meant, and yet she did, in some subconscious corner of her mind, just as she had always been able to grasp the sense of a difficult poem before its words were explained. The Song of Shakespeare must be the ring of young men's voices as they armed for war, the chime of a rhyming couplet, the clanking of goblets at an inn, the flutter of brave banners against the sky – and willow-trees dappling in water and the silent purring of old houses like black and white cats settled into their places in the sun, and the joy in Miranda's own heart at these things. So she said, wondering a little at herself, 'Yes, I've heard the Song.'

'Good, splendid.' He gave her his sweet remote smile. 'Constance, we must take her.'

'We shall need a few details first.' Constance was seated in a business-like manner at a davenport, with an inkwell and paper before her. 'You know the amount of the premium, Miss Heriot?'

'Premium?'

'You have to pay us a premium,' Constance explained patiently, 'before you can join the company as a student. £25 for twenty weeks. You did know this?' Miranda's widened eyes and appalled look suggested that she did not. Her hands tightened on her ugly steel-grey handbag.

'No,' she answered miserably. 'I thought . . . I thought I would be working. But I've saved five pounds out of my wages, if that would do . . . only I'd have to pay for a room somewhere.'

'Dear me, what have we here?' Constance's eyes asked her husband's. She knew, better than anybody, that he cared not at all for money; it meant nothing to him. When he needed it for a production it came, more or less to the amount he wanted, and that was that. She could be stern with him at times, but this was not one of them; he thought he had found something. His face was bright with discovery, and she would not spoil it for him.

'You'll recite something for me? You have a piece prepared?'

Miranda had not. In the instant of shaking her head, dumb with mortification, she knew the extent of her wild folly in leaving her home and her job to come to Stratford with no clear idea of what service she might give. Pieces learned at school flashed through her mind, all dull or inappropriate or both. She sat, feeling foolish, wishing herself anywhere else. Constance, who on the whole preferred the nervous students to the brash ones, suggested, 'Perhaps you could read something.'

F.R. beamed. 'Of course she must! Here.' He handed her his book, open at *All's Well*. She regarded it with cold horror. To sight-read was bad enough, but from a play unknown, and before England's greatest actor-manager – that was the stuff of nightmares. But she had not made her break for freedom, and got into the Presence, to be beaten at the first fence. She ran her eye down the page until it came to a passage spoken by a woman, Helena, and rhyming; and whatever angel favours the brave directed her to pause, scanning it, before attempting to read. Then, taking a deep breath, she began.

'*Our remedies oft in ourselves do lie*
Which we ascribe to heaven; the fated sky
Gives us free scope; only doth backward pull
Our slow designs when we ourselves are dull.
What power is it which mounts my love so high –
That makes me see, and cannot feed mine eye?
The mightiest space in fortune Nature brings
To join like likes, and kiss like native things.
Impossible be strange attempts to those
That weigh their pains in sense, and so suppose
What hath been cannot be: who ever strove
To show her merit that did miss her love?

The king's disease – my project may deceive me,
But my intents are fix'd, and will not leave me.'

She had stumbled over some of the awkward phrases, and
wished she could go back and read it again. But Mr Benson was
nodding his shaggy brown head.

'A most interesting passage. The whole character of Helena
is there, don't you think? Courage, resource, virtue,
philosophy . . . There are those who dislike her, but to me she
is one of Shakespeare's most admirable women. Wouldn't you
agree?'

Constance replied, 'Certainly. But more to the point, Miss
Heriot read quite well, for sight unseen, though of course she's
completely untrained. Perhaps the passage appealed to you,
Miss Heriot? You seem to have acted more or less on Helena's
principles, what with your "strange attempts" and "fix'd
intents", or you would not have got here at all.' For the first
time she smiled, a wide merry smile, and Miranda smiled back,
no longer afraid of her.

'So will you take me, please?'

'Well . . . ' She glanced at her husband, who was looking
wistful. 'Without a premium, it's difficult. This company is run
as a training-school, you know, we can't afford to subsidise
students, especially those with absolutely no experience.'

'I could pay you something – I don't know how much and
I'd work – I'd do anything.'

'You'd be prepared to super, understudy, double, learn your
part – if you were lucky enough to get one – at an hour's
notice? Because that's what all our students have to do. And if
there's something heavy to shift on the stage, and you're near
it, you help shift it.'

'Oh yes, yes, I would.' Get up at dawn and scrub the boards,
any unimaginable job. She cursed herself for not having found
out more about the Stratford company earlier, and come
prepared. Mrs Benson was looking at her watch. Any minute
now the unsuccessful aspirant would be politely ushered out.
Mr Benson had concluded that the whole matter was settled,
and was again deep in *All's Well*, deep in the character of the
comic coward Parolles; he would play that, of course, not the
tedious dying king. There would be time enough to play dying

kings when he was past his best.

Miranda said desperately, 'I'm very strong. And I can be useful in all sorts of ways – I've been working as a shorthand-typist . . .'

The noble head came up sharply. 'But that's splendid!'

Constance said, 'You interest us strangely, as they used to put it in the old melodramas. If you could undertake some office work, contracts, letters, that sort of thing, we might *just* manage without the premium – even a very modest salary. We don't do this often, I may say, Miss Heriot. It would be a relief, I must say, to get some order into things at the beginning of the season. My husband has a secretary, of course, but there is so much to do . . . We might get a second-hand typewriter, don't you think, F.R.? And you'll need a lodging, Miss Heriot, a nice cheap lodging. Leave that to me.'

Miranda was alight with joy. 'Oh, thank you, thank you, Mrs Benson! I don't know what I can say, I'm so happy.'

'Don't say anything, child, just prepare yourself for some hard work. For it *is* hard, make no mistake! Now go away, take yourself down to the Theatre, ask for Mr Fleete, tell him I sent you and do whatever he says.' As Miranda turned towards the door the loud incisive voice followed her. 'And Miss Heriot – with minors we do like to have an assurance that the family doesn't object. Perhaps you'll ask your grandmother to send a letter of consent, authorisation, that sort of thing.'

Miranda's heart sank, but only momentarily. There was Editha, her delight in playing games with authority and her cleverness at mimicking style. A letter from her, purporting to be from Grandmother, would be most convincing, if she could restrain herself from making it funny. Not even the thought of Grandmother could spoil that gleaming spring morning, as she ran rather than walked down Chapel Lane, past the gardens which had once been Shakespeare's, rich with the heavy scent of wallflowers and the honey-breath of alyssum, perfumes that would always bring back to Miranda, as long as she lived, those minutes of her youth; the ring of her light footsteps on the road, the sight of the bright red and blue of the theatre: *her* theatre.

It was quite some time before, after trying various wrong doors, and finding herself first in an outhouse full of empty crates, then in a boiler-room, she was directed into Mr Fleete's presence, on the stage, where with a great deal of noise and activity the scenery for *A Midsummer Night's Dream* was being set. Painted trees, a bank of wild thyme for Titania's bower (which at close quarters looked extremely uncomfortable), green matting for the forest floor, were being hauled into place by overalled men who conversed in shouts against a background of hammering. Miranda saw no hope of attracting attention without standing in front of the first row of stalls, which she did, until one of the scene-shifters, burdened with a large clump of wooden ferns, saw her and shouted something which was lost in the general din. At last she managed to convey that she wanted Mr Fleete.

He appeared beside her with astonishing speed, a lean wiry man with a Cockney accent so strong that Miranda had difficulty in understanding a word he said. 'It's not me yer want, love, Mrs B. ought to a' told yer they was over the road. You nip off there, nah, yer'll find 'em hard at it.'

Miranda managed to elicit that "they" were the company, or some of it, that the road was Waterside, which ran by the Bancroft Gardens, and that the place she should make for was mysteriously called the Duck. Having imparted this, Mr Fleete vanished as befitted his name.

The Duck proclaimed itself from across the narrow riverside road; but it was a swan, a black swan, painted on a signboard. On a small paved terrace in front tables and stools were set out, inviting drinkers. Miranda, who had never tasted alcohol in her life, went up the steps guiltily. Perhaps she was now about to see the theatre's darker side.

There was nobody in the little low-ceilinged bar parlour, furnished with wooden settles, and having on its walls a number of photographs of smiling handsome people in striking poses. Behind the bar a stout girl was washing glasses and humming cheerfully.

'If you please,' Miranda asked, 'where are the – the actors?'

The girl grinned broadly and pointed to a latched door. Miranda went through it, into a scene of fantasy. She was in a kitchen garden. Young beans were beginning to climb their poles, onion sprouts pierced the earth with their fronds, infant cabbages were like small green roses. And among all this, on a small patch of grass, the Athenian lovers quarrelled while Oberon and Puck looked on, all in modern clothes of a carelessly stylish kind which made Miranda realise that her own were ugly, towny, and in no way appropriate to this country scene. She leaned against the wall, feeling the sun on her face, infinitely happy. The quarrel reached its height, Lysander and Demetrius marched off glaring at each other, tall Helena ran away from short Hermia, fetching up, laughing, against a door.

'Hello,' said a voice, 'where did you spring from?'

Miranda turned, and looked up into the sunlit face of Hotspur. There were differences – the short hair and open-necked sports shirt – but she would have known him anywhere. A blush spread swiftly from her brow to her throat, and she felt a strong urge to run away faster than Helena had done. But, summoning what self-possession she could, she answered, 'I'm joining the company. Mrs Benson told me to go to the theatre, but Mr Fleete said I should come here . . .' It sounded dreadfully flat and lame.

Hotspur said, 'Well, well. Jolly nice for us.' The blush suited her admirably, wild-rose colour setting off the young face. His practiced gaze took in the off-the-peg flannel costume of a gun-metal grey which would have been unbecoming on Helen of Troy, and the awkward, unprofessional stance. It made a delightful change. He decided to frighten her, just a little.

'You'll be on tonight, then,' he said lightly.

'On?'

'In *The Dream*. Pa won't tolerate anyone sitting around, you know – people come here to work.' He had the satisfaction of seeing the blush drain away, leaving her cheeks white. Her hands went, very prettily, to her heart, and he noticed that they had dimples where older hands had knuckles.

'But . . . but I don't know anything. I mean – Mrs Benson said I should have to understudy, and double, and something else –'

'Super. Well, you'll be supering tonight, make no mistake.'

'You're joking.'

'Not a bit of it. And as for understudying, Mrs B. must have been joking. Nobody needs an understudy because nobody's ever off.'

'But – surely, if one's ill . . .'

'One isn't ill. One makes a point of not being ill. Pa's been known to go on with two teeth knocked out by a cricket ball. One goes on if one's just died – they wouldn't even notice in some cases, anyway. Ah, but you may say, there are other things – moving accidents by flood and field, as 'twere. And you'd be right. There was a time when we were playing Manchester – Pa missed his train, and Desmond there went on for him in Lear. Lear, I ask you!'

'Without learning it?'

'No time to learn it, my love. One knows quite a bit of the fat parts from hearing 'em so often, of course, and the rest of us help out. Little Alice James – that's her over there – had to go on for French Princess in *Henry Five* at half an hour's notice. Didn't know a word of it – made it all up out of her head from what she could remember of school French grammar-books. Nobody noticed a thing.' Then, because he had scared her enough, he patted her hand and said, 'Don't worry, little one, we're very kind to new faces – especially such pretty ones. Sorry, I ought to have introduced myself. Godfrey Arnold.'

'I know. I saw you as Hotspur.'

'Did tha, bonnie lass?' he said in Hotspur's voice, tenderly and suddenly was her hero again, no longer the teasing stranger who had alarmed her so much. She looked up at him with naked adoration, and received the smile he kept for attractive girls. Then, knowing the right moment to make a strategic retreat, he moved away, leaving her looking after him. He might have asked her name, she thought. Perhaps she was too unimportant for him to bother with further. Somebody indoors was playing a march on a piano that wanted tuning.

The scene being rehearsed came to an end. Somebody shouted 'Break!' Among cheers, a young woman appeared at the back door of the inn, bearing a tray containing a large jug and a number of glasses and cups, and the entire company fell on it. There was pouring and drinking and laughter. Those who had been graceful Athenians or nobles of the fairy kingdom sprawled and lounged among the vegetables, chattering, while Miranda stayed shrinking against her wall.

'Hello!' The pert face of Puck laughed up at her. 'You look terribly on your own. Are you new? Have a drink. Don't neglect this unique opportunity. Here.' A striped kitchen cup was pushed into Miranda's hand, full of something brown and curious-smelling. She tasted it, and shuddered. 'Ugh. What is it?'

'Beer. What's the matter, don't you like it? It's the Duck's best bitter. Go on, be brave.'

Bitter it was, and sour, and altogether nasty, thought Miranda, who had expected lemonade. But she drank it, making a face, so as not to seem out of things. Somehow it improved, half-way down the cup. Her braced shoulders relaxed. She found herself perched on a sawn-off tree stump, watching the animated faces, pretty or handsome, rugged or secret. A tall thin man with a long chin and a dreamer's look was talking to a gravely beautiful red-haired woman, a boy who seemed barely out of school was bowling a ball to a slight plain girl. A short tubby man – Miranda recognised Falstaff – had an arm round the waist of the girl who had brought out the beer, and a particularly large mug was at his lips; how he must enjoy playing Sir John. In a clematis on the wall behind Miranda a huge velvet-brown bee was lazily hovering, humming his tune; on a path a thrush was vigorously breaking open a snail's shell with ruthless blows against the stone.

Suddenly the lull was over. Mrs Benson, gorgeous in something purple, was among them, smiling, nodding, brisk as a young girl. Titania summoning her fairy people and those of coarser clay.

'Bottom? Where's Bottom? All right, Bill, you've had enough ale, you'll be asleep. Fairies? Haven't we got any fairies?'

'Children called for two o'clock, Mrs Benson.' This was the plain girl.

'Bother, so they are. Well, we'll have to do without them. Someone give me the lines – Alice, you'll do, it's only "ready" three times. Harry, you aren't on for ten minutes – go in and practise the dance. What are we going to use for a bank? Well, I suppose that will do if it's clean. Ready, Charley, "Come, sit thee down upon this flowery bed, While I thy amiable cheeks do coy . . ." Miss Heriot, please find something to do.'

That was Miranda's last clear recollection of a day which

escalated into a frenzy of activity. She found herself fetching, carrying, obeying commands she did not understand. At the Windmill Inn, up the lane and round the corner, a bevy of children surged, in the care of far too few grown-ups, who had to be schooled to flit about imaginary glades, singing or making noises like birds or insects and lisping the chorus of the fairies' lullaby. Trouble of various sorts erupted. Smaller children had to be removed, from one cause or another, and returned. A six-year-old with the pointed chin and square fringe of a Reynolds cherub burst into a roaring passion of tears because she had been promised wings, and given none; a little boy of astonishing ugliness, whose ears stood out from his head like vase-handles, seemed to be at the front of any grouping, and could only be moved back with pushes and shoves. A squad of mules would have been more manageable, Miranda thought. In a refreshment break she said to Cecily Hurst, the buxom assistant stage manager, 'How are they ever going to be ready for tonight?'

'Tonight? I don't know what you mean, dear.'

'It's the first night, isn't it?'

'Bless you, no. That would be a fair old disaster, for sure. No, we open on Wednesday. Who told you it was tonight?'

'I don't remember.' She was not going to say that it was Godfrey Arnold; that would have been a betrayal of Hotspur. Better to take the lie as a piece of thoughtless teasing. Probably all newcomers were told the same thing, unless they had taken the trouble to find out the facts beforehand; it must be a standard company joke.

'We'll have our work cut out to get this lot on stage by then,' Cecily was saying, 'they're worse than last year, if possible.'

'Who are they?'

'Children of locals. They get a shilling each for going on. *That*,' she nodded towards the boy with the ears, 'is the son of some bigwig on the Council – he's been told to put himself forward, and does. That one,' indicating a tall girl with elaborate corkscrew ringlets, 'wants to be an actress – probably will be if cocksureness is anything to go by. Besides, Mrs B. likes her.'

'If you call Mr Benson Pa,' Miranda said, 'why don't you call Mrs Benson Ma?'

'Try it,' Cecily replied tersely. Miranda decided not to.

The rehearsal came to an end in time for the children, many now in a state of whining tiredness, to go home to bed with their waiting mothers. Cecily and she went back to the Theatre. Mr Fleete and his minions had finished setting the stage, which now bloomed with artificial vegetation. Back-drops representing Theseus's Palace and Another Part of the Wood descended and ascended. In the Green Room F.R. called a full dress rehearsal for the following day, starting at ten o'clock. The company dispersed, chattering. Miranda watched Godfrey Arnold go off with the red-haired beauty, without a glance towards herself.

Suddenly a leaden heaviness possessed her. The day had been long, confused and tiring; she had eaten very little. The enchantment of Stratford was fading with sunset, leaving it a cold, unfriendly place. Once it would not have seemed possible to long for the familiar kitchen, the table laid for tea with cold ham and bread-and-butter, and, upstairs, her own bed, with the nightdress-case in the shape of a fluffy pink kitten, the gift of Editha, the print of Margaret Tarrant's Fairy Piper over the mantelpiece, a framed postcard of a Mabel Lucie Attwell child, all rolling eyes and fat knees, which nobody could have thought beautiful, but which was a part of Miranda's growing up, something of her own. Here was nothing of her own; even her well-stuffed suitcase had been left at the station. She was very much afraid that she would not be able to stop herself crying, and what a humiliation *that* would be.

'Still here, Miss Heriot?' Mrs Benson was beside her, picturesquely hatted, an unfashionable but splendid hand-woven cloak of many colours over the flowing purple gown. Miranda tried to smile, but decided against it as being too perilous.

'I . . . I've nowhere to go, Mrs Benson.'

'But why not? Oh, good heavens, I remember now, I promised to find you somewhere. Let me see – if all else fails I'm sure Nancye Justins will find you a cubby-hole or something at the hotel, but there must be . . . Ricky!' At her shout an actor who was leaving, winding a muffler about his neck as he went, turned. He seemed older than most of the Company, though his look of middle age may have owed something to his down-drawn mouth and the deep lines surrounding it and the baggy eyes. He seemed far from pleased to be summoned back.

'Ah, good, I've caught you. Rick, will you take this young lady home with you and ask Mrs Tibbs to find a bed and some supper? I expect she's got a spare room, hasn't she?'

'As to that, I don't know. No information,' he replied in a gravelly voice as unprepossessing as his face.

'Well, go and see, there's a dear man, as a particular favour to me,' said Constance with a winning smile. 'This is her first day with us, and I'm sure she's very tired and feels a complete stranger.' This was so true that Miranda had a strong impulse to throw herself on Mrs Benson's handsome bosom. 'I know Rachel and Polly will look after her beautifully. Go along, dear, you'll feel quite different in the morning.'

Murmuring thanks, and profoundly hoping that the prophecy was correct, Miranda followed the actor. Together they walked along Waterside, in silence. He appeared lost in his own thoughts, gloomy ones at that, and Miranda neither dared to speak nor wished to. It was like being conducted to one's execution; she hoped the journey would end more pleasantly.

CHAPTER FOUR
This is Illyria, lady

The house at the end of their silent journey was one of a terrace built perhaps thirty years earlier, of the red brick which covered the industrial Midlands. The name-plate on its iron gate said PANDARUS.

'What an odd name for a house,' Miranda said, breaking the silence.

'Character from *Troilus*. Don't think they knew much about him, or they'd have called it something else.'

He opened the door, half-panelled in secular stained glass, and gave a harsh cry which obviously signalled his return home. Into the narrow lobby there bobbed, like a cuckoo from its clock, one of the smallest women Miranda had ever seen. Hardly more than child-size, she was hairpin thin and grey all over: grey dress, with a discreet touch of greyish lace beneath the chin, grey wizened face and grizzled hair parted in the middle and scraped back, a *Punch* landlady to the life. But her smile was joyful and her steel-rimmed spectacles glinted with welcome.

'You're nice and early, Ricky. Brought someone for supper, have you?'

'That's right. And a bed if you can manage it. Mrs B. asked me to fix her up. She's new.'

Well, you might introduce us, you disagreeable man, thought Miranda. Aloud she said, 'I'm Miranda Heriot. How do you do, Mrs . . .?'

'Tibbs, dear. Very pleased to meet you, I'm sure. Was you wanting to stay?'

'If I possibly could, Mrs Tibbs.' The disgruntled manner of the actor and the ugly house could not weigh against the kindliness of the tiny woman and the thought of somewhere to eat and sleep. 'Only,' she added, 'I've just remembered my case is at the station. Shall I go and get it?'

'If you're thinking it's not respectable to turn up at lodgings without luggage, just you forget it, dear. In the Profession we takes as we finds, and you've got a good face; I always goes by a good face. We're not five minutes from the station, so the boy can fetch your stuff if you'll give me the ticket for it. Now you come upstairs with me and I'll show you where everything is.' Miranda, following her up the narrow stairs, noticed that the ungracious Rick had vanished, taking no further interest in her.

They passed a large sepia engraving of *The Light of the World* and another of *Hope*, perpetually strumming her lyre untroubled by the disadvantage of bandaged eyes. 'Nice, aren't they,' observed Mrs Tibbs, seeing her glance at them. 'Always cheer me up, them two pictures do, not that I believes in getting down-hearted, it don't do in this world – nor the next, I don't suppose, not that we know much about *that*, do we, and just as well. Now this is your room, my dear, and I hope it'll do for you – you see it's at the end of the landing and very quiet, and I hope you don't mind attics.'

The room was, in fact, reached by five twisting stairs. It was indeed small, and rather dark, papered in brown sprinkled with a busy pattern of blue and purple flowers. But it had a dormer window with a pointed roof, built out in a bay, an utterly romantic window, from which Rapunzel might have let down her hair or the Countess of Moray waited in vain for the Bonnie Earl's return. Miranda went to it and looked out. Beyond the houses opposite the flat land was a gentle haze of green, and beyond that a hill rose, blue in the growing dusk.

'That's Borden Hill you can see. There's a nice walk up to Luddington, if you like walking. That footpath, over there, that's the way to Shottery, over the fields. They say he wouldn't have gone that way to court Anne, but by the Salmon Jowl, that's the Alcester Road now. I hope the bed's right for you, it's narrow but it's feathers, and here's where you wash, I expect you'd like a wash and so forth.' Mrs Tibbs drew aside a curtain, disclosing in a corner a basin of canvas slung on a metal tripod, an enamel bowl under it; in case, Miranda supposed, the canvas didn't hold the water. Timidly she indicated her urgent interest in 'so forth'. Mrs Tibbs replied that the convenience was out in the back yard, but she supposed young legs didn't mind about that.

'I'll bring you some water up.' She turned, but Miranda stopped her.

'Oh no, please! Show me where the tap is and I'll fetch it myself. You mustn't carry it all this way up, really, Mrs Tibbs.' The landlady gave her an appraising look. She was used to lodgers of all sorts, but very few ever offered to save her a hand's turn of labour.

'That's right, Miranda. You do, there's a dear.' Strangely elated by the homely use of her name, Miranda followed her to the tap in the back kitchen, where an almost tangible smell of cooking made her realise that she was ravenous.

The boy appeared with her suitcase in time for her to put on a clean blouse and wash with her own soap. He proved to be a youth of uncertain years, unnaturally tall, with a disproportionately small head and a vacant expression. Encountered in the dark he might have been frightening, but under this roof his good nature and willingness were all that mattered. Now, clean and tidy, Miranda presented herself in the basement kitchen. Mrs Tibbs arose from bending over a huge, fragrantly-steaming pan, like a fourth member of the culinary team on the blasted heath, and led her along a passage to the back parlour.

It was not a large room, and it was crowded to its capacity, on first sight. Rick was there, sitting at a small table playing spillikins with a woman not young, not conventionally beautiful, but radiating such an impression of beauty that Miranda found herself staring. 'Actressy' was the word which came into her mind, yet the complexion of dazzling fairness bore no trace of make-up, and the pale blonde hair was simply dressed, swept from a side parting and gathered into a knot on the nape of the neck. The soft pink mouth was permanently a little open, as though its owner had difficulty in catching her breath, showing perfect teeth and giving her the look of a very pretty rabbit. At Miranda's entrance she looked up, and her grey eyes were the dove's eyes of Solomon's beloved. Rick glanced up, displeased, Miranda thought, and down again.

By the fire sat an older woman, so fat that she resembled an outsize cottage loaf. Her face was as round as her form, as round as her spectacles, unlined and cheerful, the face of a chubby schoolgirl. Her looks were quaintly echoed in the boy who sprawled on the couch. Fair as a well-scrubbed young pig, he might have been a slighter brother of Billy Bunter, Fat Owl of the Remove in *The Magnet*. In a shabby comfortable easy-chair sat a grey-headed man, newspaper in hand, his knees accommodating a huge tabby cat with a villainous expression.

For a moment they were all looking at Miranda, and for the second time that day she was among complete strangers.

'This is Miranda, dears,' Mrs Tibbs announced, 'and Mrs B. says as you're to take as good care of her as if she was Royal Doulton. Now then, let's give you all a name, so she can settle down and be comfortable. This lady,' indicating the beauty, 'she's Rachel, and this here's her sister Polly Porter, and he's Polly's old man, Edward, and that's their little boy Harold.'

The 'little boy', who was all of seventeen with the shadow of a moustache, protested, 'Oh, I say, Tibby! What a liberty.' But he scrambled politely to his feet, as did his father. His mother put down her sewing, and beamed.

'Well, how nice. Miranda, too, "indeed the top of admiration". Come in, dear, and sit down, and tell us all about yourself. Ricky did say he'd brought a new young friend home.' Ricky's expression suggested that he had said something quite different, but by now Miranda would have been surprised by any sign of amiability from him. She moved into the family circle, and more quickly than she would have thought possible was talking away to them as if she had known them all her life, so friendly they were, Rachel and Polly chatting away in voices pleasantly tinged with a native Yorkshire accent, Edward very slightly Cockneyfied, Harold emerging from boyish tenor into baritone manliness; only the actor silent or monosyllabic.

Over the enormous meal presently served to them in the front kitchen, tripe and onions and mash followed by a sponge pudding with treacle and a pot of tea brewed and drunk in the parlour, Miranda learned that Edward was a schoolmaster, teaching mathematics at a boys' school on the southern outskirts of London, where Harold was in the sixth form. On holiday at present, he would go back with Ted when term started, while Rachel and Polly remained at Stratford, Rachel to be with Rick and Polly because Shakespeare was, she said, the means whereby she lived. Miranda was at first baffled by the extraordinary phrases Polly used for the most ordinary things, until a familiar ring to one of them enlightened her to the fact that they were all Shakespearean quotations tossed lightly into everyday speech. Nobody else seemed to find this at all odd, but Miranda was relieved when she was able to understand without having to do a rapid mental translation. Polly had no function in or about the company. She was simply there, in Stratford, rejoicing in it – the gossip, the excitement, the glamour, the sweet air and country food, unashamedly lazy. London was good, Stratford was better, in her opinion. If her husband and son lived on boiled eggs and tinned sardines in her absences from home, they never complained; in any case they had Mattie, their faithful lady-of-all-work, to look after them. They were all happy, or seemed so.

Edward was, as his wife would have said, a creature of more common earth, a simple, slow-spoken man who was content to live on the edge of her world without being part of it. Fishing was his hobby. Every morning he would go off to some chosen stretch of the Avon and stay there all day with a box of sandwiches and a flask of coffee. He was a very nice, very dull man; Miranda was not surprised that Polly sought compensation in stage glamour.

She noticed that Harold's round blue eyes were constantly fixed on herself. He was at the susceptible age when girls are no longer other boys' sisters, but mysterious alluring beings. He had hung patiently round most of the available girls in the company, without reward, and here was a new one, actually under the same roof. Harold visualised romantic evening walks by the river, even hand-holdings or a chaste kiss or two; he was not unduly demanding, but he longed for a girl to call his own. Very fortunately for him, he was not aware on this first evening that his looks failed to stir Miranda's heart at all, or that it was already occupied.

As for Rachel and Ricky, Miranda found them fascinating. It was hard to imagine how a man so ugly and cross-grained as the actor could have attracted such a woman; how, indeed, he could ever express emotion, wit or charm on the stage. She studied Rachel's white-rose complexion, her pale flaxen hair, that looked almost too good to be true – was it possible that in some way Art had assisted Nature? Miranda was aware that the lacy blouse, of a becoming blue, was made of something cheap, and that the many rings on the delicate white hands were not set with real jewels. Among them the broad gold wedding-band stood out, dignified and eye-catching. It was hardly possible to believe that this fairy-tale creature and the fat Dutch-cheese of a woman, Polly, could be sisters; yet something about voice and manner confirmed it. They were not very different under the skin, these two, close and protective to each other and each other's men.

There was talk of the theatre, Edward taking no part, Harold looking from one to the other, but mostly at Miranda. She found herself telling them her story, only editing out the darker elements of it, and the revelation of her parents' tragedy. It was too hurtful to speak of, and as yet she could not tell them. They reacted to her adventure like people of her own age.

'But of course you were right,' Polly said. 'The Bard summoned, and off you went. "My master calls me – I must not say no."'

'It wasn't exactly like that, Mrs Porter. I don't know what it was.'

'Stratford,' said Rachel. 'It has a magic like nowhere else. You feel it, and sense it, and smell it, and you're never the same again, like the girl, Whatsername, who was whipped off to Fairyland.'

'"Late, late in the evening, Kilmeny cam' hame,"' added Polly, who made occasional excursions outside the works of the Bard.

'That's right. You're lucky it's happened to you so young, Miranda. Think of the years you could have wasted.'

'I know. I could have been typing inventories of goods and chattels until I fell to pieces with old age, instead of . . . this. I do think it must be the most wonderful thing in the world – isn't it, Mr, Er?' She realised that she had never heard Ricky's surname.

He supplied it, flatly. 'Savage. Richard Savage. Called after some old scribbler or other. He was a bastard.'

'A real one, you know, not just in the naughty sense,' Polly explained. 'He used to say he was the son of Earl Rivers, wrong

54

side of the blanket, of course, which would make him a great-great-something of the Rivers Richard Three polished off, wouldn't it? Fancy being descended from someone in the Plays.' She sighed ecstatically. 'I wish I was. But there's nobody in them called Outhwaite.'

Ricky, who had opened and drunk a bottle of light ale while the rest of them were disposing of the tea, addressed Miranda. 'As for what you were saying, young lady. No, acting isn't the most wonderful thing in the world. It's bloody hard work, bloody badly paid, and anyone who thinks it isn't is a bloody fool.'

Miranda gasped. She had never been spoken to so in her life, or heard that word spoken at all. But Polly remarked playfully, ' "Rudesby, begone", ' and Rachel, laying a hand glittering with Woolworth gems on Ricky's, cooed, 'Now, darling, that's simply not true. You know you adore it and you wouldn't do anything else if they paid you a fortune. Besides, think what a waste of you it would be.' She stroked the buttons on his cuff tenderly, deliberately, as though touching skin; Miranda stared. It was the most erotic gesture she had ever seen. Something like a smile twisted the long hard line of Ricky's mouth.

Edward gave an enormous yawn, then said, 'Sorry, chaps.' Miranda glanced at the clock on the mantelpiece, a bulbous composition of imitation marble and ormolu, presented, according to a brass plate, to the late Herbert Tibbs on his retirement from the London, Midland and Scottish Railway Company. It said a quarter to one, and though Miranda's own plain little silver watch disagreed with it to the extent of twenty minutes, she was conscious that the hour was the latest she had ever kept. But none of the others seemed to notice. An animated discussion had started up about a darts match to be held on the following Sunday at a pub in a nearby village, with the prize of a pewter mug offered by the landlord. Should they rely on the horse-bus which ran twice daily, for the con-venience of churchgoers in outlying hamlets, or persuade a farmer friend in Shottery to loan them a pony-trap which would take the ladies? The general opinion ran in favour of the trap, as being more fun. The two sisters turned simultaneously to Miranda.

'You'll come too, dear?'

'Oh, do, you must!'

'Well. Is it – all right, on a Sunday?'

They looked blank, and Ricky guffawed. 'Sunday?'

'I mean, church . . .'

'Oh,' said Polly enlightened, 'if you want to go to *church* we could drop you off and pick you up again. Some people do, I know – Mrs B.'s a most devout Catholic and never misses Mass – perhaps you're one, too.'

'No – I'm not anything, really.' Miranda was pleasantly shocked to hear herself making this bold statement. But it was true, she had never belonged officially to the Peculiar sect her grandmother had favoured, and the only other form of service she knew was school prayers, with hymns on which the girls had sung facetious variations. Her question about the all-rightness of going into public-houses on the Sabbath had not been answered: they had simply not understood it.

Harold cleared his throat. His voice shot down into the bass register as he said, 'I shall walk. Like to come with me? It's only four miles.'

Miranda looked down at her town boots, tightly buttoned and uncomfortable from newness and day-long wear. 'I don't think I could. But thank you, Harold.'

'I bet,' said Harold, a treble again, 'you haven't played darts before.'

'Well, no.'

'Don't worry because you've got such little wrists. It's all a matter of throwing, you know, not strength.' He made a daring grab at the wrist nearest to him. Miranda, embarrassed, let him keep it for a moment, then snatched it away. His mother watched benignly. Her boy had developed another attack of calf-love, conquest again to a white wench's black eye. But this time the girl seemed nice, gentle, less likely to mock the poor child than some of the saucy pieces in the company.

Edward rose, suddenly, expanding to his considerable length of limb, and yawning fearsomely. The cat, Timon, which had been sitting on him most of the evening, slid off and stalked away, giving Edward a look of concentrated venom as he left. As though on cue the door opened; Mrs Tibbs's head came round it, without her false teeth and decked with two tiny grey pigtails in place of the bun.

'Goodnight, lovies, sleep well.'

The sisters lingered on the landing outside their bedroom doors.

'Such a nice child,' said Rachel. 'So fresh. And so utterly stage-struck.'

'Yes. Poor worm, she is infected. I suppose we were the same, at her age. Remember the stage door of the Lyceum?'

'Shall I ever forget? The dustbins!'

'Trying to touch Irving's cloak – and the night we did, and he turned round and bowed!'

They laughed, and sighed. 'Young Miranda has all that to come – lucky her,' said Rachel.

'Lucky her. Though it's very painful at times . . . Funny, she reminds me of somebody.'

'Who?'

'I don't know – I've been wondering all evening. It'll come to me. Goodnight, Rachie.'

'Goodnight, Poll.' They kissed warmly, and parted.

Miranda's watch, when she woke from a deep sleep, told her that it was half-past eight. Horrified at having overslept she leapt from bed, washed and dressed, and within minutes was down from her tower room. The other bedroom doors were closed, the house quiet. They must all be at breakfast. On her way to the kitchen she opened the door of the sitting-room, and jumped back with shock. There were two people on the floor, comfortably tucked up in a bed improvised from cushions, a travelling-rug, somebody's coat and a Spanish shawl which had draped the piano the night before. The fair head remained half-buried, but the brown one stirred. A young man's voice said sleepily, 'Morning.'

Too unnerved to reply, Miranda shut the door and hurried away, towards the kitchen. No sound of breakfasting came from it. Understandably, for only Mrs Tibbs was there, dressing-gowned, pottering about at the gas-stove, on which sat a huge black kettle just beginning to boil. She greeted Miranda cheerfully.

'My word, you're bright and early, you are.'

'Early? But I thought – where are the others?'

57

'Bless you, they ain't up yet. Only Ted, he's gone off with his rods. I'm just going to take their teas up. Here, you can give me a hand, seeing as you're so willing.'

'Of course. Mrs Tibbs – there are two people in the sitting-room, on the floor.'

'Ow yes?' She was busy laying out cups and stirring the brown pot.

'In – in a sort of bed.'

'Ah, that'll be Eric again. Every now and then he takes up with a new girl, and they runs off together. Well, young folk, it seems more romantic-like than just courting, don't it? They usually comes to Rachel and Polly and tells them all about it, how cruel her parents is and that sort of thing, and they stays till they has a row and then goes off again. Well, fancy, Eric's back. That'll mean two more teas.'

'But,' said Miranda, trying to take in this curious situation, 'how did they get in?'

'Back door, I expect. I always leaves it on the latch. Mind you don't fall over Timon, he *will* eat in the middle of the floor just where people walks.'

Miranda picked her way round the cat, who appeared larger and more disreputable than ever by daylight, and seemed to have been in a recent fight. 'Is he yours, Mrs Tibbs?'

'Mine? Lor, no, he's theirs. 'Least, he's more Ricky's than anybody's, or he thinks he is – Ricky picked him out of a dustbin outside the stage door at the Royalty when he'd barely got his eyes open, Timon, I mean. Meself, I'd have had him doctored, but they don't hold with that, so he gets out and fights.'

'Why is he called Timon?' Miranda asked.

'Oh, *they* could tell you that, I can't, dear – I think it's after some man in some play or other. They travels him everywhere, Ricky and Rachel, wouldn't part with him for the world. More like a baby to Polly than what Harold was, that cat is. Here you are, dear, that's for Rachel and Ricky, front room at the end of the landing.'

Miranda tapped nervously at the bedroom door; a soprano voice summoned her in. To her embarrassment, here was yet another couple in bed. Ricky, villainously unshaven, regarded her sourly, Rachel with a radiant smile. Her silvery hair was spread over the pillows, the lacy frills of her low-cut nightdress billowed around her white shoulders, on one of which Ricky's head was pillowed, and somehow Miranda guessed that they had been even closer to each other not long before. She tried to avert her eyes and at the same time find a place to put down the tin tray.

'Just here, pet, on the chair. Aren't you a kind, helpful girl, then? Come on, darling, sit up and have your tea, Tibby's done us some nice toast.' Miranda, anxious to get out, was unable to stop her eyes roving round the room, collecting a pretty frothy robe hung on the door over a shabby old check coat, a scatter of dainty cosmetic containers on the dressing-table, a scent-spray such as she had always envied, porcelain, painted with a Watteauesque scene, the bulb encased in a silk net, next to a tin of cheap cigarettes and an ash-tray full of fag-ends. Beauty and the Beast, thought Miranda. How can she stand him?

'Mrs Tibbs said I was to tell you Eric's here,' she muttered, backing towards the door.

'He is? Not alone, I suppose? No, I thought not. Drat! Did you hear that, darling? Still, Pa will be pleased – he can use all the supers he can get. That means you, Miranda – you do realise you'll have to be a courtier or an attendant or a grown-up fairy, and possibly all three?'

'Somebody did say.' She blushed, remembering who the someone had been. Rachel saw; she hoped it was not Godfrey again.

The next two days passed in feverish activity. There was no time to rest, collect one's thoughts, or eat properly; Pa didn't permit idling. Miranda found herself rehearsing child-fairies in their dance (which they knew much more about than she did), standing in for the actor who played Snug the Joiner, uncomfortably aware of the critical eye of Ricky Savage upon her, frantically sewing, with cobbled stitches, in Wardrobe, fetching for Pa the lettuce sandwiches he had left behind at the hotel; which she must remember to call the Wagstaff, not the Shakespeare, just as the Falcon was referred to as the Canary. Everybody else was as frantically busy as she, but remarkably kind and tolerant.

In the general chaos she was thrillingly aware of the presence of Godfrey Arnold. At the Wednesday dress rehearsal he appeared in the semi-Jacobean costume of Duke Theseus, doublet and breeches of white and gold. It looked shabby enough on its hanger in Wardrobe, but in stage lighting attained magnificence, as he did, with a curled dark wig and small Imperial beard. For the first time Miranda heard his stage voice without a Northumbrian accent, pure, strong and beautiful. She was enchanted by him, more enchanted than ever, longing to be near him yet ashamed to let him see her dishevelled and in her ugly town grey, with a flopping overall protecting it. For most of the rehearsal, which went on all day, she had nothing to do but lend a hand wherever it was wanted. Then, before the palace scene of the last act, Benson's gaze, roving among his extras, found her.

'You. I want another court lady. Attendant on Hippolyta. Different in some way . . .' He was thinking out a new approach to the scene, as he liked to do, even at this late hour for the production. 'Bored! That's it. She can find the Mechanicals dreadfully dull, and yawn.'

'Won't that be a little dangerous?' suggested Constance. 'It could start an epidemic in the audience. Not to mention on the stage.'

'Ah, yes – true. We must think of something else. Different . . . different . . . I have it – black. A Nubian, unable to follow the language, bewildered, yes, that would be highly comic. So that's decided.'

'Weren't the Amazons from Scythia?' asked a young man who had come to the company straight from Oxford, and was full of learning. 'They wouldn't be black, you know.'

'Well, never mind,' said F.R. testily, 'it's a moot point. She can be brown, dark brown. Go along and get made up, Miss Er.' Dutifully Miranda departed to be made up dark brown, with Leichner No. 10, and her lips vermilioned to look twice their size. She was fascinated by the stranger's image looking out from the mirror.

And, after curtain up, deeply thankful to have her shame hidden behind that mask. For she had not guessed what might be the impact of finding oneself, for the first time, behind real footlights on a real stage with a real audience out there; to have to make movements not rehearsed or thought out, to be ignorant of how to manage her limbs or her expression. Even to stand still required a certain art. Finding herself standing on one foot, crowded by the other girls round her, she moved and was immediately hissed at furiously by Fay Brinks, the beautiful red-headed Hippolyta.

'Get away, you're masking me!'

A sharp push sent her recoiling against another attendant, so violently that both almost fell, and she received several glares. It seemed a lifetime, an age, before Egeus's exit in company with the ducal train. Offstage, she was rounded on.

'I say, you'll have to be careful – you nearly had us both over! Don't you know you must never move suddenly unless you've rehearsed it?'

'But there wasn't time . . .' Miranda hurried away in the opposite direction from the stairs up to the dressing-rooms, not caring where she went so long as it wasn't back to the stage. The corridor she followed led to Wardrobe; she avoided it, blindly making her way through the back of the theatre until a door let her into the fresh air, on the river bank. There she plumped down on the grass, her head in her hands, and began to cry. The evening was still light, but nobody was near to see her, so she wept with abandonment.

She had disgraced herself in the most public manner possible. After so much boldness in escaping to Stratford and forcing herself into the world of theatre, she was not worthy to inhabit it. Through her tears she glanced down at the water, dark silver, deep, cool. A swift slide down the bank and she would be in it, unable to swim, Ophelia borne down by the weight of her garments, down to muddy death. It would be horrible, but so was life.

It was thus that Godfrey Arnold found her, crouched among reeds. He knew at once who it was, for he missed very little and had noted with amusement, out of the corner of his eye, the confusion of the black attendant and Fay's anger. He put a hand on the bowed and shaking shoulders, making her start and look up.

'Good God, little Thing from Birmingham! What in heaven's name's the matter?'

Gasping, choking, forgetting in her misery even her idolatry of him, she told him. He listened gravely, standing in the

61

graceful attitude that was second nature to him, a shadowy figure who might have come haunting from the Bard's own time. Then, with equal grace, he lowered himself to kneel beside her.

'What a terrible tale. But my dear, do you know how funny you look? like a Christy Minstrel. Wait . . .' He swooped down to the water's edge and returned with a handkerchief sopping wet. Wringing it out, he gently tilted her face up and wiped it. 'That's better, most of it's off.' (It was not, but it would make her feel better to think so.)

She was indeed feeling better, the touch of her god working healing on her. She tried a smile.

'Thank you, Mr Arnold. You're – so kind. How did you know . . .'

'That you were here? I didn't, of course. I always come out after Scene One on a fine evening and take a boat out – I'm not on again till the end. Neither are you. Why don't you join me?'

Miranda was nonplussed. 'Oh. But . . . I'm not going on again. I can't. Not after I've made such a fool of myself. I'll go in and change and write a note to Mr Benson saying I'm no use to him. What else can I do?'

'You can stop being such a silly little girl. You were no worse than anyone would have been, pushed on in a hurry. I'm surprised Pa let you go on at all, let alone blacked up . . . No, I'm not, but that's another story. I tell you something – if you leave like that, he'll think you're a dreadful coward. And he'll be very, very disappointed that you let his production down by not being there for the Pyramus and Thisbe scene. Do you want to disappoint him – or me?' he added gently, with a smile that seemed to turn her heart over.

She whispered, 'No.'

'All right. Then come and help me get the boat out – it's moored only a few yards up river, by the ferry – and I'll row you up to Alveston, and talk to you like a Dutch uncle on the way.'

But in the boat, gliding under the willows' trailing hair, under a darkening sky and a young moon, Miranda heard very little of his words of encouragement. She was aware only of his presence, his voice, the wonder of being with him alone (though other boaters were around them). He showed her the island where the swans nested, still white shapes, the arch below Clopton Bridge under which Shakespeare himself must have boated, for he mentioned the strange eddy beneath it. Bats squeaked and darted above, the lights of the theatre shone like the portholes of a great ship, then were lost behind the bulk of the bridge.

Like one in a dream, Miranda asked, 'If you'd rowed the other way, where would we have gone?'

'Over the weir into eternity, at a guess.'

'Oh.' Someone, somewhere in the Plays (which she had been reading in bed every night), said, 'If 'twere now to die, 'Twould be most happy.' Or something of the kind. Miranda knew exactly what they meant.

CHAPTER FIVE

Oh, how this spring of Love resembleth
The uncertain glory of an April day . . .

There had never been such a spring, people said. The Vale of Evesham shone like a bride in its heavy veil of blossom, promising rich fruit; nightingales sang boldly close to the centre of town, the cuckoo called all day in defiance of the rhyme, and in a nest under the bridge a black swan was hatched, a thing so rare in England that naturalists travelled from far to see it. A flurry of spring-cleaning swept Stratford; washing-lines sagged under laundered linen, folk on ladders whitewashed plaster and painted timber, reviving the faces of ancient cottages. The voices of the Folk Song Society were heard through open windows, rehearsing. In shop windows new bonnets and dress-lengths of coloured cloth tempted women and girls, children appeared in fresh print pinafores; it was festival time, the birthday of the Bard, and Stratford was in its best to pay him homage.

But on the day, St George's Day, April 23, it rained. It always did rain, said Stratfordians. At the first Birthday Celebration it had snowed as well. From a dark grey sky a steady downpour rattled on roofs and turned flagstones to mirrors. As noon struck from the tower of the Gild Chapel, and painted banners were unfurled from tall masts down each side of Bridge Street and outside the Birthplace itself, the rain promptly did its best to furl them again. As the Porter family, Ricky, Rachel and Miranda left the house in Alcester Place Polly observed soulfully that the heavens were like Niobe, all tears, in mourning for the Bard.

'Damn it, Poll,' snapped Ricky, 'feller was born in 1564 –

he'd have to be dead by now! What the hell's the point of mourning for him?'

As they walked along Church Street, each clutching a bunch of flowers or a posy, other macintoshed figures emerged and joined them, also carrying flowers. At the Grammar School the town band was waiting, and the masters and boys of the school, who would by tradition head the procession behind the band. The hour chimed, the musicians struck up their version of the March from *Scipio*, and the procession moved off; first the dignitaries, Sir Percy and Lady Eggleston, beadle, mace-bearers, gold-chained Mayor and the town's most honoured visitors, including the Bensons, then a straggling, unordered train of townsfolk, actors, and anyone else who cared to join them. Slowly, yet cheerfully, they wound through the streets towards Holy Trinity. Miranda turned her face up to the rain and let it cool her cheeks. The fresh, new-washed air mingled with the scent of thousands of flowers, daffodils, primroses and violets, early blossom, hothouse blooms carried by the Mayor's lady and others who must be seen to carry only the best. It was better than sunshine; Heaven had, as usual, done the right thing.

The limes that arched over the path to the church were in their tenderest young green, dripping gently on the heads of the already sodden votaries. At the door the vicar greeted them: it was his great day. The procession took an astonishingly long time to file up the north aisle towards the Shakespeare tombs. Miranda was able to look round, without seeming to, in search of the tall Hamlet-like figure who had been walking some distance behind her, unseen but constantly in her mind. Yes, there he was, the black velvet of his coat-collar dank with rain, some drops clinging to his brown hair; she hoped he would not catch cold. He was talking to somebody; Miranda craned to see whom, and was relieved to see fat Cecily Hurst, not the beautiful Fay, at his side. She looked quickly away, pretending to study the old glass in the Clopton chapel, hoping that none of her companions had noticed the direction of her gaze.

They had politely said nothing about the number of times she managed to drag his name into conversation, always with a betraying blush. She had not mentioned the idyllic voyage on the opening night of *Dream,* or her disappointment that Godfrey had made no further approaches to her, though there had been looks and smiles to encourage her hopes. There had been no chance to linger by the stage door for him: Harold was there already, every night, to escort her back to their lodgings, chattering in his amiable boring way. He was not objectionably amorous, but determined to cling to her side on all possible occasions. Poor, plain lad, it was his ambition to have a pretty girl all to himself; Harold's girl. Determinedly he walked her by the river and along the canal, taught her to throw a dart, bored her at length with such fascinating areas of chemistry as the formation of sodium iodide by dissolving methyl iodide in an inert solvent and treating it with metallic sodium. He intended to be a chemical engineer, he said, dwelling lovingly on the charms of such a life, and not noticing Miranda's suppressed yawns.

Harold was desperately dull because he didn't belong to the world of his mother and aunt. He and his father inhabited a quite different one, a place of blackboard chalk and pints of mild-and-bitter and Rugby played on wet muddy afternoons. It could be quite a pleasant world, Miranda thought, if one were not infatuated with the theatre, and if the men in it could be as exciting as actors. There were moments – only moments – when she thought wistfully that it would be nice to be an ordinary person again, not obliged to hang about the Theatre every night in case one were required to rush on in an ill-fitting costume at a moment's notice or take part in a general dance, court scene or affray. Was it, perhaps, that a little – just a little – of the illusion went when one was actually part of it? That ought not to be the case with her, whose own father had been not quite an actor, but at least a performer; had he ever, when the seaside wind was cold and someone in the troupe was surly, felt that he would have enjoyed it all more in a deck-chair? Miranda put the thought away. Of course his heart had been in it – of course he was a professional. Would she ever know more about him – was there anyone who still remembered a dead pierrot and his pierrette?

Perhaps she had not inherited his professionalism. Perhaps things were better, for some people, on the other side of the floats. There was that line of Romeo's, when he has doubts about attending the Capulets' ball: 'I'll be a candle-holder, and look on'. Suppose he hadn't gone to the ball, he wouldn't have met Juliet, and then of course there would have been no play . . .

Godfrey had moved out of her field of vision, concealed by a pillar. The Bensons had passed the place of pilgrimage and were returning down the south aisle. Miranda's gaze dwelt affectionately on F.R. If the truth were told, she enjoyed the peace of the secretarial work she did for him more than the turmoil of the stage and the wings. His affairs were in such a tangle that it was quite a challenge to attempt to sort out letters from the managers, lists of bookings, applications from would-be company members, bills and salary details and students' fees. He had no sense of business; God, and Constance, alone kept him from financial ruin. He was touchingly grateful for any suggestion given, any problem solved, like a nice child being helped with its homework. It was not always easy to judge him as an actor; was he a great one without being a good one, or the other way round? But as a man, he was beloved of everyone, it was impossible not to like him. Kind, generous, without vanity or pomp, he was a surrogate father to his students, the 'Puddings' in company language, who came to him raw in experience, turning under his mild surveillance into 'Earwigs', creatures with small speaking parts. Slowly he moved down the aisle, looking amiably about him, his ruffled hair wild as ever, his clothes suggesting that he had dressed to the summons of a fire-alarm.

Of Constance, progressing with stately grace at his side, one had to be a little wary. She took dislikes and she was no fool. When Miranda had presented to her a letter allegedly from her grandmother, consenting to her enrolment as a student, written with high enjoyment by Editha, Constance's heavy classic eyebrows rose a trifle as she read and re-read the forged document.

'Your grandmother writes a very youthful hand.'

'Er, yes. She's always been known for it.'

Constance pretended to ponder. 'Don't I remember you saying she would not have approved of your writing to us?'

'Well – yes. That is . . . she would have thought I should apply personally, because that would be more enterprising.

Braver.' It sounded feeble to a degree, and very faint twitch of a smile touched Constance's mouth.

'In that she was quite mistaken; we always like to have notice of people arriving, though sometimes they do just turn up.' To Miranda's infinite relief, she handed the letter back without more comment.

With the letter, a note from Editha had been enclosed.

'I snooped about a bit to find out what Mrs H. had been saying since you left, and it seems she's said absolutely nothing. Miss Teasdale asked me, because she'd called at the house and had the door slammed in her face. People are probably saying Mrs H. has done you in and buried you in the back garden, ha ha. Can't wait to know how you're getting on, shall come down the first chance I get. Good luck, old thing.'

The procession was moving quite quickly. Miranda was standing before that slab of stone with its cryptic rhyme. 'Curst be he yt moves my bones,' indeed; as though anyone were likely to. Polly had lent her a modern *Life*, full of theories about the man whose stone bust looked down placidly on his gravestone, the very image, as someone had said, of a prosperous Jacobean grocer totting up his week's accounts. Were you really like that, she silently asked the bald, bearded effigy; could you really have looked so stodgy? Did you have that doggerel inscribed on your tomb because you had a horror of your bones being thrown into the charnel-house in the churchyard, because you had looked in there as a boy and been frightened by the heap of anonymous bones and skulls lying all higgledy-piggledy? Did you love Anne Hathaway as Romeo loved Juliet, or did you have to marry her because you'd got her with child, like Claudio and the other Juliet in *Measure*, and did you leave her the second-best bed as an insult or because it was the custom to leave the best bed to the heir, your daughter Susannah Hall? Was your heart broken, when you were young, by a false wanton Dark Lady, and was she Mary Fitton or Elizabeth Brydges, or who?

Her turn had come to throw her posy on to the glorious heap of flowers covering the grey stone, spilling over Anne Shakespeare's and Thomas Nashe's in a coverlet of colour outdoing the jewelled stained glass of the east window above them. 'Sweet flower, with flowers thy bridal bed I strew; oh woe, thy canopy is dust and stones.' It was a curiously personal ceremony, just as she would have felt strewing flowers over her young parents' graves. But where were they? In some London churchyard, perhaps, with London dust and stones above them. Frank and Grace Forbes, the inscriptions would say, for nobody would have been so unkind as to bury Grace under her maiden name; actors were kind people not given to making moral judgments, consigning others to everlasting fire and undying worms, ugh, because they hadn't got married. I wish I knew, she thought; I wish I could find them.

The lime-trees' green was blurred to Miranda's eyes as she emerged from the church, and her cheeks were damp. Harold, who had caught up with her after strenuous pushings and manoeuvrings, glanced at her sympathetically and pushed into her hand a large crumpled handkerchief. She blew her nose, murmuring, 'Sorry.'

'It's all right. Mother always cries, lots of people do.'

Ahead of them the procession had broken up. The civic dignitaries, the Bensons, a distinguished London actress-friend of theirs, and Miss Marie Corelli, a dumpy figure almost extinguished under a huge hat made of velvet violets, were walking together, followed by the company's leading players, Fay Brinks at Godfrey's side costing Miranda a piercing stab of jealousy. Then came top people from behind the scenes, Mr Fleete, Cecily Hurst, Alan Dobbs the master carpenter. They were making for the same point, it seemed, passing the house where Susannah Hall had lived, through Old Town and turning into Church Street.

'Where are they all going?' Miranda asked Harold.

'The Birthday Luncheon. Sir Percy gives one every year in the Town Hall. Roast chicken and lots of speeches. Company and bigwigs and anybody who matters. Special plates with the Wagstaff crest on, and a bit of rosemary-for-remembrance for the chaps' buttonholes, and a bunch of primroses for the ladies.' Sir Percy Eggleston was the local squire, a man who had retired on a great quantity of Birmingham 'brass' which he liked to spend on a high country lifestyle and extensive patronage of the arts. He had married a baronet's daughter, thereby further establishing his claims to the squirearchy. Locals knew him as Pompous Percy or The Egg.

Miranda scanned the people strolled behind the favoured few. 'But,' she said, 'Ricky's not with them – look, he's with Rachel and your mother and father. Oughtn't you to go and remind him?'

'Not really. Lady Egg won't have him, you see.'

'Won't have him?'

'Well, no, because of Rachel. I mean, *she* couldn't go.'

'What? His own wife?'

Harold looked embarrassed. 'Auntie isn't exactly his *wife*. I thought you knew.' Seeing by Miranda's blank face that she knew nothing of the kind, he explained, 'Ricky's got a wife and kids – well, not kids, there's a boy older than me. He hasn't lived with them for years, but she turns up now and then and gets a sub off him. She pulled Auntie's hair down once and slapped her face, so we have to get her out of the way when danger looms. Old Tibby knows the way she knocks and rings, so it's all right here – not so good in London, though.'

Miranda was utterly confused. Rachel and her uncouth Ricky in bed entwined like Titania and Bottom, the broad genuine wedding-band among the gimcrack rings . . . and not married? So what had seemed to be wedded devotion was – what? Illicit passion, and at *their* age. She remembered that she had never actually heard Rachel referred to as Mrs Savage. But to live with such a man, to put up with his moroseness and ungraciousness, without the tie of marriage to keep her at his side; to let herself be banned from great occasions because of the shame of her position. She opened her mouth to say all this, then shut it again with the sudden conviction that Harold, for all his moon-face and darts and chemistry, understood these things, and other strange countries of his family's world, far better than she did. Shame on you, she said to herself, what do you know about it? (But it can't be love – the sort of love one feels for Godfrey. Love's for the young.)

Harold and Edward went home to London at the end of that week. Polly and Miranda saw them off at the railway station, Polly bouncing about the platform like a bright blue rubber ball in her flowing folk-weave cloak. 'Rather you than me, dear boys. It truly hurts me to watch all the lovely names sliding past, and Great William's green country, and all that dirty red brick rolling up. Thank the Lord there's a summer festival now, not just a fortnight in spring. Come on, Harold, let's get you some chocolate to cheer you up on the way.' Harold tore his wistful gaze away from Miranda and followed his mother. Chocolates, especially milk ones, were not complete anaesthetics against the pain of separation, but they helped.

Miranda found herself standing alone with Edward, wondering what on earth they would talk about till the others came back. His taciturnity reduced her, as a rule, to making inane general remarks for the sake of breaking the silence, or simply saying nothing while trying not to appear rude. This morning, astonishingly, he cleared his throat and addressed her.

'Don't think I'm interfering, my dear. Don't want to shove my oar in. But.' He struggled for words. 'Polly and Rachel, they're strong women, both of 'em. What I mean is, they know how to deal . . . it's a funny old life, this theatre business, takes hold of people and makes 'em behave the way they wouldn't, normally.'

'Yes,' said Miranda, baffled.

'Now you're a nice girl, very. The sort of girl we'd be pleased for Harold to bring home.'

Oh dear, he's trying to talk me into Harold.

Edward stared at distant signal lights, struggling for expression. 'You don't always know – just how people are when they're . . . well, not acting. Now I daresay you've been brought up with ordinary chaps like, well, like me. But actors, they're . . .'

Miranda tried to help him and enlighten herself. 'Mr Benson's certainly different.'

'F.R.? Splendid fellow, one of the best. Head in the clouds, of course, but a really good influence on the boys and girls. No, that's not quite what I mean. I . . .' Polly and Harold appeared from the refreshment room laden with chocolate creams, and the homily, or whatever it was, ended, to the relief of both. Miranda, waving, watched the London train disappear in billows of acrid steam, and wondered what on earth Edward's warning could have meant.

The play that night was *Dream*. The black-faced Scythian

attendant had been scrapped, F.R. having reluctantly had to admit that she made no impression, or the wrong one, and Miranda now wore a fuzzy wig she had acquired for six shillings from another girl, as a beginning to the personal wardrobe every member of the company was required to own, and a yellow robe artistically draped with the aid of seven large safety-pins. She had learnt a few lessons now about stage deportment, and was able to relax enough to enjoy the lovely lyrical end of the play. Tonight it seemed to hold a special magic. Charles Law's wistful half-memory of Bottom's fairy visions: 'Methought I was . . . and methought I had . . .' brought an unexpected prick of tears. Theseus had gained – was it possible, when he had been so splendid before? – in nobility and grace. Never had Godfrey spoken so earnestly, so movingly, the Duke's

'For never any thing can be amiss,
When simpleness and duty tender it.'

Fay Brinks, wearing the pearl crown that set off her sunset hair, looked so beautiful that Miranda forgot the niggling jealousy which always attacked her when she saw Godfrey at her side. Plain little Alice Bengough, who in private life wore spectacles that almost obscured her small pale face, was an unearthly Puck, her skin a delicate whitish-green blending into the green of her tunic, her ears extended to elvish points, her large short-sighted eyes gazing past the human scene to the kingdom of spirits.

Now it is the time of night
That the graves, all gaping wide,
Every one lets forth his sprite
In the church-way paths to glide.
And we fairies, that do run
By the triple Hecate's team
From the presence of the sun,
Following darkness like a dream . . .

Behind the fairies' blessing of the bride-beds stole in the music of Mendelssohn, echoing the music of the words. Just for once, audience and players were under the same spell. When the curtain came down there was the slightest of pauses;

then, as though waking from a dream, the house broke into a storm of applause that went on through call after call.

Miranda came off in a happy daze, not caring even when she saw that one of the safety-pins had come undone and bared her shoulder. In the dressing-room there was laughter and chatter. The borrowed children were mercifully removed at once by their mothers, F.R. complimented the musicians, Constance in her dressing-room, disentangling artificial flowers from her hair, was regaling visitors with her favourite story of the Singing Fairy overcome with nerves who inadvertently changed the words of the Lullaby to "Ye potted snakes with ham and tongue." 'Hungry, I suppose, poor thing.'

'She tells that one all the time,' Alice informed Miranda, as she removed the moulded tips of her ears. Ella Makepeace, craning over for a look in the mirror, put in, 'And the one about First Witch drying on his entrance and coming out with "The cat's mewed three times". Pa nearly got the bird that night.'

Alice shrieked. 'Hush! Don't you dare quote That Play in here. You know it always brings trouble. Go out and turn round and come in again.' Ella meekly obeyed.

From the heat and excited chatter of the theatre Miranda emerged into an enchanted night. A full moon bathed Stratford in light; across Waterside the shapes of old roofs were outlined against a sky of dark pearl, the river was silver sheen and mysterious shadows of willow-tresses. The air was soft, piercingly sweet; running water had a scent of its own, and somewhere wallflowers were sending out their perfume.

Coming down to earth, Miranda looked round for Harold, who had always been there, relentlessly waiting. But he was gone, of course, back in Morden, in the family home. She was free. Among those coming out there was no sign of Ricky. Doubly free, then, to enjoy the night by herself.

Then she saw him, under the dim lamp above the stage door, smiling the half-mocking, half-charming smile of Hotspur; Godfrey, alone for once and looking only at her.

'"On such a night,"' he said. 'No, that's hackneyed. Let's just say it's beautiful.'

Shyness overcame her. She nodded silently. He saw the bloom on her moonblanched face, the dark lustre of her eyes, her pretty figure in the second-hand cotton poplin dress, damson-coloured, cut on classic lines, that Rachel had found for her in the Rother Market. While awarding her only the slightest acknowledgment in the past three weeks, he had watched her carefully, so fresh, so new, lacking the ambitious arrogance of so many would-be actresses, an Easter chick just out of the egg. *And one that adores me*, he thought wryly.

'Where's your young man tonight?' he asked her.

'Oh, he's not my young man – just Ricky's nephew.' It was almost true. 'He went back to London today with his father.'

'So, may I have the pleasure of walking you back to your digs?'

Her face answered him. He put a hand lightly under her elbow, drawing her away from the Theatre, from others who might join them.

Southern Lane was dark and quiet. Godfrey talked and Miranda answered, almost too overcome with joy at her good luck to speak at length. She might say something boring, and then he would tire of her company and leave her quickly.

'Nice warm house tonight, wasn't it.'

'Lovely. Everyone seemed happy.' Then, emboldened, she repeated the "Constance stories" Alice and Ella had told her. Her performance was very bad and she missed the point of the second one, but Godfrey, who knew them well, laughed convincingly. He gave her the shortened version of *Hamlet*, cutting from Francisco's 'Give you good night' in Act One, Scene One to Horatio's 'Good night, sweet prince, and flights of angels sing thee to thy rest', and Miranda laughed obediently. They were under the magnificent avenue of chestnuts, whose red and white candles were now in fullest flower; in a minute they would turn the corner, and he would go. She sought about in her mind for some way to keep him. At Mrs Tibbs's gate she said breathlessly, 'Would you – like to come in and have supper with us? I'm sure Mrs Tibbs wouldn't mind, she always has plenty. It's often tripe, but I think it's hot-pot tonight.' The invitation was rash, for she had no idea how Rachel, Polly or Ricky viewed Godfrey; her artless artful remarks designed to bring his name up in conversation had met with only vague responses. But he said, 'Thank you, that's awfully kind, but I wouldn't like to trouble the good lady.

Besides, I've had another idea – why don't we walk over the fields to Shottery and look at Anne Hathaway's in moonlight? The path's only just across the road there.'

'Oh *yes*! I'd like that so very much. But – oh dear, isn't it a bit late?'

'Not at all. The Gild clock hasn't struck half-ten yet.' (It had.) 'Quarter of an hour there, quarter back. You'll be home by eleven.'

She would yield, of course; she would have yielded had he suggested walking to Birmingham. The path over the stile across the meadows to the village of Shottery was moonlit, but Godfrey chivalrously held her arm, and she half-swooned with bliss at his nearness. On each side of them spread open fields, with here and there a vegetable garden or a small orchard, where white blossom shone still whiter in the moon. Godfrey could have come out with a troop of apt quotations, including the one about the silvered fruit-tree tops, but wisely he kept silent, except to sing snatches of evocative ballads every now and then. None knew better than he the power of music, or the charm of his own voice.

They reached the tiny village, with its one shop, inn and chapel, and turned up the shadowy lane to the rambling thatched house set in its Elizabethan garden, quiet and brooding now that the trippers were all gone, giving away none of its secrets.

'I wonder,' Miranda said, 'if he . . .' But Godfrey was leading her away from Anne's, into a little wood through which ran Shottery brook. They walked more slowly now, his arm round her waist; she felt he must hear and feel the beating of her heart, now that her head lay against his shoulder. The wood was a wood of Paradise, and she had no more to wish for.

But there was more. In a little clearing where last year's leaves made a rustling carpet, dappled with the shadow of the new leaves above, Godfrey gently drew her down and lay beside her, looking down at her, then bending to touch and kiss, tempt and excite. He was a past master at the game, a sport he excelled in.

And yet she was shocked and frightened when he ventured too far, and cried out, 'Don't! You're hurting!' Godfrey sighed inwardly: these virgins . . . He released her and rolled over on to his back.

Miranda was shivering from shock. Memories of those obscure lectures on Life at school came dimly back, but surely the thing the Scots doctor had been attempting to describe was to be expected only as the climax of a wedding ceremony, reception, and honeymoon journey. What place could it have in a woodland, on a night stroll? She and Editha had giggled about it as all the girls did, and speculated on how it felt, and whether it was as marvellous as it was made out to be, but the whole subject had seemed very remote from them, and they had not pursued it.

It had not been at all marvellous, but distinctly disagreeable. The person who had been her idol had changed into someone else. In every sense, she felt outraged. She said in a shaking voice, 'Why did you do that?'

Godfrey, who was sitting up lighting a cigarette, paused in surprise. 'Didn't you like it?' He was used to an enthusiastic response even from first-timers, but this one evidently needed a bit of jollying along.

'No, I didn't, and I think you should have asked first.'

'Ah well, couldn't help it – a lovely little girl like you can drive a man mad, you know, so that he forgets himself. Sorry, darling.' Gently he stroked her cheek and dropped a quick kiss on her brow. 'Come on, time we were getting back.'

Their return to Stratford was almost silent. Miranda rejected his arm, keeping as far away from him as she could. Godfrey occasionally whistled, to cover his annoyance that the pleasant little expedition had been a failure. What else had the silly little cat expected, after making eyes at him for weeks and keeping him at bay with that goggle-eyed fat boy always at her heels? He had thought her a better actress than she was, putting on those coy airs. Besides, he had done her no harm. Her squeamishness had seen to that. He quickened his steps, anxious to get rid of her as soon as possible.

At the gate he said blithely, ' 'Night, see you again.' But not if he could help it; he hoped she wouldn't go complaining to Mrs B. or anybody, spoiling his chances and getting him into trouble with Pa, who didn't at all care for that sort of thing.

Mrs Tibbs was waiting up, toothless and pigtailed. Her usual genial face was solemn. 'You're very late, Miranda. They've all gone to bed but me. You didn't ought to be out so late at your age.'

'I went for a walk.'

'Ho yes?' Sharp eyes did not miss signs of dishevelment; dead leaves, applied to a coat, are hard to dislodge, and there is a certain flush which betokens guilt or shame, or both. 'Doesn't seem to've been a very nice one, by the look of you.'

'I lost my way, Mrs Tibbs. At least I went the wrong way.'

Absent-mindedly, and trying not to catch the landlady's sharp glance, she stroked Timon, curled up on a chair. He opened one eye and gave something between a growl and a snarl, and Miranda hastily withdrew her hand.

'I shouldn't touch him, he's had a rat tonight, it fought him somethink awful. I kep him down here, or he'd have bled all over their bedclothes. Oh well, 'spect you'd like a cup of cocoa.' Mrs Tibbs had seen everything in her time, and knew that this girl probably deserved a scolding less than whoever had been with her.

In bed, thankfully, Miranda gave herself up to wild speculations. The worst part of the whole thing was that Godfrey had not said he loved her – not once. Yet he surely must, or why would he have dared . . .? It was maddening to know so little about men, but there might be those who unleashed their passions first and did their courting afterwards. It was probably quite romantic in its way, though it had not seemed at all like that at the time. Nobody as thrilling as Godfrey (had she even called him by his name yet?) could be ignoble. Her own raw ignorance had been to blame; how callow and unresponsive he must have thought her. Next time they met she would apologise, and be very understanding and grown-up, and he would say all the things she had longed to hear that night. As she slid into sleep, her sense of outrage faded; daydreams merged into real dreams, in which she and Godfrey were married at Holy Trinity by Pa in the robes of Cardinal Wolsey, and the effigies from the Clopton tombs came alive and joined the congregation, gracious and gorgeous in their Tudor dress.

A small snatch of one of the tunes Godfrey had whistled

came back to her, lilting through her half-conscious mind, and making her smile, half asleep. It was, had she but recognised it, 'A Little of What you Fancy does you Good'.

CHAPTER SIX
I call'd my love false love . . .

Two days passed, one of them a long Sunday full of the sound of bells, before Miranda saw Godfrey again. Everybody in the house was invisible until Sunday lunchtime, as was their way; even Mrs Tibbs, who had gone early to spend the day with her married niece at Wootton Wawen. No dinner would be required, since the family was invited to the home of a wealthy Stratford citizen with a taste for theatre folk. Miranda was not asked, not being family. She made herself sandwiches and took them out on a long walk to Bidford, the village where Shakespeare was said to have caught his last cold while drinking at the Falcon.

The sandwiches tasted good, as they do in the open air, eaten on a sun-warmed table-tombstone in the churchyard. The congregation had streamed out some time before; Miranda shared the peaceful place, and her sandwiches, only with a family of importunate blackbirds, shining cock-tailed parents and fluffy brown young, gaping pinkly for crumbs. It was luxury to stretch out in the sun (surely the long-gone person beneath the stone wouldn't mind) feeling the sun's heat, looking up through the boughs of a great tree to the blue, cloud-flecked May sky, knowing herself a woman now, desired, possessed, soon to be claimed.

For he would claim her. Perhaps he was thinking of her at this very moment, as he studied for the new production, *All's Well*, for which the Bensons had finally decided. He was to be the noble, haughty Bertram de Roussillon, adored by the humble physician's daughter Helena, rejecting her, yet won in the end by a woman's trick, the bed-trick of substitution, a true wife for a light-o'-love, in darkness and silence.

It was not, on reflection, the most romantic of plots, or Bertram the most admirable hero. But he was real, human, passionate, beautiful with his hawking eyes and his curls (very like Godfrey) and Helena as ardent as Miranda herself. She had read the play over and over and knew a lot of Helena's part already. Suppose Mabel Delaville, who had come from London to play Helena, were to be taken suddenly ill? A desperate situation, no understudy, F.R. about to cancel the first night, Godfrey helpless; then she, Miranda, the unknown, would step forward modestly to announce that she knew the part perfectly. Surprise, joy, the day and the play saved, herself an instant success, hand-in-hand with Godfrey for the curtain calls.

Children began to gather in the churchyard for Sunday school, looking curiously at the bold young lady lounging on a tomb. Hastily Miranda slid off it and pretended to read the lichened inscription. It was time to take herself off, back over the ancient buttressed bridge to the quiet lanes that led back to Stratford; dreaming, every step of the way, of what had happened and what was to happen. Perhaps Anne Hathaway and her Will had walked those very lanes, dreaming too; perhaps they had known that little wood where the brook flowed, Will's mind a-throng with midsummer fairies and Anne's beauty. The memory of what had happened there to herself was rapidly misting over, the ugly embarrassing details veiled.

That Monday morning Miranda should have attended a dancing class held in a small rehearsal room at the theatre. She hovered near the door, hearing the high precise tones of a local dancing teacher instructing students. Then, furtively, she moved away and darted across the road to the Duck, where a very few early drinkers watched her from their benches under the fig tree. In the back room voices could be heard, F.R. using high blustering tones for the coward Parolles, Constance dignified and mellow as the Countess, Mabel Delaville fluting for Helena. Miranda pushed open the door a crack. Godfrey was leaning against a wall, gracefully, negligently, in the attitude of Nicholas Hilliard's poetic 'Young Man among Roses', one long elegant hand holding the script to his breast, while he soundlessly murmured his next lines.

She sidled in and slipped into a corner, crouched on a stool half-hidden by a hanging coat. Nobody would mind her being there. It was Benson's strongly-held belief that acting was learned by observation; watch me long enough, then go thou and do likewise. The scene broke off, F.R. commented, Delaville made pretty apologetic faces and obedient noises. They went back: 'Save you, fair queen! And you, monarch.' Miranda mentally spoke every line, proud of being a little ahead of Delaville, always conscious of Godfrey's presence and least movement.

Then he saw her. The faint smile he had worn, watching dark brilliant Delaville, part Frenchwoman, part English Jewess, flicked off, to be replaced by something else; displeasure, hauteur, the very look of Bertram. 'A poor physician's daughter my wife! disdain rather corrupt me ever.' Miranda blushed and smiled, but met no answering warmth. For a second she wondered whether he were short-sighted and had mistaken her for someone else. Impossible, short sight always betrayed itself on stage. Disturbed, puzzled, she sat out the scene, then slipped away, back to the dancing lesson, where they were thumping and jumping in a *coranto*.

Their next meeting was not so much contrived as fortuitous. Shopping in Sheep Street, she saw him across the road talking with old Andrew Durant, who played kings, dukes and venerable courtiers. A bag of buns in her hand, she lurked in the bakery doorway until they parted; then was over to the other side like a lightning-streak, a step or so behind him on the downward slope towards Waterside.

'Godfrey! Wait for me.'

He turned sharply, his face suddenly blank and cold.

'Ah, Miranda. Sorry, must rush.'

'I'm going to rehearsal – aren't you?'

'Oh. No, got to see about something.' In a flash he had turned into a haberdasher's, shutting the door behind him. Miranda stared for a moment at ties, socks, tapes, buttons and handkerchieves. To follow him in would be too brash. Reluctantly she moved on, troubled, glancing back in the hope that he would emerge and hurry after her, mercifully unaware that he was watching her retreating back from a corner of the shop window.

After that she kept out of his way, giving him time for whatever mood was on him to pass, and earning herself a rare reproof from F.R. for muddling up letters to two correspondents and offering each the other's salary, the salaries being so glaringly different that even he noticed. At night she sat through the entire Folio version of *Hamlet*, a stock Benson production which F.R.'s slow enunciation and melancholy reading justified the irreverent description 'Hamlet in its Eternity'. Godfrey's Laertes was not exciting, though he fought the duel well, as he needed to, with so athletic a Hamlet. To watch him was a painful pleasure; Miranda was glad when all the principal characters were dead and it was time to go home.

She confronted Godfrey at last in the cobbled yard of the Windmill inn. F.R. had suddenly gone off on one of his trips to London, without explanation and in the cheerful confidence that everything would go on without him exactly as it should; which it did, with the exception that hard-worked and hungry actors allowed themselves something nearer to the usual idea of lunch than a ham-roll eaten in a corner. So, passing the entrance to the Windmill's inn-yard, Miranda saw Godfrey standing in the sunlight, a mug of ale in one hand and a piece of bread and cheese in the other, laughing. Alice Bengough was with him, and a pretty dark girl who had just joined the company. She was wearing a sort of gipsy or peasant dress, patterned skirt and gold blouse embroidered with beads, and a red satin ribbon round her head. Godfrey, looking down into her eyes, said something outrageous, at which both girls shrieked with laughter and Alice playfully struck him.

Miranda, after a second of hesitation, joined them. The white doves which haunted the Windmill flew up in the air with a rush, as they did at any new entrance. None of the three seemed particularly pleased to see Miranda, who hovered on the edge of the group, unwanted and uncomfortable but determined to speak to Godfrey alone. At last Alice said, with a malicious note in her voice, 'Come on, Rosa. Three's company, four's none – or is it the other way round?' They vanished, chattering, into the bar parlour.

Miranda said in a rush, 'I wanted to speak to you.'

'You made it fairly obvious.'

'Well. I thought I ought to tell you – it was all right.'

'*What* was all right?'

'I mean, I didn't really mind. I wasn't really cross, it was just

82

– you startled me.'

'My dear girl, what in Heaven's name are you talking about?' Godfrey's tone was wearily patient, his eyes roving wistfully toward the street. But if he made a bolt for it she'd follow him.

'The other night.' Miranda could not look at him. She said to the cobbles, 'You must have thought me very silly. I do understand now. So can we – well, start again?' As she said it she knew the words were all wrong, but she trusted to Godfrey to understand and help her out.

And he, quite appalled, was temporarily stricken silent. The awful truth dawned on him that she had taken seriously his casual little adventure with her, quite meaningless to him except as a brief pleasure, another notch on the stick. Now there would be tears, reproaches, a public scene – perhaps a series of them; his luck with women had run out. At a window he glimpsed the dark pretty face of Rosa, marked down for his next conquest, and he guessed that she and Alice were thoroughly enjoying the scene. He thrashed around for what to do. Whether he were sweetly understanding or uncompromisingly brutal, the result would be the same, he was sure. He decided on brutality.

'I don't know what you've got into your head, Miranda, but I hope it's nothing too serious?'

'Well. I thought . . . you wanted us to be engaged.'

He laughed, genuinely amused at last. '*Engaged?* My dear, stupid child, hasn't anyone told you I'm married? I've got a perfectly charming, beautiful wife, and I intend to stick to her. She's up north touring at the moment, so you needn't think of running to her with any tale. You're not used to the theatre and its ways, my dear, and it's about time you grew up. You'll have to learn to accept flirtation for what it is – just that. Right? No hard feelings?'

Miranda said nothing. A qualm of self-reproach touched Godfrey, but he was too embarrassed and annoyed to try to smooth over the hurt he had given. He turned and vanished into the bar. In the yard, the doves returned one by one, to pick about the cobbles for scraps of food. On a deal table lay the remains of the bread and cheese Godfrey had been eating before her arrival interrupted him. Mechanically she picked it up and scattered it for the doves, who flocked round her feet. It was something to be approved of, even by birds, in a world suddenly full of cruelty and rejection.

It was true, then, that at such times one's heart was literally heavy, weighed down with lead like a drowned sailor, in some fathomless pit. She lay on the narrow bed in her tower room, from which all romance had gone. The Warwickshire land-scape beyond the roofs out there was only a reminder of what the footpath to Shottery had led to, and the long, dreaming Sunday walk from which she had returned over Borden Hill. Nothing was left of illusion and beauty. The house was utterly quiet; a deathly hush. Miranda had let herself in soundlessly, had reached her room without seeing a soul except the boy, mending a chair out in the yard.

Nothing had ever been so bad before, even with Grand-mother at her worst. To have got away from Chamberlain Road – for this! Her mind travelled over and over the folly, the humiliation, the pain of it all, trying to extract some measure of comfort and finding none. If only she had had more sense, had never let him charm her on that enchanted river journey, had resisted the invitation to that late walk, had known what would happen in the woodland . . .

And, thinking over that experience, a cold horror crept upon her. It was unthinkable, yet she must think of it. One dreadful picture after another flashed through her mind. It was too much to bear alone. She left the bed where she had lain for almost three hours, and went downstairs. If they were all there, she would still have to tell them. No, not Ricky. The withering sarcasm he would bring to the news would be a public execution.

But only Rachel was there in the parlour, sitting at a table covered with cut-out cloth and sewing materials. She made all her own clothes, from the cheap materials which were all she could afford from the little money that had come to her from her mother's estate. The lilac blouse which she was now trimming with lace would have cost many shillings less than in a shop, yet would charm the eye like its wearer. She looked up from the intricate pin-tucking of a sleeve as Miranda entered the room.

'Well, how nice! Company. Come and talk to me.' She patted

84

the chair by her side. In the grate a cheerful small fire burned, for Rachel loved warmth, as did Timon, curled up before it like a large, mangy muff. Then Rachel took in the tragedy-face.

'Good God, what's the matter, child?'

Miranda dropped into the chair and began to cry with loud abandon. Rachel let her weep until the worst was spent, then said quietly, 'All right. Now tell me all about it.'

Miranda told. At the end of the sorry recital she said, 'And now I'll have a baby, won't I.'

'Just tell me again what happened. All the details. No need to blush, I've heard it all before. Only I must know exactly, you see.'

Miranda did blush, painfully, but managed to explain to Rachel's satisfaction. She nodded. 'I see. And that's all?'

'*All*?'

'Yes, all. It is? Good, then. You can mop yourself up and stop worrying, because you haven't lost your virtue, only your dignity. You see, men . . . dear me, how can I put it for your delicate young ears? They don't risk awful consequences, if they're experienced, as experienced as Godfrey Arnold is.'

'Experienced? I know now he's *married* . . .'

Rachel laughed. 'Marriage, darling, has nothing to do with it. You ask nine out of ten girls in the company, and if they're honest they'll tell you they've been for walks with Godfrey Arnold, too. Don't look so shocked – it's not half as shocking as if you'd been pounced on by a real villain, the sort that doesn't care. Godfrey's a terrible one for the girls, but he's not bad – just selfish and thoughtless.'

'Oh. But Rachel, why didn't you warn me? You or Polly, or somebody?'

'Because there was nothing serious to warn you about, love. We knew you were as green as grass, but you had to take your chance and learn. Nobody's ever going to warn you about the nasty things that happen to you in this life.'

'Even you?'

'Especially me – and Polly. We were stage-struck from the time we could walk, and oh, my dear, the situations we got ourselves in, I can't tell you. We fell in love all the time with the most unsuitable people. It's glamour, star-dust in the eyes – you can't see properly for it. Next time it happens to you, blink hard, and you'll find it'll go away.'

Miranda wanted very much to ask where Ricky and Edward fitted into this philosophy. Had they been figures of glamour to the sisters, transformed by hard blinking into solid earthy men?

'I don't see how I can go on here,' she said, brooding, 'after I've made such a fool of myself. Those girls know, Alice and what's-her-name, Rosa Something. I expect they've told everybody by now.'

'Rubbish, of course they haven't. They had a giggle over it, no doubt, and Godfrey's made capital out of showing them what a feller-me-lad he is, and that'll be the end of it. This is a family company, you know, and families don't crucify each other, or shouldn't.'

Miranda was still contemplating disaster. 'Suppose somebody tells Mr Benson?'

'They won't, and if they did, all that would come of it would be a severe wigging. He isn't called Pa for nothing, you know. Come on, child, do you want to stay here for the rest of your twenty weeks or don't you?'

'Well . . . yes.'

'All right, then. Go and wash your face, ask Tibby to put the kettle on, and while it's boiling slip down to Winter's and get me two more reels of this turquoise cotton, will you? There's a good girl.' Suddenly, Rachel swept aside her sewing, and picked up the sleeping Timon from the rug and held him to her breast. On her face was the maternal, Madonna-like expression with which she sometimes looked at Ricky. As she hugged the cat a flea hopped from his fur to the cream of her skirt, and he gave himself a hasty scratch with a back leg, drawing back his lip to show one yellowed tooth as he did so.

Miranda, running to the draper's, reflected that she had perhaps just learned something about the nature of love, though she would have been hard put to it to say just what it was.

The shining days of May gave way to high summer. Rachel's prophecy came true – Godfrey pointedly avoided Miranda's company, and when on stage together each behaved as though the other were invisible. Miranda's vanity was too bruised to

86

let her seek consolation from anyone else. Perhaps they were all the same, and it was not worth risking further disillusion. Only one pursued her, a very young and raw recruit just down from Cambridge. Walter Bean, weedy and unalluring, hung round her and haunted her as Harold had done, waylaid her into teashops and poured out the story of his life, which included a stepfather who disapproved violently of Walter's disinclination for the law and passion for the stage. Miranda took his seeming devotion to her not at all seriously; she heard plenty of life-stories. She spent more and more time in the office and less in the theatre.

For instinct told her that she was not cut out to be an actress. She had not yet been promoted from a Pudding to an Earwig, had not spoken a line on the stage, and had, to her own surprise, no real wish to speak one. The time was coming when she must either finish her twenty weeks' course, or leave. But leave for what way of life? She brought the problem to the parlour at Alcester Place, where everything that needed talking out was talked out after supper, over a huge brown teapot inscribed with the invitation, 'Du 'ee zit down an' 'ave a cup o' tay'. The room, fireless for once, was full of the warm scent of lavender, which Polly was preparing to lay among bedlinen for the winter. Miranda was aware of the objects on the walls, beloved of Mrs Tibbs and not rejected by her lodgers: a large photograph of a wistful-eyed young man in uniform, her nephew Ernest killed at Mafeking years ago, a sampler quoting painfully in bad stitchery the praises of My Mother ('Who ran to catch me when I fell, and kissed the place to make it well? My Mother'), a woolwork picture some day to be a collectable antique, showing a red and white young woman draped round a cross against a green background – 'She's a bride and something's 'appened' was Mrs Tibbs's explanation. On the sideboard, flanking a china parrot startlingly coloured, a Dresden-inspired shepherd and shepherdess who could never have been mistaken for the real thing, their clothing covered with raised gold dots, a glass bell over each of them through which they must eternally yearn at each other, until some careless hand shattered the glass. It was all stuffy and in bad taste and old-fashioned and sweet and cosy and a haven such as Miranda had never known before.

'I don't think I ought to go on, you see,' she said. 'I haven't the talent. If I had, they'd have made me an Earwig by now.'

'No, you haven't,' Ricky said gruffly from behind his ale-glass. 'That sticks out a mile.'

'Darling!' reproachfully from Rachel. 'He doesn't quite mean that, Miranda dear –'

'Yes, he does,' Ricky said.

'I think you're right.' Miranda met his cold gaze, neither liking nor disliking him, aware that he resented her as he would any intruder into the circle that he jealously prized as his own, though he had no legal right to it. 'I know I'll never make an actress. I suppose I could hang on. I've got enough left to pay Mrs Tibbs for another fortnight, as Mrs Benson kindly let me off half of my £25 for helping out in the office. Then I should get a salary for touring, but the question is, am I worth it?'

'"O wise young judge!"' Polly observed, a length of lilac ribbon between her teeth, ready for winding among the lavender stems.

'Not really wise at all, not a bit. But I have to think about it, because I can't go back to – to Birmingham.'

'Are you sure, dear?' Polly was ever ready to believe the best of anyone. 'Surely time will have softened your grandmother up a bit?'

'No, it won't. When Editha came down last Saturday she said she'd met Grandmother in a shop and asked her, sort of innocently, if she'd heard from me, and Grandmother walked straight out without waiting to be served. She would – I can just see her.'

'Oh dear. How peculiar people can be.'

Ricky lit one of the cheap cigarettes whose pungent smoke fought with Rachel's delicate perfume, and won. 'Talk to F.R.B. Ask him. He'll tell you.'

Rachel leaned across and kissed him. 'How clever you are, darling. Of course that's the best thing.'

Benson listened, in quiet stillness, as Miranda outlined her doubts. His grave, visionary eyes seemed to look at something far away, but she knew he gave her his full attention. He had not said, when she humbly asked if she might speak to him, 'My leisure serves me, pensive daughter, now,' but she knew she would get as attentive a hearing from him as Juliet from

Friar Laurence (and better advice, considering what came of the Potion plan). When she paused, running out of words, he said abruptly, 'Do you lose yourself?'

'Lose myself?'

'Forget yourself utterly in the play, in the part.'

'I haven't exactly *had* a part yet, Mr Benson, only walk-ons, and it's not easy . . .'

He waved a long, muscular hand. 'No matter, no matter. Whether you are representing Eighteenth Citizen or some other nameless personage, that personage should be the whole of your life, until you are off. You should be all-absorbed, so that if a telegram were to be handed to you containing the news that your house had been burnt down you would merely scan it and throw it away. Act from the spirit, from the heart; act for Shakespeare! He has suffered so much, you know.' He leant forward, all earnestness. 'Butchered in the schools, anatomised by the pedants, made a mockery by those who thought they knew better.' He discoursed at length of the happy endings given to *Lear* and *Romeo* ('She lives! she lives! and we may still be blessed'), the pranks of against-the-text enthusiasts in search of something novel: 'Thersites cast as a woman – can you imagine what *he* would say to such language from feminine lips? And yet it has been done.' A vast melancholy clouded Benson's Roman features. 'I would like to lay a wager with you that the time will come when we shall see boys once more playing women's parts, because, forsooth, it was so in his time – as though he would not have rejoiced to see true women as his Rosalind, Imogen, Cleopatra – you remember how she feared to see "some squeaking Cleopatra *boy* my greatness, I' the posture of a whore"? No, no, if he were with us today he would seize joyfully on all we can give him, lifelike sets, properties, costumes, gas-lighting . . . we who hold the mirror up to nature, here where Avon sings to the stars the Song of Shakespeare; we happy few, we band of brothers . . .'

Like one awaking from a dream, he blinked and shook himself slightly. Miranda wondered whether he thought he had been addressing her or a public meeting; she would like to have applauded, but instead said, timidly, 'I should love to act for Shakespeare, sir, indeed I should. But I don't think he would care for me at all.'

The strange eyes widened, then he laughed, a ringing laugh that might have been heard across a county cricket ground. 'So, you don't think he'd care for you. Then you must be content to be a candle-holder and look on.'

Miranda started. 'How did you know I thought of it like that?'

'As I know many things, by *his* light, my dear.' She was conscious that for once he was looking at her, studying her face, not some remote prospect, so keenly that she wondered whether she had suddenly come out in a rash or turned a curious colour. Nervously she asked him if anything were the matter.

'Nothing, nothing at all. Just a fancy. What did you say your name was?'

'Miranda Heriot.' (And really, Mr Benson, you ought to know that, after all this time, she added mentally. But he was known for remembering faces and not names.) 'Mr Benson, please tell me what you were thinking – I'm sure it was something interesting.'

'Of thee, my dear one, thee, my daughter, who
Art ignorant of what thou art . . . he said.

'Well, perhaps you should leave us, though we shall be sorry to lose you,' he said politely, giving her his delightful smile. 'If one has not the theatre in one's blood – '

'But I have,' she said hastily, anxious to justify that laughing young man in the long-ago sunshine, 'my father was an – an actor and a musician.'

In time to come she wondered often what would have been said if the conversation had been allowed to continue. But at that moment Benson's valet put his spherical face, adorned with flourishing handlebar moustachios, round the door, requesting a word, and she quietly slid away.

So that was settled, she must leave the company, and go – where?

It was Polly Porter who supplied the answer, beaming with pride. 'I've been thinking, love, and we've all talked it over, and we're sure we're right. When the season's over you must come back to London and live with us. Ricky and Rachel will be touring, there'll be just me and Edward and Harold. You can get a job to use your typing and shorthand, which will cover what you pay me for your room and something to live on besides. Everybody will be so pleased, especially Harold, poor boy. There! Isn't that a good idea?'

Miranda waited for a few words from the Bard to round off the proposal, but for once there were none.

'Yes,' she said, 'I think it is, Polly.'

CHAPTER SEVEN
Sergeant Death

Harold Porter rearranged the knife, fork and spoon more to his liking. They were special ones, chosen for Miranda's use from the others in his mother's cutlery drawer as being rather shinier than the rest. He had tried cleaning them with silver polish, but it had left such a strong odour behind that he had hurriedly washed them in hot water. He stood back to admire his work.

The table was laid for high tea, as well as Harold could lay it. Not all the cup-handles pointed the same way, he had not been able to find the best sugar-bowl, so had substituted a basin from the kitchen; the tablecloth was one of his mother's best, put aside regretfully as being too stained by years of tea-spillings to be presentable. But Harold had unearthed it from a top drawer and proudly laid it out. It had a beautiful lace border.

In the middle of the table, bravely peering over the objects around it, was a bunch of marigolds from the small back garden, crammed into a narrow silver vase which Harold had painstakingly polished (after all, nobody would have to drink out of it). He was annoyed to see that a number of small black insects were crawling over the flowers. Hastily he removed the vase and threw the marigolds away. Ideally they would have been a spray of exquisite roses, tied with ribbon, at the side of his lady's plate. There was nothing wrong with Harold's sense of romance; it was just that no roses grew in the back garden.

The kettle had been simmering for an hour and a half, though she – they – could not possibly arrive until at least four o'clock. Twice he had put more water in it, several times looked under the milk-jug cover of net fringed with beads, to make sure that nothing was floating in the milk – a fly, for instance. No, all was well. The butter had liquefied slightly – he took it into the kitchen and ran cold water over it, giving it a curious dew-pearled look perhaps not quite right for butter. Nervously he dabbed it with a tea-cloth, then washed his hands yet again. How considerate it had been of his father to stay out of his way, in the little room at the back of the house that was called his den, and was so full of books, papers, pipes, ash-trays, and other objects personal to Edward that no duster nor sweeper could get near it; not that Polly had ever urged them on him.

Harold entered the den.

'What time is it, Dad?'

'Same as your watch says, I expect.'

His son consulted the School Boy's Keyless nickel watch which he earnestly hoped to have replaced by something more sophisticated and flashier when he reached his eighteenth birthday. 'It loses a lot,' he said hopefully.

'The time,' Edward said, looking at the large silver turnip fettered to his watchchain, 'is precisely three forty-six and twenty-seven seconds. I could do with a cup of tea. I suppose there isn't . . .?'

Harold sighed. 'If I make it now it'll be cold when they get here. There's a little silver pot in Auntie's room, though, if you *very* much want one.'

'Oh no. No, no, no, no, no. I can very well wait.' He returned to the contemplation of a large stuffed carp in a glass case on the wall. At that moment a bright rat-tat on the knocker was followed by the sound of a key turning. 'There you are,' Edward said, 'they're here. Now I shall get my tea.' Harold's face turned a hot pink, so hot that his spectacles misted up. He snatched them off, wiped them, jammed them back and rushed out of the den. At the dining-room door he paused, quickly surveyed the table, ran in and gave the cloth a quick tweak, straightened his tie, gulping, and appeared in the hall as his mother and Miranda came through the door. Thus were completed Harold Porter's rites and ceremonies for the welcoming of his love.

'Phew, what a journey. Home at last, though,' Polly said, bestowing a peck on Harold's cheek. 'Hours and hours of sitting in Sunday trains and then we had to wait for ages for the tube, hadn't we, Miranda.' She pulled the pins out of her hat, flung off her coat, and in less than a minute had reduced the narrow lobby to a state of chaos, talking all the time. Harold heard without listening, his eyes on Miranda. In the weeks since he had seen her she seemed to have grown more fascinating. She wore a dust-coat he had not seen before, ground-length and sweeping, of a dusky pink that made her look interestingly pale. There were smudges on her cheeks and her gloves were dirty. Harold longed to put his arm round her and say in his gruffest voice, 'There, there, little girl, I'll look after you now.' Instead he said, at the wrong end of the register, 'Hello,' and got a tired smile as reward.

'Now then,' Polly said, 'get our bags upstairs, there's a good boy – the trunk's coming c.o.d. from the station. You come with me, Miranda, and we'll both have a really good wash and change.' Harold murmured that tea would be ready any time, but was brushed aside. 'We'll be down with all convenient speed, dear, just be patient.'

The room Miranda had been given was the one used by Rachel and Ricky as a sitting-room, next to their bedroom. In contrast with the shabby, happy-go-lucky appearance of the rest of the house, which was very like a Metropolitan Pandarus, the room had charm and taste. Furnished in shades of grey and soft blue-green, its walls bore a few good prints and some costume designs, one with the face of Ricky as a young man. Photographs of him filled all the other spaces. On the mantelpiece a single porcelain figure stood, an Italian Madonna serenely smiling. The divan bed was scattered with satin cushions. It was a room of peace and beauty, a refuge.

The bedroom next door also breathed of Rachel in its pretty drapes and furnishings. Over the brass bed, inset with a mother-of-pearl medallion, Raphael's roguish cherubs gazed pensively out from the edge of Heaven. A trouser-press, a wig-stand and a faint hangover from the smoke of many Woodbines evoked Ricky, as did a battered cat-basket the absent Timon. Most welcome of all to Miranda was a small, plumbed-in washbasin.

She sluiced the grime from her face and body; there was plenty of it. The departure from Stratford had been lowering to her spirits. The company had left, packed into labelled carriages, excited, laughing, bound for new theatres, new adventures, F.R. running up and down the platform, hair streaming, long legs going like pistons, Constance enthroned on a hand-cart piled with luggage. If Godfrey noticed Miranda slinking, as she thought of it, behind a notice-board, he gave no sign. He was in the middle of a bunch of colourful, expensively-dressed young women, none of whom Miranda had ever seen before. Even Walter seemed not to see her. At length they all piled in, heads crowded at the window, waving, smiling and shouting to well-wishers on the crowded platform, as the train began to chug and clank on its way to Birmingham. By nightfall they would be in the north, almost at the end of England. Miranda watched the tail of the train disappear, utterly forlorn and depressed. She had let them go without her, when, with a little contriving, she could have stayed with them. Even before their going she had been forgotten; soon they wouldn't even remember her name.

Polly, immersed in magazines, seemed not to notice her companion's dejection as Warwickshire was left behind, or perhaps she knew better than to comment. The passing landscape grew flatter and duller. Here was Oxford, its lovely spires clustered. Entering the Home Counties the train passed village after village, sunk in Sunday sloth, a few gardeners raising their heads to watch it go by, cows or sheep running frightened from the noise. Then they too disappeared, lost behind the frontiers of London, a sprawl of new buildings and engineering works arrested for the Sabbath. The skies grew heavy with smoke, patches of green became fewer and fewer, houses taller and dirtier; it was nothing like Birmingham, or anywhere else. Miranda reflected, on first glance, that whoever had called London the 'Floure of Cities all' had needed stronger spectacles.

'Well, here we are,' said Polly, suddenly shutting her magazine and busying herself with luggage, 'Paddington.'

In fact, the platforms and arches of the Great Western Station were all Miranda was to see of London that day. They were swept along in what seemed to a provincial girl a great crowd of people, though it was a mere scattering, all walking very fast, down stone stairs into a brilliantly-lit underground passage where people stood and waited, patiently, gazing at huge hoardings, until a glittering electric monster rushed out of the tunnel, paused to collect them in its maw and tore off again

95

at its frantic rate.

Miranda was enthralled by the speed, the brightness, the exotic air which smelt like burning brown paper, and which Polly said was caused by sulphur. On rattled the train to a station where they had to get out and change, hung about with their luggage like pack-mules. As they subsided in the Northern Line carriage which was to be their last conveyance that day, Miranda realised that she was tireder, dirtier and hotter than she had ever been in her life, yet tingling inwardly with the excitement of being in London. It was a new beginning to life, the homely house in Erasmus Avenue, Morden, as Stratford had been. Perhaps life was full of new beginnings.

When she came downstairs Harold was hovering, anxious for his preparations to be a success. Polly surveyed the table, so meticulously laid, the boiled eggs in their little knitted jackets, the best tea-cosy dotted all over with bright woollen flowers, the pink ham laid out in neat slices, the thick chunks of bread and butter, the shop-bought Madeira cake.

'Very nice, dear, you *have* been busy. We're absolutely starving – I wish I'd let Tibby do sandwiches for us, but she'd so much work with getting Rachie and Ricky off and Timon being so naughty about going into his basket . . . oh dear, I do miss him. Do you suppose he'll be all right in the Newcastle digs, Ted? They've not stayed there before, and you know what landladies can be like.'

'I should think so – he's used to all sorts.' (Yes, but are they? Miranda wondered.)

'Women always like bad lots,' said Harold. 'Look at Bill Sikes.'

Polly poured the tea. 'Come on, Miranda, be as ourselves in Denmark. Let good digestion . . . good gracious, no, what am I saying? Such a pity that play's full of splendid things. Pass the salt, dear.'

Harold, while eating as heartily as he always did, managed at the same time to watch Miranda with untiring devotion. The eyes it shone from may have resembled gooseberries, but the devotion was very welcome to a heart still sore. She smiled at him, her warmest smile.

'It's a lovely tea, Harold. Thank you.'

His face was a study in embarrassment and rapture.

The days that followed were pure holiday. Breakfast was taken in bed, from a tray brought by Mattie, the cook-general who was the Porters' only servant, a cheerfully impassive Cockney for whom nothing was too much trouble. The Porters provided her not only with a livelihood but with endless entertainment. She lived round the corner, arrived in time to get Edward and Harold off to school, and departed after tea. Only on Sundays was she absent. With Mattie about the house, there was no washing-up, tidying, dusting, food preparation or cooking: Polly lived a lady's life, and Miranda shared it, for, Mattie said, with her theatricals out of the way there wasn't enough to do about the place to pass a person's time. Her wages were twenty pounds a year, on which she managed to dress more smartly than her mistress, even to an orange-dyed feather boa and a motoring veil, which she affected on windy days though she had never been in a motor-car in her life.

Polly said that Miranda must take a week to do nothing but discover London; not that it was enough, or anything like, but it was as much as a foreign tourist would get, and with an experienced guide she could see a lot in the time. The experienced guide was Polly herself, briskly indefatigable, and what her companion saw most of was the London theatre in all its aspects. They paid swift visits to the National Gallery, the Tower, and Madame Tussaud's, but every day, after a quick cheap lunch at an A.B.C. or Lyons' teashop, they were to be found perched uncomfortably on rickety collapsible stools ranged in twos under the lee of a theatre.

There might be an hour to wait after lunch, or more, but there was no danger of boredom. The entertainments outside were continuous and varied. If it was not the one-man band, operating drum, cymbals and concertina, it was the hurdy-gurdy with a miserable, flea-ridden monkey in a red coat ringing a bell on top of it, or the lugubrious trio of two blind men and a sighted woman, who took the money; or the felt-hat manipulator who transformed himself comically from Napoleon to a Westminster dustman and from that to Nelson. The fire-eater and the escapologist each demanded their money before the performance, the man who cut skeletons out of lengths of newspaper was gloomy enough to have chosen that profession, of all others.

At first Miranda felt bound to give each performer a penny, whether the turn was enjoyable or not. But Polly said, 'Kind of you, dear, but you'll break the bank if you go on like that. Just smile, or look the other way.' Uncomfortably aware that any pocket-money she spent was provided by Polly, Miranda obeyed, though it was hard, particularly in the case of the monkey and the blind men. It would have been pleasanter to sit and gaze at the passers-by, entertainments in themselves, these Londoners, so rich and so poor, so swift-footed and pushing, so much at home in their huge noisy city, unafraid of hoof or wheel, conscious of their heritage of London, with a special look about them. Even the man with no legs who danced a jig on his hands for the benefit of the playgoers had it, as much as the grand lady in furs who stepped out of her carriage at the front of the theatre, proudly aware of the gallery queue's eyes on her and her liveried footman.

'They're so different,' Miranda said. 'Not like people in Birmingham, at all. I think – yes, I do believe they frighten me a bit.'

'You'll get used to them. We did, Rachel and I, and we came from a village near York where everybody was Quaker and worked in a chocolate factory. You can't be much more un-Londonish than that.'

Polly was faintly disappointed in her protégée's reaction to London theatre fare. It was the Silly Season, so all that fare was light, musical comedy about a Girl from Nowhere, a burlesque on the story of Pygmalion and Galatea, a high society play featuring a nobleman suspected of some mysterious crime and his remarkably silly young wife who believed everything people told her, however unlikely. Miranda laughed politely in the right places, but not heartily, and Polly's instincts told her that no magic was getting across from the stage to a mind that had been so eagerly receptive at Stratford. True, *The Girl from Nowhere* wasn't Shakespeare, but to Polly just being in a theatre was better than anything else in life, and she assumed that all right-thinking people felt the same.

The subject came up as they sat over tea and scones in that Lyons' Corner House which allowed the customer a fascinating view of Soho and Rupert Street in particular. Polly said wistfully, 'I do hope you're enjoying it all. There isn't anything else you'd rather do, is there? Museums and art-galleries, and things?'

Yes, Miranda thought, there's Kew Gardens and the Zoo and the river-steamers. She replied no, of course there wasn't, and it was very kind of Polly to take her to so many shows.

'But it isn't like Stratford?'

'Well . . .'

'No, of course it isn't. You probably haven't got the taste for theatre, pure theatre yet. After all, it was a closed book to you until this summer – how dreadful! But it will probably come.'

'Oh, I'm sure it will. It must, because . . .' Suddenly, without meaning to, Miranda began to tell Polly the history of her mother and father and the reason for her own restrictive bringing-up. As she told it, she felt a burden slipping away from her. It was like letting daylight into a nightmare, and she wondered, even as she talked, why she had not let Polly into the secret before. There was no reason why it should be a secret; she was not ashamed of being illegitimate, after all, only of her grandparents' cruelty.

Polly's round face, that lent itself so readily to beaming smiles, grew as grim as it ever could. When Miranda finished the story she broke out, 'I never heard anything so shocking. The woman must be more than wicked – mad. Or there was more to it . . . Could it have been some sort of revenge – Lear in reverse? "How sharper than a serpent's tooth it is to have a thankless child." Could your mother have been thankless, in some way?'

'I can't imagine her or anyone having much to thank Grandmother for, so perhaps she was. But even that wouldn't be enough to make Grandmother act so cruelly.'

' "Dead to me",' said Polly thoughtfully. 'That was how parents in the old melodramas put it. Erring daughters were dead, as far as they were concerned.'

'Only my mother was really dead . . . I wonder why they even bothered to take me? I should have thought I'd have been looked on as the Fruit of Shame.'

'You were to be brought up in the way you should go, the way your mother didn't go. Oh dear! What a horrible story. I don't think I can eat another scone now. What did you say about the inscription in the Bible?' Miranda repeated it.

'"Concubine of Frank Forbes . . ." Why concubine? It's a nasty word anyway, but why didn't he marry her? I shall find out.' Polly's spectacles flashed determination. 'It was a long time ago, but someone will know. Ricky has friends who work the concert parties. A lot of those pierrots and minstrels come to nothing, but some get into the music hall – there's dear old Jimmy Pleasants, he's about Ricky's age, which would make him, let me see, about twenty-five when you were born. No idea where he is now, but Ricky may know. I'll write to him tonight, my dear, I promise.'

'Thank you, Polly. I should have tried to find out for myself, but I didn't know where to start.'

'Better leave it to me. It seems to me a great wrong's been done, and I want to redress it, for the sake of you and those poor young things – for never was a story of more woe, than this of Juliet and her Romeo. It's my belief,' said Polly as they collected their gloves, handbags and theatre programmes, and she searched for two pennies to leave under the plate, 'that the whole shocking thing comes from people belonging to these ridiculous sects that call themselves Christian and aren't. I was brought up a Quaker, of course, and I suppose the Friends were once thought of as something very out of the way, but my dear parents were extremely broad-minded and quite understood when I took myself off to the Church of England because it was so much – well, prettier. The tongue of Shakespeare, beautiful old choral tunes, and no rubbish. Where in the Bible, I should like to know, does one read of Our Lord being forbidden to go to the theatre? His mother would never have done that; I've always thought of her as a very sensible woman, keeping out of the way as she did and asking him to perform a really practical miracle when the wine ran out at Cana . . .'

Miranda reflected that the rights and wrongs of theatre attendance were unlikely to have arisen in Nazareth, unless King Herod had brought a touring company with him from Rome. But Polly's burning enthusiasm was infectious. She was glad to have told the story, excited at the thought that at last some sort of justice might be done for Grace and Frank.

Harold was deeply envious of his mother's freedom to show Miranda the sights. School would not end for another week. For the first time in his conformist life he toyed with the idea of playing hookey. But it would never do, for the son of a master. 'As soon as we break up,' he told Miranda, 'I'll take you to all the places you ought to see. Crystal Palace – Windsor – Hampton Court – the Oval – the Science Museum . . . We'll have a really ripping time, you'll see.'

'Harold, dear,' said his mother, 'don't build too many castles in the air. Miranda will have to get a job, you know. I've spoken to Mr Knight, the solicitor in Morden Hall Road, and he's hoping to find some secretarial work for you, dear. It's a splendid place to be, right opposite Morden Hall and the park, and there's an old gardener who swears he remembers Nelson visiting the Hall and giving him sixpence when he was quite a boy, though he'd have to be Methuselah for that to be quite true.'

But there was to be no ripping time, no legal work, no reminiscences of Nelson. On the Saturday morning a letter addressed in Editha's large pale blue script was on Miranda's breakfast tray. 'My word, you've got friends that write nice,' Mattie commented. 'I wish I'd been learnt proper, but I never got no further than A for apple, B for bat, D for dog and C for cat. Good news, is it?'

Miranda looked up from the letter, frowning. 'Not exactly good Mattie. I'll tell you later.'

Dear old girl, not just a letter for fun, though I've got lots to tell you, chiefly this marvellous Scottish boy who came to Amanda's tennis party last week and invited me to his twenty-first next year – they live in a castle, imagine it, such splendour! He really is very sweet. But what I wanted to say was that Mummy heard, in a sort of roundabout way from one of the servants, that your grandparents are both very ill, quite frightfully, with this influenza thing which is apparently quite serious when old people get it. Mummy felt she ought to ring up Doctor Stubbs, who's our quack as well, and he said it was most important that you should be sent for at once, as there seem to be no other relatives. Sorry about this, when you must be having such a gorgeous time in

London (and how's the lovelorn Harold?) but you do see how it is . . .

Miranda's first thought was that she couldn't, wouldn't go. Sitting up in bed, her hands round her knees, she saw neither the delicate prints, the little French writing-desk, nor the calm face of the porcelain Madonna. Instead, there in front of her was the grim bedroom where the dusty box and its contents had shocked her out of what remained of her childhood. To return to it would be like going back to prison after months of freedom. Grandmother might be ill, but would certainly recover quickly once she saw her victim again, and that was a thought not to be borne. She rushed to Polly's bedroom with the letter.

Polly, girlish with plaits over her shoulders, put down *The Stage* and listened. The plaits were solemnly shaken.

'No question of not going, dear child. Suppose they both died – how would you feel then?'

'Relieved,' Miranda muttered.

'Nonsense – don't be naughty. Our natural feelings are much stronger than we sometimes think. And there must be things that need looking after – money matters, the house . . . Of course you must go, now.'

'Now? But I can't!'

'Why not, pray? The wind sits in the shoulder of your sail, and you are stay'd for, and the Birmingham trains are very frequent on a Saturday. Run along and pack your bag, and Mattie will make you up a lunch box, and once you're there you'll be so glad you made the effort.'

'I doubt if I shall be glad at all, whatever your mother said,' Miranda told Harold as they stood dismally on the platform at Euston Station. 'I expect I'll find them fighting fit, eating egg and chips, and Grandmother all ready to chase me with a hairbrush again. No, I shan't be glad at all, and I *hate* leaving London and not being able to go and work for Mr Knight next week and – oh, everything.'

Harold waited wistfully for her to say that she hated leaving him, but the words were not spoken, his longing not even noticed. 'You'll come back?' he asked. 'You will come back, promise?'

'I promise. I'll be back as soon as ever I can. Oh, and thanks for seeing me off and carrying the bag.'

As the guard's whistle was blown she wound down the window and leaned out – he hoped, to give him a kiss. But he only got a firm handshake. When the train had gone he went out disconsolately into the dusty, unpleasant afternoon, walking slowly through the great Euston Arch and looking up at it, because Miranda had said she admired it. London was horrible, life was horrible, and rather surprisingly for a great boy of nearly eighteen he felt very much inclined to cry. Instead, he walked very fast through the streets and squares to the British Museum, where he spent two hours among statues, mummy-cases, idols, fossils and autographs. If one could not be happy, the next best thing was to be usefully occupied.

Chamberlain Road had not changed at all, but then there was no reason why it should. It was almost deserted this Saturday afternoon. Two children were bowling a hoop; in some of the small front gardens people were tidying the heavy summer growth. They glanced up as Miranda passed, with a half-smile or a face of non-recognition. She had changed, even in the short time of being away, in looks, dress and bearing, and they had not known her well before.

In front of the familiar house she stopped, looking up at it. It stared back blankly. The bay window on the first floor with the heavy lace curtains hiding it was her grandparents' room. There was no sign of life at it, or any other window. Very reluctantly, longing to turn and run away, she approached the dark-green front door with its black iron furniture. Then the thought struck her – how to get in? The key she had once carried was in the grey handbag, now exchanged for a new raffia one, left behind at the Porters'. Steeling herself, she rang the bell.

Nobody answered. A second ring, after a minute or so, brought no response. Miranda tried the side gate, leading to the back garden; it was, as she had expected, bolted. She measured with her eye the height of it, and was looking round for something to climb on when the door opened.

'What do you think you're doing?'

A short woman in nurse's uniform stood there, glowering.

'Oh.' Miranda abandoned the dustbin she had been dragging

out of a corner. 'I was trying to get in, actually.'

'If you don't leave this instant I shall send for the police,' snapped the nurse, beginning to shut the door.

'No, don't do that – I'm Mr and Mrs Heriot's grand-daughter – I've come to see them.'

This information brought no smile to the nurse's grim, pouchy little face, but she opened the door again. 'If that's true,' she said, 'you'd better come in. I was told you'd run away,' she added disapprovingly.

Miranda ignored this. 'Didn't Dr Stubbs tell you friends had got in touch with me?'

'He did mention it. But that was no guarantee you'd come, was it?'

The hall smelt just the same, of turpentiney polish, now blended with a strong odour of hospitals. There was no sound from upstairs, no sound at all but the slow tick of the long-case clock. The nurse, bent on making the visitor feel as uncomfortable as possible, made no gesture to invite her to sit down or enter one of the rooms. Her arms folded in front of her starched pinafore, she stood at the foot of the stairs like Horatius keeping the bridge, challenging Miranda with her small snapping eyes. People who ran away had no rights in a house of sickness.

Miranda stared her out. 'How are my grandparents?'

'Since you ask, very poorly. Very poorly indeed. It's turned to pneumonia with both of them, and Mr Heriot's heart's affected. I ought to be with him now, not wasting time down here.'

The frustrations of the day rose up in one of Miranda's very rare surges of temper. 'I've come here from London,' she said loudly, 'because I was told I was needed, and I intend to stay as long as I *am* needed. I don't know who's employing you or paying you, but while my grandparents' illness lasts I shall be looking after all that sort of thing. Now I'm going upstairs to wash and unpack my bag, and after that I want to see them both – please.'

Faint surprise at this defiance crossed the nurse's face; she nodded curtly and ran upstairs on silent rubber-shod feet. Later, over the tea Miranda had made, she stiffly unbent enough to reveal that she was Nurse Davis, employed by an agency and summoned by Dr Stubbs for day duty, being replaced by another nurse at night. The doctor himself was paying her fees, for which he had assured the agency he would be reimbursed later (Miranda wondered what made him so sure of this). The cleaner, Alice, had been asked to come in every day, since no professional nurse would tolerate a household where no domestics were kept. Dr Stubbs was going to be in for a sizeable reimbursement.

Still crackling with disapproval, she preceded Miranda to the main bedroom and ushered her in, with a hissed warning not to make a noise. There was no temptation to do anything of the kind, in that gloomy place. There was the bed with its triple-tombstone head-board, there was the lowering ward-robe that housed the box of secrets. And in the bed, a tiny figure under hospital-neat bedclothes. Loud rasping breaths came from it, as the head turned fitfully from side to side. The fallen-in face was a grotesque mask, like an African shrunken head. A table by the bedside was covered with medicine-bottles and appliances. Miranda stepped back from the reek of carbolic, watching Nurse Davis examining her patient, feeling the hot skin, taking the pulse, rearranging the sheet.

'Where's my grandfather?' she asked.

'Sssh! Next door.'

Albert Heriot lay in the narrow bed of the spare room, which had been a repository of suitcases and out-of-season clothes. Now all such things were swept out of sight or shrouded under covers: just the ugly iron bed, which might have come from a hospital, though it had not, and the old, old man in it, muttering, coughing, groaning, his face open-eyed, wild-eyed, the chin thick in white stubble. Nurse Davis gave an exclamation Miranda could not catch, and hurried her out of the room.

'He's worse,' she said, 'lot worse. A sudden change. I'm going to telephone the doctor.'

'But we haven't got . . .' Miranda began. A moment later she heard the bang of the front door. Some up-to-date neighbour with a telephone must have agreed to act as a link between nurse and doctor.

Unconsciously tip-toeing, she went back to her own old room and shut the door. The room had been cleaned but not changed. There was the Fairy Piper, piping eternally at the foot of the tree, there was the Mabel Lucie Attwell child, on the bed the night-dress case. Her clothes were still in the wardrobe, her dressing-gown hanging on the door. 'Dead to me,' Polly had said. How right; it was as though she had died and the room had been kept just as it was. A wonder they hadn't hung a wreath on the door and sealed it up.

But that night it was Albert Heriot who died, watched by the doctor and the nurse, while Miranda sat downstairs, unwanted, unable to help. She wished Polly hadn't insisted that she should come back; yet it had been the right thing to do, the responsible thing.

As though Death had stalked from one room to the next, a change came over her grandmother on the following morning, while Miranda discussed with a tall-hatted undertaker the arrangements for the funeral. All through that day and the next night the two nurses took turns to watch, boiled water, administered stimulants, piled on blankets, and Miranda lay awake listening. She knew they thought she should not have gone to bed, it showed a disgraceful lack of feeling, but neither would they have thanked her for staying up and getting in their way. It was impossible not to fall asleep, in the end. She woke with a start at the abrupt opening of the door, to see dawn-light outside, and hear the night-nurse saying, 'Your grandmother's passed away.'

'So I never had time to ask her.' Miranda and Editha were sitting on the bedroom floor, surrounded by clothes and small objects. The solicitor had said that the rental of the house was to cease a fortnight after the death of the two Heriots, and the furniture and effects to be stored until the wills could be found and proven. In the meantime Miranda might lay claim to any minor objects she considered to be her rightful possessions.

'Ask her what?'

'About my parents, of course. What it was all about, why she treated them so badly.'

Editha shrugged. 'You wouldn't have got much intelligent conversation out of her when she was dying of pneumonia.'

'Oh. I thought people often had flashes of clear-mindedness at times like that, and understood things they'd never understood before.'

'Did she seem as though she might, when you saw her?'

'Well, no. No, I suppose it wouldn't have been any use.' Miranda forebore to add that she was sorry she had not been able to make some real, human contact with her grandmother that would banish the nightmare image and bring them close together, for the first and last time. She thought of her own childish shortcomings: how she had never tried to understand the two old people, never made any appeal for affection, never stood up for her own rights to know why she was not treated like an ordinary beloved grandchild. Now it was too late. They said that when people died one wished one had been nicer to them. In a way it was true.

'I'm going to take the little coral twisted necklace,' she said, surveying the contents of the top drawer from her dressing-table. 'And the forget-me-not beads, and this bangle.' She held up a slender wrist-band from which five golden hearts, of graduated sizes, depended. 'It was among Grandmother's things, but I swear it wasn't hers – she simply wouldn't have worn it, ever. I think it was my mother's. It was in its own little box in cotton-wool.'

'Perhaps it was a present she wasn't allowed to have.' Editha picked up a dress lying limp and crumpled over a chair. 'This used to be your best, didn't it?'

'Yes, but it's much too small for me now, they all are. Just a few petticoats and things will do. I don't want the dresses, anyway, they're not my style any more. When I get a job I'll buy some others.'

Editha was getting bored. She wanted to talk about herself, about Colin, the boy with the castle, about the holiday she was to have in St Tropez. 'Is that all, then?'

'Except for this.' The heavily-carved oak box was worm-eaten with age. Once it had been locked, but the key was gone. Miranda lifted from it the thick, musty-smelling volume bound in calf, much of the skin flaked away into dust. She laid it on the floor, and opened it at the title-page, elaborately engraved with twin vertical scrolls flanking the lettering, each scroll holding twelve cameos, of tents on one side, portraits on the other. Editha peered over her shoulder.

'"The Holy Bible, conteyning the Old Testament and the

New: newly translated out of the original Tongues . . ." Not all that newly, by the look of it, must be hundreds of years old. Yes, look – 1611. What do you want this for? It might have grubs in.'

Miranda had given no thought to the old book itself, only to the savage inscription at the end of it. She had told Editha only something of the story, not all, friend that Editha was.

'It's the family Bible,' she said. 'Grandmother showed me the . . . details about my parents. It's probably got more information about us in it.'

'If your grandparents were Nonconformist, very Nonconformist indeed, by the sound of it, why did they have a proper C. of E. Bible?' enquired Editha. 'Perhaps they came from – well, respectable stock, and just turned peculiar. Can I see the thing about your parents?'

'No. Sorry. It's too personal. Let's see if there's anything else.' She turned over the bulk of the thick pages, avoiding the last one. Editha exclaimed, 'Crikey!' Where the printed text ended there began pages of manuscript, the early ones on paper contemporary with the printed matter, followed by pages of different texture, in varied styles of writing and colours of ink. It was quite clear that they were entries of family births and deaths. Editha pointed to one page written in a delicate italic hand. 'Look, they've given the time of birth, and the sign of the Zodiac – "At half-past five of the Morning, under Leo, the Moon ascending". How extraordinary.'

Miranda turned back to the first page of entries. Apart from a letter and a figure here and there, it might as well have been in Hebrew, so indecipherable it was, so old and faded the brownish ink. 'No good,' Miranda said disappointedly. 'It needs a magnifying glass.' She turned over carefully, smelling the stuffiness of centuries, the peculiar staleness of old paper. The next page began with the same intricate, unreadable writing; then came another hand, less scholarly but clearer, and a legible date: 1613. The entries were in Latin, a language both girls had learned since they were in the fourth form together. They read out words, names: Margarita, Georgius, Johannes, Anna, Tobias.

Suddenly Editha let out a shrill squeal and pointed. 'I don't believe it! Can you see what I see?'

'What? Where?'
'There, look, there!'
Miranda read the name beneath Editha's finger. *Shakspere.*

CHAPTER EIGHT
The Heart of my Mystery

'Well, how amazing,' Miranda said. 'But don't get excited, it was a terribly common name. There was a man before the Bard's day who changed his name from Shakespeare to Saunders, to avoid getting confused with all the others. But it *is* odd. What's the rest of it say?'

She carried the book carefully to the table in the window, where the better light showed them the entry more clearly. It was longer than the others. *Joanna filia Mariae Curtis et Guilielmi Shakspere ex vinculum matrimoniae O dies infaustus Nov 3 1613.*

'There's somethng written in the margin,' Editha said. Miranda stooped closer. 'It looks like *Eheu.*'

'*Eheu*? That isn't a word, is it? Unless it's Greek?'

'I don't know.' Miranda stared at the letters, written very small in an ink different from that of the entry, and somehow pitiful-looking, as though the person writing had contrived to slip in a personal, rueful comment, perhaps much later, on the fact that one Joan had been born to Mary Curtis and William Shakspere outside the bonds of matrimony, O unhappy day – for that was what *dies infaustus* looked like.

It no longer seemed important to sort out trifles. The mystery of the name had eclipsed everything else. They went slowly through the heavy pages. As the handwriting grew less crabbed various surnames could be read: many Curtises, records of some children born to Curtis women, presumably in lawful wedlock. Sometimes a large blank occurred, followed by an entry at a much later date than the last. A pedantic eighteenth-century hand had inscribed a long text from Deuteronomy, with profound comments of the writer's own, and further on, perhaps early in the nineteenth century, a dissertation half a page long on the nature of moral duty.

Miranda skipped entries until a familiar name caught her eye.

'1834, Dec. 17. Bedelia, daughter of Bertha and Frederick Soarfleet. That must be Grandmother. I never knew anybody else called that.'

'I should hope not. Editha's bad enough, but Bedelia . . .'

'1834,' Miranda reflected. She remembered very well the dates mentioned on the last page. 'So when my mother was born she must have been about thirty-nine or forty. Quite old.' The near-middle-aged woman with the new baby, the background of religious gloom, three hundred or more years of it. Some kind of pattern seemed to be emerging to explain what had so far seemed only senseless cruelty. She shut the Bible and began to heap the clothes and trinkets into a suitcase.

'Do you think your mother will mind if we go back to your house now, and if I don't come back here, at all?' Editha said her mother would be delighted, never having cared for the idea of a young girl in what was not only a house of death but had never been much of a house of life. They went round it together, about the satisfying task of tidying up and throwing out – ashes from grates, old food, anything perishable, fastening windows and locking doors. The beds in the main bedroom and the spare one had been stripped down to the mattress, the bed-linen taken away to be burnt by the order of Nurse Davis, the whole house permeated with the lingering reek of fumigation. Of the personal possessions of the Heriots nothing remained, their toilet articles destroyed, their clothes disinfected and given to the Salvation Army for distribution among the poor. Miranda shut the front door after her with a bang, and double-locked it. On the way back to the Finchs' she would drop the keys in at the house-agent's. Soon it would be empty, redecorated, changed, with new people living in it. Behind that door was a whole section of her life.

'Won't Mummy be intrigued when we tell her!' said Editha. 'Guilielmus Shakspere, what about that?'

'Don't tell her, please, Edie – don't tell anybody. I don't know why – it's just something I want to keep to myself for the moment. For one thing, people would be funny about it – I don't mean your mother, but other people, whether there's anything in it or not, and I don't see how there can be.'

'But you're not going to leave it like that – without finding out? It just *could* be true, and it would be so exciting. I'm sure I couldn't be as cool about it as you, if I thought I was descended from – oh, I don't know, Chaucer. That's it – Editha Chaucer sounds quite too mediaeval.' They strolled on, talking, speculating.

Mrs Finch was sorry to lose her guest. But Miranda was determined to get back to London. 'I have to earn my living,' she said. 'I can't live off the Porters – they're not at all rich.'

'Perhaps you will be, when the wills are proved,' Editha speculated. 'You might have untold gold in the bank, who knows?'

'As they can't even find the Wills, it might be years before I can touch any money there is. And I don't think there'll be any – for me. Grandmother was just the kind of person to disinherit me when I ran away, and persuade Grandfather to do the same.'

'Then what would they do with the money? There must be some – your grandfather didn't exactly spend his all on drink and the horses. Perhaps they left it to a cats' home.'

'Grandmother didn't like cats, couldn't bear animals at all.'

'Oh. Then perhaps it's hidden in a secret place, like a priest's hole.'

'In Chamberlain Road?' It was certainly strange that no Last Will and Testament had been found. Dr Stubbs had traced a firm of solicitors who had dealt with the Heriots in the past; one of the older partners thought he remembered a will being drawn up, but nothing of its terms, and the young man who had searched the house, with Miranda's permission, had found no trace. She had been sure it would be in the box in the wardrobe, the box where the photographs had been. But when she opened it, with the key which in itself had been hard to find, it contained only those two faded pictures, the Heriots' marriage certificate and the certificate of Grace's birth, besides a quantity of old documents, receipts, insurance papers, household trivia. The photographs she kept to treasure; they could be restored one day by an expert. The rest didn't matter, nor the wills. Better to be going into the world to make one's own living than to have begrudged money in one's purse.

On the last night of Miranda's stay the two girls talked in the bedroom they shared, Editha's room, crammed with knickknacks, dolls, theatre programmes, dance cards, and sweet with the heliotrope perfume which was peculiarly Editha's. Miranda had already heard all there was to hear about Colin McAndrew, his stately home, his university, his beautiful American mother, his sister's impending presentation at Court. A photograph of him, slightly pompous, Miranda thought, in Highland dress, stood in a silver frame on the mantelpiece.

'Do you think you'll marry Colin, Edie?'

'Oh. I hadn't really thought about it. Not yet, at any rate. It's such fun, just flirting, isn't it . . . I'm going to be "finished" you know. At a rather grand place near Lausanne. 'Randa, did you – in Stratford – did you fall in love?'

Miranda hesitated. 'Yes. Yes, I did.'

'There, I knew I was right! You were different, when I went down to see you. Do tell, who was it – not Frank Benson?'

Miranda laughed. 'Good heavens, no. He's a great dear, but not the sort of man one falls in love with. Constance has a story about a rather raffish young woman who joined the company once – she used to boast that she always mashed the leading man, but certainly wouldn't try it with Benson. " 'E's too 'aggard," she said. He's very handsome in his way, of course, but well, too 'aggard, I suppose, and a bit old.'

'Don't prevaricate. Who was it?'

Miranda found it impossible to form the words that would give away the Godfrey episode. It should have been a relief to tell about it; but a bitter disappointment that might, disregarded, be forgotten, is made real and lasting by the telling of it, as a bad dream is when recounted over breakfast. Rachel knew and would never tell; Polly almost certainly knew, and would never tell either.

So she said lightly, 'Oh, it was one of those silly things. Just a rave, an infatuation. He didn't mean it and neither did I.'

''Randa,' said Editha thoughtfully, 'how far did it go? Because you *have* changed . . .'

'Quite as far as was proper.' She gave an artificial yawn. 'I'm going to sleep now. Good night.'

'Good night.' Editha's tone was still thoughtful. There is a quality about lost innocence which is unmistakable, even to those who are themselves still innocent.

Mrs Finch exclaimed next morning at the enormous brown paper parcel which sat ponderously among Miranda's luggage. 'But what a monstrous thing – how on earth will you manage at Paddington? Can't you leave it here? We'll look after it for you.'

'Well, no, Mrs Finch, thank you very much. It's the family Bible, and I have to take care of it myself.'

As the train was about to move out Editha said urgently, 'You'll let me know, won't you, about . . . that name. As soon as you find anything out – promise?'

'I promise. But don't get too excited. The explanation's probably utterly boring. It could even have been written in afterwards by someone who wanted to brighten up the family tree. Polly will know . . .'

Polly Porter had always dreamed of going to university: Oxford, of course. Flowing gowns, secluded cloisters, earnest evenings of talk and cocoa, unlimited wonderful hours of research in ancient books, green lawns and Gaudys, the slow, detailed delicious compiling of a thesis on one's pet subject, Shakespeare, the weighing and balancing of facts and probabilities and the disproving of myths: how splendidly fulfilling it would have been. But instead, she had teacher-trained for two years at a college in Wimbledon, and then Edward had appeared, and after years of waiting for him to be appointed to a post that would keep them they had been married. In the course of time Harold had come along, and been somewhat absent-mindedly brought up, none of this being very real or important beside the fantasy-world of theatre which Polly shared with her sister, or that other olive-grove of Academe where part of Polly's spirit belonged.

She sat at the kitchen table, the great book carefully propped up with others flanking it. She had looked at the entry until it danced and blurred before her eyes, for the pleasure of re-focusing and finding it still there. An interested group watched her – Miranda, on a leather fender-seat, like Cinderella, Harold as near to her as he could get, Edward sprawled in his sagging old armchair, neither reading nor meditating for once, but watching his wife with mild, temperate admiration.

'The script looks right to me,' Polly said. 'No, Miranda, it couldn't have been put in later, or the whole page would have been spoiled. I don't know about contemporary inks, but I'll find someone who does. As to the Latin, it was less and less common as a language for making up registers. We'd been Protestants for seventy years or so – nobody used Latin much apart from scholars and lawyers. So whoever wrote that was probably elderly and set in their ways.'

'What about the word in the margin?' Miranda asked.

Polly looked over her spectacles. '*Eheu*: alas. A sad little comment by somebody. Perhaps the wretched Mary, or Joanna herself, if they kept her long enough for her to learn to write. The important question is, where did the family live, and where was the Bard at the time?'

Miranda had the Works open at the list of Plays. '*Henry VIII* was put on in 1613. He'd probably have been in London for that.'

'Don't we want to know where he was, er, nine months earlier?' Harold suggested delicately.

'True, dear.' Polly consulted her notebook. 'He wrote *Winter's Tale* in 1611, and *Tempest* the same year – well, it looks like that. How curious – both plays centred on daughters, Perdita and Miranda. Perhaps he had daughters on his mind – he was seeing a lot of his own two round about then. Miranda . . . Now why did they call you that, I wonder?'

'I've no idea,' Miranda said. 'It isn't the sort of thing Grandmother would have told me even if she'd known. It means "worthy to be admired", so perhaps my parents thought I was a pretty baby.'

'All parents think that. I expect we thought Harold was.'

'Oh, we did – he wasn't half-bad,' put in Edward loyally. Harold blushed.

'Well, then,' said Polly, thinking aloud, 'as Miranda isn't at all a usual name, let's suppose your parents were thinking of the Bard's girl. Now why should they do that? Presumably your mother had been brought up like you, not allowed to attend wicked playhouses, so she wouldn't have seen *Tempest*. Read it? Perhaps. Not everybody does. Now, my dear, do you suppose your poor mother would have been shown that 1613 entry, just as you were shown the one about her? There must have been some reason, you see, for that inflexibility about theatres. Could it have dated from the time of the family scandal, when a daughter of the house had a baby by a married playwright?'

'Seems a long way back to remember,' Edward puffed at his pipe. 'Things have changed a bit since then, people got more broad-minded.'

'Of course, dear. Darling Ellen Terry had two children outside marriage, but nobody seems to have said a word about it, even Queen Victoria. If Rachel and Ricky had had babies I'm sure we'd all have been delighted, and everybody would have been very nice to them. But – a big but – some families are different. Old wrongs and feuds can be kept up a long time. I think that's what happened here, and I'm going to find out.'

'But we don't even know the family name,' said Miranda. 'I've sat for hours over those first pages, and I can't read more than two words of that writing – it might as well be hieroglyphics – and they didn't put surnames in often, in the later pages. Anyway, the names must have kept changing, as the girls married.'

'That's true, but there are ways of solving puzzles like that.'

'Come to think of it,' Harold said, 'it's like a detective story, isn't it. Austin Freeman's *The Red Thumb Mark* – Dr Thorndyke solved that one without much more to go on, and I bet he could solve this. What we need is a key to the mystery.'

'I know a chap . . .' Edward began, and stopped to tamp down the tobacco in his pipe. 'Well, do go on,' his wife prompted, 'what chap?'

Harold interposed. 'Sykes-Harker. Used to teach History. Retired when I was in the Fifth.'

'Oh, him – yes, I remember him. You got a few bad reports when he was teaching you.'

'Trust you to remember that, Ma. The trouble was, we couldn't hear a thing he said – he mumbled into his waistcoat all the time.'

'Very clever, for all that,' Edward said. 'Makes quite a living transcribing documents and translating stuff from Greek and Latin.'

'Then he can transcribe this document.' Polly shut her notebook. 'That should keep him happy for a week or two. I'm going to miss trying to make it out myself.'

'Only an expert could ever make it out,' Miranda said. 'I really shall hardly sleep until I know what it's all about.'

The firm of Knight, Ashe and Stephenson was as unlike the Bromsgrove Household and General Insurance Company as one firm could be unlike another. It occupied two floors of a Georgian house, ground and first floor; lofty rooms whose ceilings were still proud with plaster cornices of acanthus leaves, rams' heads and sea-shells. The fine mahogany stair-rail was no longer kept highly polished, the tall twelve-paned windows were dirty and harboured spiders' webs in their corners, the Cupids carved on the marble mantelpieces sported with goats and lambs over wrought-iron grates that were never black-leaded, and whose fires warmed clerks instead of gentlefolk.

Miranda found it charming. From the window of the room where she worked it was possible to see the stately Hall to which Nelson and his Emma and her Sir William had driven to dine with the rich and genial Abraham Goldsmid. Perhaps that good man had in his time visited the house across the road, for something warm and gracious permeated the shabby rooms. Miranda, who had been a drudge, a misfit, and the target of unwelcome attentions in Birmingham, was here the pet of the firm, their young lady typist, the only female to adorn it, apart from the elderly widowed caretaker who lived in the basement and was not much of an adornment. Old Mr Knight was now too infirm to attend the office, only visiting it occasionally to nod and smile deafly, and to reassure himself that all was as it had been and would be for evermore. Young Mr Knight, in his fifties, spent much time in Gray's Inn, where he had offices; he was a kindly, quiet man whose lively wife was a friend of Polly's. Mr Ashe, for whom Miranda worked, had a sharp manner but a soft heart. The clerks, from a pimply boy to old Walter who had been with the firm for fifty years, were polite, well-conducted and admiring towards their young colleague.

Strange words and phrases were the everyday language of the Law. But, once met and mastered, torts and malfeasances and their fellows were harmless enough; Miranda grew quite fond of them, and of the many documents relating to property.

Behind the screen of 'a certain messuage or tenement and premises with the appurtenances thereof', what real building was hidden? What was the truth about that night 'when a certain Accused, on the 18th day of June, with force and arms etc. broke and entered the close of the Plaintiff, in the County of Surrey, and other wrongs to him did'? What past horrors could have led to the prohibition on newly-leased premises of Butchery, Gaming, the Manufacture of Bricks, or the Keeping of Goats for Milk? The Law was said to be dull and prosy; in fact it was full of romance and mystery.

Miranda's own mystery was taking time to unravel. Old Mr Sykes-Harker was working hard, Edward reported. It was several weeks before Polly and Miranda were summoned to the little house in Merton.

Whether the old schoolmaster's sight was as bad as it appeared to be, from his thick-lensed spectacles, or whether the little room at the back which he used as his study was perpetually overshadowed by the next-door wash-house, a stranger could not have said; but gas illuminated the hall at ten o'clock in the morning, and in the study a bracket was lit on either side of the fireplace. The small, bent old man was almost submerged under the mass of books surrounding him. They covered the furniture, lined the walls, and filled the fender. From a shelf picture-rail high they threatened to topple down and crush him. Centuries of mustiness breathed out from them, clouds of dust rose into the air when they were moved. Fascinated, Miranda watched a mouse emerge from a gap between two volumes on the floor, sit up to wash its face, then calmly turn and begin to nibble a binding.

Polly moved eight or nine books from a rickety chair, dusted the seat and sat down. Miranda looked round for a seat for herself, but there was none, only a book-crammed crate. She perched on it, hoping no further mice lurked within it.

Mr Sykes-Harker, behind his desk, looked at them as blankly as though he had strayed into the wrong classroom and recognised none of the boys.

'Miss Heriot's Bible,' Polly prompted. 'You were going to tell us what you'd found.'

'Ah. Was I? Yes . . .' It was not surprising that Harold had complained he was hard to hear. His voice was as thin and reedy as though one of his books were speaking. He was a great scholar, a master of research, and the life of the man had gone into his work.

When they had almost given up expecting him to say any more, he dived at the littered top of his desk, pushed piles of books and papers aside, and revealed the Bible, on which he laid his hands, as if taking oath.

'A most interesting business,' he said. 'Sometimes I wish I had the novelist's art. Perhaps I should be a richer man, eh? Well, well.' He lapsed into silence again. Miranda stole a glance at Polly, who shrugged. Be patient, her look said, he'll speak in his own time.

When he did, it was with deliberation. 'I am not used to talking, these days, ladies. Since I gave up the teaching profession my labours have been largely silent. When I am forced to talk, I become breathless very easily. The dust, I expect, the dust from my volumes.' He caressed a calf binding with a lover's touch. 'And so – to make it easier for all of us – I have written down my findings.' He picked up a sheaf of papers. 'Here you can read all there is to be learned from your Bible, Miss Curtis.'

'Er, Heriot.'

'Ah, yes. So many names.'

Miranda rose from her uncomfortable perch. 'It's extremely kind of you, Mr Sykes-Harker. I'm very glad you've saved yourself the trouble of telling us about it, and I'm sure it will be most exciting to read. The only thing is – and I'm sure Mrs Porter will agree – you can't do all this work for nothing. I mean, I'd like to pay you for your time, and your skill.'

He shook his bald head. 'No need to pay me for the pleasure of solving an absorbing problem.'

'In my firm we're always solving people's problems, but we don't do it for nothing. Please, do let me pay you.' Polly was nodding in approval.

The old man looked at her for a long moment, scanning her features, smiling faintly. Then he put out a withered hand to her; she clasped it with her own firm young one. 'You are very kind,' he said. 'You may pay me at some future time, if I am here. You will be able to afford it better, then.'

She did return at a future time, when she could indeed afford it better: but the old man was gone, and his books scattered over market-stalls and second-hand shops. Only the fruit of his labours remained, the thesis he had painstakingly written down for her to read.

CHAPTER NINE
I could a Tale unfold . . .

'I do not intend to weary you (began Sykes-Harker's narrative) with an exhaustive account of the steps by which I assembled the facts and theories I have put down here. The transition from the Secretary hand to the Italian hand, shown in the earliest entries, are of striking interest to students of paleography, but to the non-specialist reader it is sufficient to say that such handwriting must of its nature provide a stumbling-block to any such person attempting to read it.

'It would have been impossible for me to deduct any coherent narrative, however conjectural, without much consultation of various works: i.e. family histories, biographical dictionaries, and contemporary accounts of the events concerned, reinforced, if I may say so in all modesty, by my own fairly comprehensive knowledge of the history of the sixteenth and seventeenth centuries. Detailed footnotes will explain and verify all my reference sources.

'Let me begin with the essential facts about the Bible itself. The volume is, of course, the Authorised Version of 1611, known as the "King James" Bible, printed in London by Robert Barker and accepted for almost three centuries as the definitive translation of the Scriptures. It was welcomed, and extensively used, in Protestant households, who frequently doubled its religious function with that of a chronicle of births and deaths within the family, on the assumption that the same volume would be used for all time. (The gaps occurring in such records usually indicate that in fact the Bible would be laid aside for a generation or more, or used for entries only sporadically, as is the case here.)

'The volume in question belonged to the family of Curtis, spelt alternately as Curteis, Curtois, and Curtoyse, squires and virtual owners of the village or hamlet of Bedington, on the river Avon some miles east of Coventry. Their home was Curteis Hall, a mediaeval structure partly rebuilt in the reign of Elizabeth, which still (I am told) stands. It is evident that during the latter part of the sixteenth century fairly detailed family records had been kept, which, when the 1611 Bible was acquired, were copied into it by persons apparently of advanced age, judging by the antique nature of their handwriting and the use of Latin.

'I come now to the members of this family of direct concern to us. It would seem (and this is verified by memorials in Bedington Church, which the incumbent has kindly inspected on my behalf) that for a large part of the sixteenth century the head of the house was Sir Roger Curtis, born in 1533 and therefore a product of pre-Reformation schooling. An engraving in *Warwickshire Worthies* shows him in middle age as a man of aquiline features and a strong cast of countenance. I can find no description of his wife, formerly Mistress Ursula Aston, but the following epitaph appears on her tomb, in contrast to the conventional Latin eulogy of her husband.

Of stedfast Purity, with no alloy,
Pious was she, in Christ was all her joy.
On Earth she suffered little weal, much woe,
But freed from mortal Maladies below
In Heavenly bliss she dwells with Saints above,
Chanting with them the Hymns of Holy Love.

'From this verse, despite its meretricious quality, I think we may gather that Lady Curtis was of a gentler disposition than Sir Roger, and had suffered considerable grief, probably caused by the deaths of many of her children in infancy, as only one survived to adult years.

'This was Edward Curtis, born in 1562. He married one Mistress Joan Baddesley, and it is clear that the same misfortune pursued them as befell Edward's parents, for the Bible records the births of no less than eighteen children to the couple, of whom only one grew to womanhood: Mary, born in 1594.

'(I am greatly tempted to digress into the studies made by

modern medical authorities of the appallingly high mortality rate among infants in the centuries preceding our own, largely caused through ignorance and superstition, and on the possible dynastic effects of these evils having been reformed earlier. For instance, had Arthur, Prince of Wales, survived instead of dying prematurely in 1502, his brother would not have become Henry the Eighth, and the Reformation in England might well not have taken place when it did. But these are byways . . .)

'Now we find our way more directly by historical records. The Dictionary of National Biography tells me that both Sir Roger and his son Edward were frequent visitors in the last decade of the century to the court of King James of Scotland. Now, the journey from Warwickshire to Edinburgh was a long, hazardous and tedious one in the 1590s. The Curtises, father and son, must have been most anxious to gain and preserve the friendship of King James, a man almost of Edward's age; no doubt because it was widely thought that he would be successor to the ageing Queen Elizabeth. This, indeed, was so. In 1603 he became King James the First of England and Sixth of Scotland. The ambitious Curtises now had their wish; they had become people of influence at the English Court.

'It happened that King James and his Queen were also sufferers from infant mortality. Only one of their daughters survived – the Princess Elizabeth, a child of great beauty and charm. On her father's accession to the English throne, she was brought south from Scotland and given into the guardianship of Lord and Lady Harington, and lodged at their principal home, Combe Abbey, two and a half miles north of Coventry. I cannot say whether the Curtises had any influence upon the decision to send her there, or whether they merely took advantage of the fact that the Second Lady in the Land was now housed only a mile or two from them, and that she was almost the same age as their daughter Mary, who was now nine years old against Princess Elizabeth's seven years.

'What is certain is that by 1605 Mary was established at Combe as one of the Princess's companions and attendants. Old Sir Roger must have been most gratified; even more so, when his son was knighted by King James. No doubt he hoped to see him, like Lord Harington, raised to the peerage.

'Delightful accounts remain of the time when the Princess, the Pearl of Britain, as they called her, came to London. Golden-haired, merry and innocent, the child Princess was as different as could be from the late Queen, that old Tudor she-dragon who had terrified everyone – even Death, people said, until they stared each other out, and Death won. I can find no record of Mary Curtis at the court of Whitehall, but she appears in a list of performers of one of the stately masques introduced by the Princess's mother, the pleasure-loving Queen Anne of Denmark, first as one of a train of nymphs, then as a "Starre" (presumably a satellite of Elizabeth as the Moon) in cloth of silver and "a ruffe of cypresse, spangled". Poets and musicians and, what we would call today, fashion designers abounded at this young Court; its atmosphere must have been cheerful, carelessly Bohemian in our sense.

'More literally, the crown of Bohemia itself came a-wooing to Princess Elizabeth in the person of Prince Frederick, Elector Palatine of the Rhine, when both he and she were fifteen. Out of many suitors this handsome, accomplished youth was accepted. He came to England, the young pair were attracted to each other on sight, and festivities began which would last for almost four months. Banquets, masques, feasts, hunting, were continuous, interrupted only by the sudden death of the Princess's beloved brother, Henry Prince of Wales.

'Such an event should have put an end to the rejoicings, in the name of decency, one would think. But it did not. A royal betrothal was a royal betrothal; Frederick was determined to take his bride back over the sea with him, without waiting for her term of mourning to be ended. Indeed, I have not been able to find any trace of actual mourning garments being ordered or worn. What I have discovered is that the Princess's apartments at Whitehall, known as the Cockpit, became filled with merchants, tailors and sempstresses, as her trousseau and that of her ladies was devised. In my fancy (for this strange tale has carried me away somewhat) I see the Curtis family – old Sir Roger, now nearing eighty, his brisk ambitious son Sir Edward, and perhaps their ladies – travelling up from quiet Warwickshire to attend some of the celebrations, rejoicing on their own behalf in the presence of Mary, now seventeen and doubtless beautiful, so close to the Princess, so likely to profit by all this splendour. Already she and the other maids had been given "medalias" engraved with the Princess's portrait: a Harington niece had received a diamond and pearl necklace. They must have seen glory ahead for their girl.

'One of the strangest things about this time of mixed grief and rejoicing is that between her brother's death and her marriage, in this winter of 1612–13, the Princess was present at the performance of fourteen different plays at the Palace of Whitehall; six of them were by William Shakespeare.

'You will wish to know what they were. We have their names: *Much Ado about Nothing*, *The Winter's Tale*, *Sir John Falstafe* (either *Merry Wives of Windsor* or *Henry the Fourth Part One*), *The Moor of Venice*, *Caesar's Tragedy* (*Julius Caesar*) and *The Tempest*, which was also given on the betrothal night, being itself concerned with a most romantic betrothal.

'There can be no doubt that the author was present. At this point in his life he . . .'

'I don't think I can stand any more without a drink,' Polly said. 'B. and S., please. You'll find the syphon on the bottom shelf in the sideboard, and if it's empty there's another in the kitchen cupboard.'

Edward, who so far knew nothing of the contents of the Sykes-Harker screed, which Miranda and Polly were reading together from a table bookstand, obediently fetched brandy, soda and glasses, and poured for them all. He was not himself unbearably excited, but sympathetic, as ever, to Polly's excitement. Miranda choked slightly on the enormous drink he had unthinkingly put before her, but unhesitatingly drank it. The occasion seemed to call for a bracer.

The readers returned to the manuscript.

'. . . was at the height of his fame and prosperity, a highly respected citizen of Stratford, where he and his family now lived in the best house, New Place, and a senior figure in the hierarchy of the London theatre. In March, 1613, he was to buy a house in Blackfriars, adding to the property he already owned. He was forty-eight years old, an age he would himself have considered verging on the sere and yellow. He may well (though this is speculation, and therefore not allowable in a work of scholarship) have reached that state of *ennui* common in men who feel they have reached the highest peak of achievement.

'It is unthinkable that he would not have wished to supervise performances of so many of his plays in such circumstances – entertainments chosen to grace the first royal wedding in England for almost sixty years. He may even have acted in them; he had never, so far as is known, played romantic "juvenile" parts, so his age would not have diminished his usefulness as an actor.

'Now we come to an area in which proof and evidence are impossible. I have said that the atmosphere at Whitehall Palace was one of excitement and liveliness; what might be called wedding fever. Elizabeth's own apartments were the centre of it. Quite possibly the plays were given there, for we know that soon after Frederick's arrival in England she invited him to witness a play performed by her own servants. Whether the professional performances were given there, or in the great hall of the palace, there would have been some social mingling between the favoured players and the Princess's personal courtiers.

'I can say no more on this subject; it is a matter for imagination, not research. What remains on record is that Mary Curtis did not marry a young lord, nor was she among the ninety-seven persons who attended the wedded Princess to Heidelberg when she left England on April 14th. Her name occurs next in the Bible entry which I have been asked to investigate, as the mother of an illegitimate daughter by one William Shakspere. On consideration of the persons involved, I would guess the writing to be that of Sir Roger, using the Latin of his boyhood, and the comment, which breathes out to us like a sigh from the past, by Mary's grandmother. But it may well be otherwise.

'Parish records and church memorials furnish all we can know of the rest of the story. Sir Roger's death is recorded in 1615, aged 82, his wife's shortly afterwards. No christening entry appears for the birth of Joanna, or Joan, as she may have been known, or any other entry appertaining to her or her mother. It appears that Mary was not buried with her ancestors, and that Joanna left Bedington. Only in 1691 there is recorded the birth of James Englefield, son of James and Mary Englefield of Warwick; I can but think this child may have been a grandchild of Joanna.

'We come thence by sparse and random entries to the marriage of one William Curtis Soarfleet, which in 1834 produced a girl named Bedelia, later married to Albert Frederick Heriot, though not christened in the parish of Bedington. A much later and somewhat incoherent note refers to a ceremony in the Nahumite Chapel of Bromshill, Birmingham, at which a daughter, Grace, born to Albert Frederick and Bedelia Heriot was baptised. (I find that the Nahumite movement is a small by-product of Nonconformism based on the somewhat savage writings of the minor prophet Nahum against the city of Nineveh, and has no true religious significance.) Then follow the unfortunately-worded entries with which you are familiar.

'I thank you for giving me the opportunity to investigate this curious and absorbing story, and I wish I had been able to afford you proof of what I feel to be the truth. I would like to draw your attention to the likelihood that the mention of the child's father's name may stem from an inverted pride that if the girl had to fall, she at least chose a spectacular way to do it.'

They all sat back and looked at each other. Miranda, who had gone very pale, reached out for her empty glass, into which Edward poured another touch of brandy.

'It all fits,' Polly said. 'The time, the place and the loved ones, so to speak. He's right about the name; if the man had been William Shakspeare, or Shagsber, from nowhere in particular they'd have kept quiet about it. But Sir Roger, or whoever the writer was, couldn't resist, even in his righteous sorrow, just mentioning that Mary had done rather well for herself, in a scandalous sort of way.'

'Which is why,' Harold said, 'the thing went on down the years, one generation telling another about it. So, when your grandmother joined this batty sect, Miranda, the old story came up again and got mixed up with the Nahumites' ideas about playhouses being an invention of the devil.' He was trying to sound bright and interested, but his heart had gradually lowered itself into his boots as the Sykes-Parker narrative unfolded. He was glad for Miranda, proud of her illustrious descent, and yet it put her a remove away from him, just when she had got away from the stage and its dangerous glamours. (His father had dropped a hint about Godfrey Arnold which had made him all the more determined to see her home from the theatre every night, until term-time claimed him.)

Miranda still looked stunned. The brandy had helped, but she was still unable to rise to the bright expectancy on Polly's face.

'I'm sorry,' she said. 'It's still a bit of a shock. I suppose . . . I didn't believe it before, at all. I thought it was just an interesting mystery. It seemed so very unlikely, when I knew the name was such a common one. But now I know about Mary and the Princess's court, and *him* being there – I have to believe it.' She was living the scenes that had begun themselves to come to life: winter at the Palace of Whitehall, the excitement and the laughter, so much that even grief for a dead prince was submerged beneath it. A man middle-aged and more by the standards of his time, perhaps blasé with success, taking what he could of pleasure, while he could; at the end of his days in the theatre, with only small-town Stratford to look forward to, an ageing wife, rents to be got in, money to be counted, a pipe and a mug of ale with visitors from London his only diversion. A pretty girl, very young – 1594, that would mean she was exactly thirty years younger than he – coming from his own county of Warwickshire, amused to test her kitten-claws on this great man, or perhaps attracted by him.

My glass shall not persuade me I am old,
So long as youth and thou are of one date . . .

And it was winter, bitter-chill to thin blood, and fires were banked high in Whitehall, flames dancing to light up fair young faces, the scents of musk and spices on the air.

Polly said, 'I don't want to claim hindsight, dear, but I told Rachel a long time ago that there was something familiar about you. Come here, look.' She led Miranda to stand in front of the overmantel mirror. There she swept back the dark fringe and held it to show the high, rounded brow Miranda had always disliked and contrived to veil with hair. In the pale face the eyes plum-dark, the soft mouth as vulnerable as that half-seen in the portraits.

'You see? Look here upon this picture, and on this. It was there all the time if we'd had the eyes to see it.'

'But it's ridiculous, after so many years – what is it, three hundred? The likeness would have worn off, with so many other strains mixing with it.'

'That's right, genetically,' Harold said.

'But,' Polly's tone was awed, 'we're not talking about an *ordinary* strain. This was the most wonderful man who ever lived. There must have been something in him that was imperishable, something he handed down through his blood to his descendants. Why shouldn't features be part of it? Perhaps the genius is there too, dear, just waiting to break out. He was not of an age, but for all time.'

'I'm quite sure it isn't, and I certainly hope not. I don't want to be a genius – it would be very uncomfortable. And to tell the truth,' Miranda turned from the mirror to face them all, 'I feel just a bit silly about the whole thing. I mean, the Bard wasn't exactly a beauty, if that poem by whoever it was about the artist having drawn his likeness so well is true. I shall start imagining I look like one of those faces in posters that boys have drawn moustaches on.'

Polly shook her head. 'You have a most marvellous inheritance, you ungrateful girl. I only wish it were mine! You'll just have to get used to it. What will F.R. say when he hears? And the others, come to that.'

It was later in the evening, when they had talked all round the situation, or rather Polly had talked and the rest of them had listened, that Miranda, who had been thinking as well as listening, said, 'Polly, can I ask you something?'

'Anything, dear.'

'Well, then. Would you be awfully kind and not tell people about this yet? Not till I've had time to take it all in, and what it implies. You see, it would mean my mother's story would have to come out, and I wouldn't like that. I need time to make up something that will leave her out of it – and my grandparents.'

'That's right,' Edward said unexpectedly. 'Go easy, Polly. Miranda doesn't want the wrong kind of talk about this. Might do harm.' He had tried to protect her once before, from a danger he could see though his wife could not, and he had a dim feeling that the warning had not been understood or heeded. Now, like others who hear more than they speak, he was again conscious of danger for this nice, pretty girl who in his view looked not at all like that very plain man of whom, in his quiet way, he was heartily sick. It would have been nice to own a daughter like Miranda, someone who would talk about the things he liked, not merely her own enthusiasms, sit by his side while he fished, make him apricot pudding like his mother's. But there had been no other children after Harold; he was not even quite sure how Harold had come into the world. On the whole he rather wished Miranda had been descended from any historical figure except That Man. Herod, or Attila the Hun, for instance.

'Of course,' Polly answered Miranda cheerfully. 'I shouldn't dream of telling anyone without your permission, dear.'

CHAPTER TEN
The Strangers all are gone . . .

'I don't believe it,' Rachel slapped the letter down on Ricky's dressing-table, under the bright side-lights, among the clutter of grease-paint tubes. 'Yes, I do, though. It's too amazing not to be true.'

The actor, who was painting lines round his mouth in addition to those already there, muttered unintelligibly that he wouldn't be surprised at anything that fool of a girl had done, after making a spectacle of herself on the stage and letting young Arnold gammon her like that.

'She hasn't done anything, except follow up a clue, and I do think you're a bit hard on her. But *isn't* it a marvellous thing! Three hundred years after, the truth comes out – and it's someone we know, someone who's actually . . .'

Ricky drew black lines under his eyes. 'Don't make a sacred cow of her, that's all.'

'Of course I won't. Polly says she's not told anybody else.'

'She will.'

'I'm sure she won't, if she says not. But she thought we ought to know.'

'Don't see why. I may make a living out of the fellow, but I don't have to fall down and worship him like you two. Damned ugly mug he had, if you ask me. Shouldn't have thought a young woman'd care to have it passed down to her. He was bald, for a start.'

'Darling, you're so ridiculous.' She picked up the lucky black cat he wore on a chain round his neck when costume permitted, and stroked it. 'Polly thinks the likeness is remarkable, but I remember Miranda's face very well and I can't see any resemblance. No, what matters is the story. That beautiful young girl from the country and the ageing Bard –'

'Thanks. He was about my age.'

Rachel slapped his hand hard, then kissed it. 'It's the perfect age for a man. Seasoned, mellow, experienced, wise, but still able to love passionately . . .'

'If that's a hint, they've just called the quarter.'

'Don't be shocking.' She leant against him, warm and scented, alluringly powdered and rouged, making herself heavy against his arm. Reluctantly he pushed her aside. He would make up for it later, in the back-street lodging where Timon surlily awaited them.

Rachel lost no time in passing on the news of the Great Discovery, as she and Polly called it, to her friend Kate who was touring with another Benson company in the south. It was in confidence, of course, but Kate's husband shared the letter over breakfast, and just happened to mention it later to the actor who was playing Ford to his Page in that morning's rehearsal. Part of the conversation was overheard by someone else, who butted in and demanded to know more. He was a young man with a well-developed streak of opportunism, in this case to be rewarded. His telephone call to a news desk in Fleet Street aroused the interest of the editor concerned.

'I want more details, mind, and I want them now, not Tuesday week. Where the girl lives – we'll have to know that.'

Young Mr Philips went back to Kate's husband and very casually plied him with questions. Possessed of Ricky Savage's London address, he returned to the telephone, and some days later received a small but welcome cheque.

It was a wintry morning, with snow in the air, when Mattie answered the door to find an unknown man on the Porters' doorstep. Used to theatricals turning up at all times (though he didn't look quite like the run of them) she asked him in and invited him into her kitchen for a sit down and a cup of tea, which he appeared to need, blue with cold as his face was.

'Ta very much, I don't mind if I do. Family not at home, then?' It was a little surprising that he spoke with a Cockney accent stronger than Mattie's own, but actors did sometimes put on funny voices.

'Not one of 'em. Mrs Porter's gone up to town to a sale – you've missed 'er by 'alf an hour or so.'

'Ah. Pity.' He drank his tea slurpingly. 'There's a young lady, though, isn't there? Forget her name. Starts with an H.

Harriott? No, Heriot, that's it.'

'Oh, Miss Miranda. She's gone to work same as usual.'

The reporter, for such he was, neatly elicited Miranda's business address from the unsuspecting Mattie, who still thought him an odd member of the profession, but very friendly and grateful for the tea. In her innocence she saw no wrong in putting a complete stranger in touch with Miranda.

The two boys who occupied the ground-floor cubby-hole which served Knight, Ashe and Stephenson for a reception area were under strict orders not to let any unknown persons upstairs to the offices of the partners. The Law affected people unfortunately, sometimes; clients had been known to behave inconsiderately when displeased with the progress of their cases. But, on the visitor saying he had particular and important business with Miss Heriot, one of the youths went upstairs with the message that a gentleman would like a few words with her. No, he hadn't given a name.

She went downstairs half-expecting to find one of their Morden neighbours, some one with a message for Polly, perhaps, who had called and found Mattie gone to the shops. But there instead was a man she had never seen before, with a perky air, a battered hat and well-worn boots, studying the framed documents on the wall with an air of keen interest; which was remarkable, as the one most commanding his interest was in Latin, and legal Latin at that. He jumped round, touching the hat.

'Miss Heriot? Very pleased to meet you. Oh yes, I see it now, at the first glance. Quite extrer-ornery.'

'What? What do you see?' She caught the eye of the youth Bertie, who nodded in reassurance that he was on guard. It seemed she might be dealing with a madman.

'The likeness, Miss. Very strong, isn't it? Oh, sorry.' He produced a well-worn visiting card. 'Pierse of the *Daily Comment*.' A thick notebook secured by a rubber band was whipped out of his pocket and a pencil poised over it. 'Now, if we could just have a few words from you about this amazing little story . . .'

Miranda stared at him. 'You're from a newspaper?'

'That's right.'

'But I don't understand. How did you get my name, and

what's all this about a likeness?'

Mr Pierse held up an admonitory and nicotine-stained forefinger.

'Ah, now, don't pretend with me, Miss Heriot. We get to hear these things, you know. Suppose we start at the beginning, with this old Bible you were left –'

'Suppose we don't start at all. I've no idea where you heard this – whatever it is – but it's my business and I don't want to discuss it. Good morning.'

Mr Pierse, watching her neat ankles in their black silk stockings receding upstairs, thought it was a pity she had been so prickly, but at least he'd spoken to her and taken a quick dekko at her face, which hadn't looked much like old Shakebag's to him, but he remembered big dark eyes and could easily make up a lively few pars., with the aid of the Dictionary of Quotations.

It was not true that Miranda had no idea where he could have heard her story. It could only have come, in a roundabout way, from Polly, who had promised not to tell a soul.

Horror and guilt chased themselves across Polly's scarlet face.

'Oh dear. Oh dear. I did tell Rachel – I thought it wouldn't matter, and I knew she'd be so interested. It can't have gone any farther from her.' Her eyes pleaded with Miranda to agree – no, it couldn't, it must have got out some other way. But Miranda had realised by now, reluctantly, that it is the breath of life for stage folk to talk, communicate, strike an attitude, if only that of one who enters, left, finger on lips, to pass on a thrilling secret. Ruefully, she wondered whether the silly little secret of her own almost-lost virginity had gone round the company.

'I'm afraid it must have been through Rachel. You see, nobody else knew at all. I haven't even written to Editha. Don't feel bad about it, Polly dear. These things happen, I suppose. Even if awful Mr Pierse prints his piece nobody's going to notice it.'

Polly brightened. 'That's true. There's so much going on at the moment, what with Polar expeditions and the Irish and something about the Kaiser which I can't be bothered to read. It'll all be forgotten in a day or two.'

But Polly was a poor prophet. The story appeared in the *Daily Comment*, four paragraphs of highly-coloured, ill-informed journalese. Miranda threw the paper down in a temper.

'I'm going to write to them and say it's all nonsense! How dare they print such rubbish about me? I shall say it's not true and they're to apologise.'

Edward, one of whose chief pleasures was his morning paper (not the *Comment*), shook his head. 'That's just the way to make them believe it is, and come back to you for more. I wouldn't.'

Harold surreptitiously bought the *Comment* every morning. He was studying at technical college now, and able to read a newspaper between classes without being rebuked. Two days after the article's publication letters began to appear: 'Dear Sir, I was very interested in your story. My mother always told me we were descended from Shakespeare. I think Miss Heriot may be a cousin of mine.' It was amazing how many readers of the *Comment* thought they were off-shoots from the Shakespeare family tree. One or two declared flatly that the whole thing was eyewash. A scholarly lady much given to writing to the papers contributed what was more of an essay than a letter, protesting against this slight on the Bard's morals (for Mr Pierse had coyly mentioned the wrong side of the blanket) and referring readers to her own pamphlet *Sweet Swan of Avon!* published in 1898.

Harold left the newspapers in the college waste-paper baskets. But his trouble was in vain. Other more serious journals picked up the story and made much of it. There was plenty of disturbing world news, but little on the peaceful, cultural front. The Porters' house became the target for representatives of the better dailies, intellectual weeklies, women's magazines and individuals anxious to write up the story for themselves.

'Thank God we're not on the telephone,' Polly said, shutting the door behind yet another caller. 'I don't know what to do, Mattie. If it were me I shouldn't mind, but Miranda does, and it's all getting too much to bear.'

'Send 'em away with a flea in their ear.'

'I do, I do, but they only go round to Morden Hall Road and

ask for her. She won't see them, but Mr Ashe is getting very annoyed about it, and I'm afraid she may be asked to leave, even though they like her so much. Oh dear, how I wish all this had never started . . .'

The crisis came for Miranda with a letter sprawlingly addressed in an envelope which looked as though a dog had had it on a muddy floor. She knew the Benson hand; there was none like it.

My dear Miss Heriot: I have been delighted, charmed, and I may say awed, by the news which has reached me of your illustrious lineage. When we were happy enough to have you in our number none of us could have realised that we daily saw and spoke with one who carried in her veins the blood of the Greatest of all us poor players, whose words are our daily bread and spirit's food. My Shakespeare, rise! exclaimed Jonson in his eulogy on his friend; but not in his dreams could he have imagined . . .

Miranda read the letter to the end; tender, naïf, over-flowing with boyish enthusiasm like its writer. He had hardly noticed her when she was in the company, but now she was a sort of goddess to him, a piece of his sainted Shakespeare. It was touching, it was funny, and it made her mind up. She told the Porters that night what she intended.

'I am going to stop fighting. If I don't, one of these snoopers is going to climb up a drainpipe and steal the Bible and find out about my mother and father, which so far nobody has.'

'We're not going to have to let those dreadful men in?' Polly cried.

'No, of course no. I'm going to telephone to the *Recorder* feature desk. They had the decency to write instead of battering on the door, and they're quite the grandest of the daily papers. I shall say that if they'll send someone who knows something about Shakespeare I'll talk to them and tell them everything I know – except about my parents, of course, because that really doesn't matter to them. After they've printed it there'll be nothing for the other papers to find out, will there. So I'll be rid of all of them.'

Harold gazed at her adoringly. 'You're wonderful. Fancy thinking all that out!'

Edward nodded. 'Very sensible.'

Polly looked less careworn than she had done since the hunt started.

'That sounds splendid, dear. We'll get rid of all the pests at one fell swoop, and then we can be peaceful again, and enjoy it just for ourselves.' She had written to Rachel reproachfully and had a contrite answer, denying that anything had been said except to one person, not counting Ricky, whose discretion she had been sure she could count on, and it was all terribly unfortunate but after all it was a thrilling romantic story, not a scandal, but Polly was to give Miranda a 'sorry' kiss and say that Rachel was in sackcloth if not ashes, and please forgive her. And Ricky had had a letter she meant to send on to Miranda, only it couldn't be found.

'Of course I forgive her. It would have come out somehow. I don't mind half so much now I've decided what to do.'

The front parlour of 92 Erasmus Avenue was always tidy when Rachel and Ricky were away. When they were at home Rachel would spread about her sewing things, while Ricky occupied the table-top with materials for the scrap-book he was compiling about the players of the eighteenth century. The wall-paper was almost hidden behind theatrical photographs; men looking stern with a pipe clenched between their teeth, whether they smoked in private life or not, men with Joan of Arc haircuts standing, hands tied, on a scaffold, looking up to Heaven as Sydney Carton, or gazing, tartan-swathed, in horror at an invisible dagger, or crowned and aloof in a lot of ermine and scalloped sleeve. Women, either smiling or soulful, in every variety of costume except the unflattering ones that signified character-parts. And, on all, inscriptions: To Rick, till Hell freezes, Yours Aye, Don't I look Sweet, Remember Clacton, Tons of Love, Darling, and even Merry Christmas.

Polly had put a vase of chrysanthemums in the middle of the table, and Mattie had built up a much more generous fire than usual (with coal at seventeen-and-six a ton economy was necessary), all for the comfort of the *Recorder* representative.

'What do you think they'll be like?' Miranda asked Polly. 'I rather fancy an elderly female with pince-nez and a Girton degree.'

'Oh. I'd thought some potent, grave and reverend signor. Or perhaps a pale aesthete with a cough.'

'Good thing the fire's drawing well, in that case.'

'Yes. You look very charming, dear. Dark blue's such a *right* colour for skirts, I always feel, and the blouse is so pretty and school-girlish.'

'Ugh!'

'Oh, not in that sort of way, just young and fresh. Particularly with that little standing frill round the neck.'

'Not too like Dog Toby?' Miranda glanced at her reflection, and was satisfied. She looked sufficiently ordinary to please even herself. To have worn anything in the least stagey or romantically-flowing would have been no less than vulgar. The only thing she had ever liked about her appearance at school had been the large ribbon bow confining her hair at the back, so that the ends framed her face, and this she had revived, even with the hair piled up and arranged on her neck in a plaited coil. She was a little nervous, but not much. There was a pleasant importance to being the heroine of this particular Winter's Tale, provided that no Mr Pierses arrived. It was unlikely. The conservative *Recorder* had a name for balanced views, sober reporting, informed criticism, distinguished contributors. The best people read it on trains. It had never figured in Miranda's life, but she trusted it and admired it as everyone did, except perhaps the followers of the Socialist Ramsay MacDonald, who read more lurid journalism.

She arranged herself by the fire, too much on edge to read, and picked up a small elastic and leather collar made for Timon, who had furiously refused to wear it, finally obtaining release from the thing by a deliberate attempt to hang himself on a bush.

Promptly at three o'clock the door-bell rang. Mattie's voice in the hall, and a man's. So it was not to be the Girton graduate.

'Mr Craigie,' announced Mattie, and retreated in a flurry of best pinafore.

Andrew Craigie came into the room as though he owned it, and looked about it as though surveying his territory. He was not at all like anyone Miranda had imagined. He was tall, taller than anyone in that house of shortish people, strongly and straightly built. His top-coat of soft melton wool was wide in the collar and revers, showing off his broad shoulders, and belted into a slender waist. Surprisingly, for that winter day and for the custom of the times, he was hatless. His hair, thick and curly, was of a singular dark red: colour of rich orange marmalade, was Miranda's instant thought.

His steely blue eyes swiftly took in the room and its details, then its occupier. As Miranda's met them a most curious sensation attacked her, as though a charge of electricity were going through her spine, followed swiftly by a cold shiver. She wondered briefly whether she could possibly be getting influenza. It struck very suddenly, she had heard. How like a germ to choose such an inconvenient moment.

'Andrew Craigie, *Recorder*,' he said. His voice was markedly Scottish, with a soft musical accent. 'Miss Heriot?'

'Yes. Do sit down.' He took off the greatcoat, under which he wore a tweed Norfolk jacket of speedwell blue, completely out of the run of the convention that men only wore sombre blacks and greys; which was why he chose to wear it.

'Good of you to talk to us,' he said, settling into the armchair which was Ricky's own, almost obscuring it, long legs negligently crossed; then produced a notebook and began to scribble in it, glancing round the room between scribbles. How arrogant, thought Miranda, like a detective taking down details of the scene of the crime. And 'us', like the royal We. Where was the respectful eagerness of the previous reporters?

Suddenly he looked up with a brilliant smile. 'You've a very theatrical home.'

'Oh, it isn't mine.' She explained, stumbling over her words under his disconcerting gaze, about meeting the Porters in Stratford and coming to lodge with them in Morden.

'You've a great admiration for the theatre and theatre folk.'

'Yes. Well, not all my life. I was brought up quite ordinarily, really. I didn't know anything about the theatre until . . .'

'Suppose you tell me about your life. From the beginning.'

'Not *quite* from the beginning, surely? It would be a bit hard to remember.' She was trying to lighten things, but he did not smile again.

'From as far back as you recall. Your home, your family.'

Nobody had prepared her for this. Nervously she began a sketchy account, unsatisfactory to her own ears, of her childhood and youth in Chamberlain Road, leaving out her grandmother's hostility and trying to concentrate on her school-days. It sounded boring, silly and pointless. She knew by the faint lift of one eyebrow that he thought the same. Then he asked the question she dreaded.

'So you never knew your parents? Tell me about them.'

A stage 'dry', when words utterly desert one, is no more agonizing than the same phenomenon in real life. After a struggling pause, she said, 'They died very young, quite close together. I'd rather not talk about them.'

'That's a strange thing, if I may say so, since you don't remember them. Why do you find it painful to discuss them?'

'That's my affair, isn't it. I thought we were going to talk about Shakespeare.'

He scribbled for some time without speaking. Then he said, 'Very well. Tell me about you and Shakespeare.'

Relieved, she launched into a version of her first visit to Stratford and her subsequent joining of the company, little knowing that everything she left out was apparent to him. 'Grandmother a dragon,' he was writing. 'Went to Stratford behind her back. Got blown up for it. Hated the typing job in Brum. Something behind all this.'

'And how did Stratford affect you?' he asked.

She glowed, forgetting to be prickly. 'Oh, I loved it. Everything about it. It was the most beautiful place I'd ever seen. The –' But this sharp man was not going to want to know about the silver river, the chestnut trees, the first words of *Henry the Fourth*. 'Everything,' she finished lamely.

'You felt you'd been there before, in a previous life, perhaps?'

Her eyes widened (and they had been large and lustrous enough before, he thought). 'I don't think so. Why should I? I don't believe in previous lives – at least I've never given any thought to such things.'

'Read any of the writings of Madame Blavatsky?'

'Who?'

He was not getting anywhere with that one; he tried another line. 'I don't think you told me how well you knew Shakespeare's works before you saw the Stratford staging.'

'Fairly well. We did him at school, of course, but I was never very interested then. It's different now, of course.'

'It is, indeed.' His tone was dry. 'You mean you had never seen a professional production?'

'No.'

'Strange. The Benson Company's been going most of your life, I imagine. But you'd seen other things on the stage, of course.' Something in her face made him press harder. 'Pantomime? Children's plays? The Pilgrim Players?' Seeing that she would rather not answer, he said blandly, 'Of course, you told me you knew nothing about the theatre until, let me see, last year. Why was that? Why had you not been taken to the theatre? That's very unusual in these days, surely.'

'My grandparents didn't approve of playgoing. It was against their religion.'

'I see. No other reason?'

Miranda burst out, 'Yes, there was. I think the story about Shakespeare and Mary Curtis had been passed down the family, and they thought it very shocking, especially my grandmother.'

'Ah. But she'd never mentioned it to you, or shown it to you?'

'No.'

'Why do you think that was?' He leaned back, perfectly at home, tapping his pencil rhythmically against the notebook.

'I don't know! I've told you what I think – what else do you want to know?'

'I want to know,' he said softly, 'whether that entry in the family Bible was ever there, until you put it there, when you acquired such a passion for Shakespeare – on a page with plenty of spaces on it, perhaps? I wonder if you'd been such a lonely child that you thought you'd give yourself the man you admired most for an ancestor? Don't look so shocked, Miss Heriot. It would have been a perfectly understandable thing to do.'

Certain freckles which had powdered Miranda's nose lightly since the summer stood out sharply against the whiteness of her face. She had never been so angry in her life, even to the point of feeling that she might be sick, which would have been the ultimate indignity in front of this unspeakable man. Taking a deep breath, she said, 'I've never been in a witness-box, Mr –

Christie? – but now I know how it feels. If I'd known I was going to be cross-questioned like this, as though I'd committed a murder, I'd never have asked you to come here. I'm sorry I did. Perhaps you'll go now. But first I want you to see something.' She jumped up and reached to a high bookshelf, standing on tiptoe so that he was aware of the pretty line of her figure, the little waist primly banded by a wide leather belt, of the whiteness of her delicate neck, tendrils of dark hair straying on it. A liar, a fantasy-weaver, but not what he had expected.

She came to him, her arms full of a large volume wrapped in cloth, and laid it on the table. Still not speaking, she carefully opened it at the page, laid it flat, and pointed to the entry.

Craigie stood beside her. His sight was extremely good, mountain-bred as he was. He took in the age of the writing, the type of ink, the integration of the entry with the others. 'Do you mind?' he asked, producing a small magnifying-glass; she shook her head. He scanned first the entry, then the whole page, then the entry again, before putting the glass down.

'Have you had this verified?' he asked, and his tone was not what it had been.

'Yes. By an expert. If you want to ask him, he lives not far away. I should go and see him if I were you. Now.'

He returned to his chair, leaving her standing defiantly by the table. 'I apologise. I came here with the firm conviction that the whole thing was a hoax. I see now that it isn't.'

'Thank you. But I really haven't any more to say to you.'

He ignored the dismissal. 'Has your expert said that this reference is definitely to William Shakespeare, playwright?'

'No, because it can't be proved. But it's more than likely, from what he's discovered. Look, here's a typed copy of his statement.' She had stayed on at the office to type it in her own time. 'Why don't you take it away and read it? Then you can make up your mind. There isn't any point in talking any more.' Not talking, but fighting, her unversed self against this hard cynical man. She held out the envelope.

Craigie rose and took it from her. True, there was no point in further talk until he knew the full story. But, much to his own surprise, he found himself very unwilling to go. She had calmed down now, but he was displeased with himself for having upset her by his casual assumption of fraud. He had been in more rooms than he could count, interviewing more people than he could remember, yet he had never felt such a curious compulsion to prolong an interview. There was something unusual about the room, an ordinary enough front parlour in an ordinary ugly house, plastered with the smirking self-satisfied faces of actors. He considered himself the complete materialist; there was an explanation for everything, and it would amuse him, going back to his office on the tube, to work out just what the attraction of the place could have been, apart from its pretty occupant. It had almost as strong an atmosphere as those rooms he had been into in his early reporting days, full of the grief of bereaved relatives whom he would have to ask unforgivably personal questions. But this atmosphere was not grievous but happy, and its effect on him was almost erotic.

As he folded the envelope and put it in his pocket an agreeable thought occurred to him.

'May I come back and talk to you when I've read it?'

'Yes, if you want to. But I work in an office – I could only see you in the evening.'

'What about Monday evening, then?'

With a shrug in her voice, she said, 'If you like.'

'Until Monday. Goodbye, Miss Heriot. And my name's Craigie, not Christie.'

'I'm sorry.' She smiled and gave him her hand. As it touched his the same startling sensation shot through her which she had felt when he entered the room, but this time no thought of influenza entered her head. They were standing very close. She was conscious of the soft texture of his greatcoat, like an animal's fur, of the dampness of rain on it. His tie was blue, echoing his eyes, which were piercing and brilliant but not cold, as she had thought. His mouth was long and firm, and yet with a sensuous look to it. Quite deliberately she looked him full in the face, the electric feeling coursing through her, and felt his hand's clasp tighten on hers. For a long moment they stood, drawn to each other by the strongest magnet in the world.

'Goodbye, then.' She was still standing in the hall, staring at the front door she had slowly closed after him, when Mattie appeared to ask whether tea was wanted.

'What? Oh – no, thank you, Mattie.'

Mattie peered into the parlour. 'Gentleman gone already?'

'Er – yes.' She went back, and sat in the chair she had sat in before, looking at the one which had held him, remembering the turn of his head, the way his hand had rested against the worn stuff of the chair's sleeve-cover. Then she went over and touched it, very lightly.

And Craigie, who should have left the tube at the Strand station, found himself at Leicester Square, the station beyond: a thing he had never done before.

CHAPTER ELEVEN

Dead Shepherd, now I find thy saw of might –
'Who ever loved, that loved not at first sight?'

When Craigie returned to Erasmus Avenue on Monday evening it was in a very different mood. He was angry with himself, and that, in Andrew Craigie, meant very angry indeed. In an inexplicable moment of weakness he had put himself in the power of another person, which, by his standards, was somewhere on the level of yielding to the effects of a drug.

He was twenty-nine years old. A very long time ago, in his Edinburgh boyhood, he had made up his mind that nobobdy at all was going to get in the way of his upward progress through life. His father, a cold, dour man, had expected the utmost of his only son, to whom, as the boy was frequently reminded, the best and most expensive education had been given. When Andrew's examination results fell below Excellent, he was beaten, painfully, thoroughly, and with righteous enjoyment, while his mother wept downstairs. Her health had been ruined by Andrew's birth; no more children were possible, and she must endure the suffering of the one she loved at the hands of the man she had come to hate. For every beating he took, the boy Andrew set up a double black mark – one on his own account, one on his mother's.

With a resolution beyond his years, he determined grimly that his father should not be disappointed. He would be successful, more successful than anyone in his family, whatever it cost him in the way of hard work and application. As he grew older he worked not only in school and at home but in libraries, in his free time; worked himself beyond the reach of criticism. The beatings stopped; he was bigger and stronger now than his father. His last term at school brought him a university place. His mother hugged him and called him her clever laddie, but his father merely grunted, without a word of praise.

In the week after he left school, Andrew disappeared. To his mother he had written a letter, assuring her that he was doing the best thing for himself and for her, that she was not to worry, he would let her know from time to time that he was well.

He kept his word. Postcards reached her, bearing pictures of Highland scenery but with assorted Lowland postmarks. All his father's attempts to trace him failed. The police were not over-interested in his disappearance. Craigie Senior's personality did not impress them. If the lad had run away from such a dour auld callant, it was far from surprising that he didn't want to be found.

In fact, Andrew was an easy train-ride away. Having made for Glasgow, he set about finding himself a job, however lowly, on a newspaper. Living in a back-street lodging in the poorest of conditions, sometimes almost starving, he went from one newspaper office to another until he found an editor willing to take him on. After that there was no holding him. He taught himself shorthand as doggedly as he had made himself perfect in school subjects. As a junior reporter he covered anything and everything, from pit disasters to weddings, always accurate, always possessed of every fact in question, always relentless in the pursuit of news. He moved on from the first undistinguished journal to a better one, then to feature writing as well as reportage; and, having no more worlds to conquer in Scotland, went south to take Fleet Street by storm.

He had not done that, but he had moved swiftly from the London office of his Glasgow paper to a more prestigious one, and upwards until he reached the pinnacle of the *Recorder*. He now had a comfortable mansion flat (not that he cared over-much about comfort) looked after by a cleaning-woman he shared with other tenants. Though in his upward course he had fluttered many women's hearts and occupied a fair number of their beds, he had always extricated himself in time from any situation which threatened his freedom. Other men might let themselves be dragged down by the heavy weights of

146

matrimony, but not Andrew Craigie. He was free and would stay free – free to leave for Tibet tomorrow, to attach himself to an archaeological expedition on the other side of the world, to give up his nights to an investigation of London's underworld, or as much of it as his paper saw fit to pass on to its public.

And he had never fallen in love. Violent attractions he had experienced, and indulged, but his heart had never been lost. Some of the ladies he had gracefully and swiftly abandoned doubted, bitterly, that he had a heart. One of them remarked that he looked romantic, but was just the opposite.

So, when he once more settled into Ricky's special chair, he viewed the room and its occupant with cold, critical eyes. How could he have felt it to be in any way erotic? It was poky, the furniture shabby, the photographs cluttering the walls might have sentimental value but certainly had no other merit, and there lingered on the air a faint but unmistakable smell of tomcat.

As for the girl, who was now wearing a soft woollen dress of deep violet, which became her extremely, she was little more than a child and living under the protection of respectable folk, actors though they might be. He had no intention of seducing her. For a moment he had felt the old familiar thrill that meant the start of an *affaire* as their hands touched and lingered. But he had felt it so many times before, and maybe now it was only because he had not had the time recently to find himself a woman.

'I don't think we can make quite as much of this as we'd hoped,' he said, crisply business-like. 'It's a pretty story, but it won't stand up to inspection, you know. There's absolutely no proof that Mary Curtis's William Shakespeare was *the* William Shakespeare. She may have met him at Court, or she may not. There must have been hundreds of Shakespeares in Warwickshire, and thousands of Williams. The theory's full of holes.'

He tried not to see the disappointment on her face, or to let himself think that it was for the way he spoke to her, not for the brushing-off of the story. 'And let's remember,' he went on, 'at the time this seduction's supposed to have happened he was a personage in Stratford, a man everybody looked up to. D'you suppose he'd have thrown all that away for the sake of a few minutes with some young wench? He'd been through all that, the fires of life, and come out the other side, hadn't he?'

'I don't know,' Miranda said meekly. 'Perhaps some people never do. Perhaps they go on getting burnt up, like Phoenixes.'

'Aye, maybe. But this man had been through all hell for love, if you can believe his own words. "The expense of spirit in a waste of shame is lust in action." If a man can almost die of jealousy, he did. It's there, time and time again.'

'I didn't know you were such a Shakespearean scholar.'

'We're all scholars, we Scots.' His smile softened the boast. 'Did you think we only study Rabbie Burns?'

'I've never really known any Scots. I'll remember in future to notice.' Miranda was beginning to pick up the art of verbal fencing. Andrew, tempted to join in, sternly got back to the matter in hand, which was to disillusion her and take himself off, uninvolved.

'Another point,' he said, 'is that even if this story could be proved, it wouldn't be all that sensational. There are other descendants alive, from the line of Joan Hart, William's sister.'

'Then why did anyone get excited about me?'

He shrugged. 'Women are news. Especially young ones.'

'So you don't think I've any resemblance to the Bard at all?'

Now he had no excuse for not studying her face, letting their eyes tangle, dwelling on the pure paleness of her skin against the purple gown, like white violets among their darker sisters. 'I would I had some flowers o' the Spring that might become your time of day . . .' Damn and blast it, he said within himself, I'm catching something from this infernal room.

But then her eyes, so lustrous, a colour indefinable, mossy green and ferny brown, eyes that a man might drown in, get lost in, as in a forest . . . mocking him a little now, surely.

'What colour are your eyes?' he asked abruptly, unable to stop himself.

'Hazel. That's another thing. The Bard's supposed to have had hazel eyes – you know he's thought to have played Benvolio, and Mercutio says "thou wilt quarrel with a man for cracking nuts, having no other reason . . ."'

Andrew said loudly, the accent very strong in his voice, 'The Devil take the Bard and Benvolio, and the whole gang of them.' He sprang up and pulled her from her chair into his arms and began to kiss her wildly, as wildly as she responded, until the

148

frenzy passed. They stood, clasped together, on the hearthrug, searching each other's faces, breathless and shaken.

Andrew put her a little away from him. 'I didn't mean this, you know.'

'I think you did. I think we both meant it.'

'Aye. Maybe.'

'No maybe about it.'

He traced the outline of her mouth with his finger. 'Where did you learn to kiss like that?'

'You taught me. Just now.'

'Havers! I'll not believe that.'

'Well, it's true. Actually there was – I've had what you might call some experiences . . .' At the thought of Godfrey Arnold and the bed of leaves in Shottery Wood she began to laugh so much that she was obliged to sit down and mop her eyes; and Andrew, catching the infection, laughed as much with relief as anything else, relief that she was not a flower he must not pick. He sat on the arm of her chair and drew her back against him to kiss her again; at which moment the door opened and Polly stood there, her mouth an O of astonishment. Andrew stood up swiftly. Miranda, very pink, said, 'Polly, this is Mr Craigie,' and to Andrew, 'This is Mrs Porter.'

Both murmured politenesses. 'He's been interviewing me,' Miranda added. Polly thought it looked as though he had been doing a great deal more, by the evidence of Miranda's tousled hair and unmistakably well-kissed face. She, so seldom morally shocked, felt as scandalised as she could be. Had they perhaps known each other before? But then Miranda would have said so. Always such a modest, well-behaved girl – and to be sitting there as wild as a Bacchante, leaning against that red-haired young man's shoulder, and his arms round her. For once Polly could think of nothing to say, no quotation that was apt.

So they remained, suspended in embarrassment, until the spell was broken by the loud banging of the front-door knocker to the rhythm of 'How's yer father? All right'. Polly, with an exclamation, rushed into the hall, where a moment later the excited tones of Rachel mingled with the deep growl of Ricky in joyful greetings.

Andrew raised his eyebrows. '*Quel* brouhaha.'

'Yes. It's Polly's sister and her, er . . .'

'Her what?'

'Her husband. They've been on tour.'

All his journalist's instincts informed Andrew that whatever relation the craggy, dour actor bore to the very pretty, alluring woman in cheap but becoming furs, with mock diamonds twinkling in her ears, it was not that of husband. He was pleased, and not only by the fortuitousness of their entrance at such a difficult moment. It gave Miranda even more of a bohemian background than her instant surrender to him and her frank confession of her own free morals. The awkwardness of Polly's discovery of them was lost in general introductions, Rachel's repeated embracings of her sister and Miranda, and the furious squalls of Timon from his basket on the floor. Everybody was very happy and very noisy. Miranda seized her chance of beckoning him into the hall and shutting the door.

'That was lucky, wasn't it. I'd absolutely forgotten they were due back tonight. Anyway, it didn't matter, did it. Nothing matters.'

'Nothing, naughty wee thing.'

'So when shall I see you again?'

His professional diary was full. He was required to sit in on a major dispute about coal-miners' hours, to report on an archaeological discovery which would shake the scientific world, and to inteveiw a certain bristly and difficult Irish playwright, to whom he had a deep aversion, about his latest work. (He looked forward to that one.) These, plus anything else which might crop up, and would.

He said, 'Tomorrow. When do you finish work? All right, I'll pick you up there. We'll go and eat and talk. Goodbye.'

'Not goodbye!'

'No, *adieu, auf wiedersehen, mizpah.*'

'But you don't know the address.'

'The office have it. Escape me never, beloved, and that isn't Shakespeare, it's Browning, of whom it was said that whenever he called for afternoon tea it was a near thing for the housemaid on the stairs.' He kissed her on the tip of her nose, because any further south was dangerous.

Much later in the evening, when Rachel and Ricky were upstairs unpacking, Edward and Harold were in the den, and Polly and Miranda were washing up, Polly asked, 'What was all that about? And don't say all what, because you know perfectly well.'

'Yes. I can't explain it, really. Just one of those violent delights, I suppose.'

'Well, mind it doesn't have a violent end. That's a very tough young man. He won't be any good to you, dear. Please be careful.'

Miranda turned on her a glowing face and eyes full of stars. 'It's too late to be careful, Polly. We're meant for each other, and we both knew it at the same time. It isn't just a violent delight, actually, I only said that. I knew at once, on Friday, when he touched my hand. It was as if . . . I can't explain. Oh, Polly don't you understand? After all, you're married.'

Polly slowly dried a dinner-plate and stacked it. Married to dear Edward, dear stuffy Ted, with whom there had never, even in the beginning, been a night of roman candles and golden rain and whizzing silver catherine wheels, just awkward silences and kindly understandings. All her romance had been channelled into plays and poetry, the expression of other people's loves, not of her own, which had known no summer flowering. Rachel's late summer of love had both delighted and hurt her, but the pain of that was over, and now another had attacked her, one which must also hurt a girl she was fond of, had dreamed of taking into her fold. 'I hop'd thou shouldst have been my Hamlet's wife; I thought thy bride-bed to have decked, sweet maid . . .'

She was too wise to scold, too distressed to reason. Perhaps Rachel, who had a lot of shrewd Quaker common-sense under her fragile exterior, would be able to sort it out in the morning.

But Rachel, warm and rested and happy from a night in her own dear bedroom (Miranda had been hastily removed from the sitting-room to a plain but comfortable attic), was too busy with her own concerns to listen. Edward listened. But he shook his head.

'We're not her official guardians, Poll. She's a pretty girl. Don't suppose the fellow's serious, but a bit of flirtation won't do her any harm.' He could not say that he preferred the thought of Miranda being wooed by a journalist to the prospect of her being swallowed up by the greedy painted mouth of the theatre. When he had met Andrew Craigie, he had been impressed by his strong personality and forthright manner. Besides, Miranda had been brought home at a decent time from the dinner in town to which Andrew had taken her.

She had expected a restaurant, somewhere smart, foreign waiters, women with bare shoulders and jewels, and had been nervous about her own best gown, a simple one of cheap black velvet with a low round neck and sleeves to the elbow. She had taken it to the office and changed into it in the dark and poky cloakroom with its flickering gas-light and stone sink. It seemed hardly the ideal boudoir in which to dress for the evening. The one dingy mirror failed to show exactly what her hair looked like.

But Andrew looked only at her face, greeting her gravely enough. His manners were unobtrusively gallant; she was protectively handed into the tube carriage, as though into the King's glass coach, placed in her seat, and assisted out at Charing Cross. The procedure was repeated in the hansom which took them to their destination. Rumour said that hansoms brought out the beast in men – venture in one, and you were set on and savaged, and the cabbie would not heed your screams for help.

It was not so. In the stuffy little compartment smelling of damp and old leather and horse, Miranda instinctively moved close to Andrew, as close as possible, touching the whole length of him, and her gloved hand found its way into his. He raised it and kissed the spot where a little island of flesh appeared above the glove's button, inside the wrist. A shudder of pleasure went through her; she wondered how she would be able to get through the evening if they were to sit on either side of a table, not touching.

He told the driver to take them to an address Miranda did not recognise, which proved to be a small street somewhere beyond St Paul's. As the cab clattered and jingled its way past shut-up, secret-faced buildings huddling behind the great Cathedral, Andrew opened the legal-looking case he was carrying and took out something encased in a sugar-loaf of florist's paper. It was a posy of white violets, their scent deliriously sweet.

'For me? Oh, how lovely.' But he silently unfastened the top buttons of her coat and slipped the flowers expertly into the low-cut bodice of her dress, between her breasts.

'"In her excellent white bosom, these,"' he said. 'Hamlet. Or shall we forget the Bard tonight?'

'Certainly. In any case, you despatched him to the Devil on Monday.'

'So I did. Here we are. Allow me.'

The place was a chop-house, and had been for a century or more, a cosy, savoury-smelling old place whose tables were divided from one another by dark green curtains on brass rails. High settles backed on to each other, so that conversation at one table could not be heard at the next. Law-clerks, booksellers and bookbuyers, and those whose work lay in and about Paul's had eaten and drunk there for so many years that they seemed to have left their imprint on those who used the place still. It was easy to imagine stovepipe hats hanging on the pegs, side-whiskers and high choking cravats on the diners, leaning chatting across the tables.

Andrew and Miranda had a table to themselves. Looking round, she saw only one other woman in the place, a young foreign-looking girl talking earnestly to a bearded man. So there were no white shoulders, no jewels, no rivals; not that it mattered, for the two of them sat closely pressed, as closely as in the hansom, and Andrew had eyes only for her.

An elderly waiter who seemed too bent to carry trays waited on them deferentially, calling Andrew by his name. He brought a great joint of beef on a wheeled trolley, which Andrew carved for them with expertise; then piping-hot vegetables, greens perfectly done, potatoes in their jackets. Miranda was simultaneously conscious that it was all delicious and hardly aware of eating at all. They drank beer, which she was used to from the inns of Stratford. It was good, the best of Barclay and Perkins, but its effects could not compete with their own exaltation.

They talked very little, and lightly, and laughed a good deal, finding the same things funny. Andrew had a fund of stories, some curious, some scandalous; he had not the actor's facility for mimicry, but a dry-point manner of his own. They were both aware that they were marking time, putting off what had to be said between them. It was when Miranda had regretfully decided that she could eat no more of the excellent Spotted

Dick pudding, with its rich veil of custard, that Andrew said, 'I suppose we must face it.'

'Yes.' There was no need to ask what.

'I can't do without you. I've tried arguing with myself, but somehow it's no good.'

'I haven't even tried that.'

'Will you leave those very worthy people in Morden, and come and live with me?'

A chill touched her, as though the cold wind outside, with its warning of snow, had got in through the thick walls and blown aside the green curtains. A memory came back that she had sworn never to recall, of dashed expectations, once before.

'Live with you, Andrew?'

'I can't marry you, my love. A man in my profession shouldn't marry. I have to be free. I might have to go anywhere or do anything. I could be killed, blown up, kidnapped . . . there's no saying. It wouldn't be fair to my wife. I could even be picked up by some island enchantress.' (Or any enchantress, he thought; there's no vow a newspaper man can take for faithfulness.)

Miranda experience a long, bitter moment of disappointment. Whatever she had expected, it was not this. She had been merely silly and naïve over Godfrey; this time was to have been something different, more real, happy and fulfilling. All her old self-criticisms rushed back, as though Grandmother's ghostly voice were speaking them: bad blood, spawn of the Devil, like mother like daughter . . . perhaps there was something about her which gave her away to men as a loose creature, not the sort of woman they would marry.

She met his eyes, and read frankness in them, not disparagement. Of course what he had said was true. His life was not like other men's – he was not free to make promises. And then, if one could look past the conventional wedding frills, bridesmaids and flowers and church, it was really a rather exciting prospect, daring and modern. 'Have you heard about Miranda Heriot? She's living with a man, *not married*,' Editha would tell girls she had been at school with. If it were Andrew it would be marvellous, divine, just the opposite of respectable and stuffy. Rachel and Ricky weren't married, and they were far happier than Polly and Edward.

'No,' she said again, 'I don't mind. I'll live with you.'

'My lovely girl.' He put his hand over hers and squeezed it tightly, a snowball melting in fire.

When the time came for her to go Andrew beckoned the waiter, and spoke softly to him. Then he turned to her.

'You'll be driven home. No need to pay the man, it's all taken care of.'

'But, Andrew – all that way! I could perfectly well go by tube.'

'Do you think I'd allow that? And I can't go with you, I have to be off by first light in the morning.'

'And they say Scotsmen are mean . . .'

The house in Erasmus Avenue was quiet and dark when she let herself in. But Harold, lying awake, heard her, and slept no more than she that night, though for other reasons. As she lay awake, staring into the spangled darkness, panic crept into her mind: how would she tell people, what would they think? Was she cutting the ground of respectability from under her feet, now that she had made her own life? Visions of unpleasantness chased each other through her thoughts, exaggerated by the lateness of the night and her nervous reaction from excitement. But, she reasoned, it could not be all that bad, Andrew would never let it be, for he loved her; of course he loved her. And in time he would come to see that she cared nothing for the uncertainty of his work, that she could be good and patient and not complain about his absences, or ask questions. And so, in the end, he would marry her. From that long-ago production of *All's Well* lines floated into her mind.

. . . who ever strove
To show her merit, that did miss her love?

She recited them to F.R. and Constance at that first audition at the Wagstaff. It had been an omen; of course.

She fell asleep, happy.

CHAPTER TWELVE
A Maid at your Window

Polly sat down very suddenly on a kitchen chair when Miranda told her.

'I've been afraid of something of the kind. But I didn't know it would be as soon or as bad as this.'

'It isn't bad, Polly dear. It's wonderful. Something I've been waiting for all my life, I think. Be happy for me, please.'

'I'd like to, but I can't be. You don't know this man, Miranda. He simply came here to interview you (and now you say he isn't even going to make much of that) and in five minutes you've struck up this . . . this relationship. Can't you see what he's after, child? There's only one thing men like him want.'

'It isn't like that —'

'It never is. They all say that, to start with. But I've seen so much of this sort of thing, and it always ends badly. Young girls simply aren't a match for experienced men like this Craigie. He'll destroy you, dear, use you and throw you away.'

'Like an old glove, I suppose. Oh, Poll, don't be so melodramatic. I'm sorry to break it to you like this, and you know how fond I am of you all and how much I've enjoyed living with you. I'm grateful, really I am, and I wouldn't dream of leaving here if it weren't for . . . this.'

'What about your job?' Polly asked coldly. 'You're not proposing to live in town and work in Morden Hall Road, I suppose?'

'Well, no. But I expect I can easily get another one in London, now I'm used to working in a law office.' She had given it no thought, but it was not important enough to worry about. 'I'll tell Mr Ashe tomorrow.'

'They'll expect some kind of notice,' Polly pointed out, 'a fortnight, or a month, whatever was agreed when you went to them.'

'Oh. Will they?' Miranda had envisaged sweeping up her belongings and flying ecstatically to Andrew. Marking time in Morden was not her idea of instant romance.

'You'd better speak to him as soon as you can – and apologise, won't you. I did get you that job, after all, and I'm sure they expected you to stay with them. There aren't many places suitable for well brought-up young women to work in, you know. And if I were you, I wouldn't explain.'

'No?' Miranda had toyed with the idea of a mysterious romantic-sounding statement of why she was going away.

'Because it wouldn't sound very well to say, "I'm leaving because I'm going to my lover who can't be bothered to marry me and doesn't in the least mind taking me away from my friends."' Polly jumped up and began noisily to clear out a cupboard, slamming its contents on the kitchen table. Unhappy at the upset she had caused, Miranda went to seek out Rachel, who was at her dressing-table absorbed in re-styling her hair into a crown of plaits round her head. She listened in silence, transferring hairpins from her mouth to her coronet. Then, after a satisfied glance in the mirror, she swung round to face Miranda.

'I'm not really surprised. You're an impetuous young thing, aren't you, chick.'

'I suppose I am. But I can't help it.'

'No. None of us can, when the cupids swoop down and carry us away. But I must confess that I agree with Polly, it's all too sudden and too soon.'

'But . . .'

'I was almost thirty,' Rachel applied a light spray of perfume behind each ear, 'when I met Ricky. I was working as a shopgirl after Mother died, because there wasn't really enough to live on, and I just happened to be staying in digs that took theatricals. Ricky had a room there. He'd just had a frightful quarrel with his wife and they were living apart, not for the first time. We sat next to each other at supper, and that was that; I don't have to tell you, you know all about it now.'

'Yes.'

'But it was a bit different, you see. We were under the same roof. We both had to queue up for the bathroom. I found out what he ate and didn't eat, and how bad-tempered he was first thing in the morning. We had one of those big-hearted landladies, so before long I found out that he didn't snore. I got to know what I might be able to change about him, and what I couldn't. And it worked the other way, as well, because he saw me when I hadn't any make-up on and found he could bear to look at me like that. You see? All those things, before we decided to pair up together. It wasn't always easy; there were times when – well, I had to work hard at being loving. I know he had, too.'

Miranda said nothing. She had given no thought to these things, any more than to Mr Ashe's reaction to her sudden departure from the firm. But it seemed nonsensical that such little things should matter.

'I'm quite sure it will be all right,' she said.

Rachel sighed. 'Are you, darling? You're looking for love, of course. You never had it at home, so now you don't care where you get it. I only saw your Andrew for a few minutes the other night, but he didn't strike me as a man who minded a lot about love. And you were wrong about Godfrey Arnold, you know.'

Miranda flushed. 'Oh, that! don't remind me. I was so silly then.'

'Then? Not all that long ago, chick.'

'No . . . But Andrew isn't an actor, he's real. At least, I don't mean that Ricky isn't. I meant . . .'

'I know what you meant. The point about Ricky is that I fell in love with him before I'd seen him *as* an actor. Stage images have nothing to do with reality. You could fall head over heels for a Romeo, and find him a cold fish with bad habits once you got him home. Beware of illusion, darling.'

'There isn't any illusion about a journalist.'

'No? Doesn't every man put on a conjuring act when he's courting a woman?'

Miranda had no answer ready. Rachel looked long into her eyes, then shrugged and laughed. 'No use talking, is it. Just be careful, that's all. And I mean careful. Do you understand?'

'No, Rachel. At least, I think I know what you mean. But not . . . well, not any more than that. Please will you tell me?'

Rachel told her. 'You mustn't risk having children. It wouldn't be fair to them. Just you be thankful I know about such things.'

Ricky, when he was told of Miranda's departure, grunted. 'Silly bitch. Good riddance.' Rachel said nothing. She knew that he had looked on Miranda as one more person to take up her time and affection. Edward sighed for the loss of his surrogate daughter. And Harold all but pleaded on his knees for Miranda to stay.

'I know what you say about not feeling I'm right for you. But I am, I am really! I may seem a bit young now, but if you'll only wait for me – only six months or a year – you'll see how much I've changed. I can give you something that rotter never will. He'll have finished with you in six months, I know that type.'

'How can you possibly know any type, when you've only just left school? You're not even grown-up.'

'What about you, then?' Then they were squabbling like children until Harold's pain recalled him to the need to plead with her. She was distressed at his distress, embarrassed for him and for herself, but quite unable to give him hope or comfort.

'Please don't go on so. It's not as if I were the only girl in the world . . .'

'And it's not as if that rotter were the only man in the world.'

'Don't call him "that rotter". For me he *is* the only man. And you'll meet lots more girls, you know – just think of the chances you've got, with different ones in the company every season.'

'I tell you I won't. I only want you.' He gulped. 'I'll – I'll marry you, if you like. I expect it could be arranged, even at my age.'

Miranda got up abruptly. 'Thank you very much. I do appreciate your kind offer, but I don't want to marry you, Harold. Nobody here's a bit pleased that I'm happy, and it seems to me the sooner I go the better.'

Harold's spectacles were misted with angry tears as she slammed the door.

To be going to live in a flat was tremendously exciting and romantic. Flats were quite different from houses; a modern, adventurous, sophisticated way of living. Miranda, who had never been inside one, was thrilled by the exterior of Kent and Sussex Mansions, many storeyed, red-brick, imposing, with a professional air to it. Andrew watched her, amused, as they waited for the lift to come down to ground-floor level, manned by the porter, who kept an old-fashioned winged chair in the entrance hall and had no hesitation about asking strangers their business.

Miranda wondered how Andrew was going to introduce her. She was hardly young enough to pass as his niece, which she understood to be the usual alias for illicit ladies. Or would he, perhaps, be terribly bold and say, 'This is my mistress' or paramour or even doxy? When one was only familiar with such things in Shakespearean terms it was difficult to guess the right word.

But he merely said, ''Morning, James. Bring Miss Heriot's luggage up, will you.'

The flat, three floors up, had high ceilings, huge windows, moulded cornices and marble fireplaces that looked back to an earlier time, though the building was only fifteen years old. Its décor was austere: heavy dark curtains, patterned Turkey carpet, upholstery of leather and stern hard-wearing fabric. There were some large pieces of good reproduction furniture. The only pictures were sepia prints of scenes featuring people wearing powdered wigs, swords, and other Georgian accoutrements, who quite plainly belonged properly to the very late nineteenth century. Miranda thought they were very boring. She was, as she looked round the living-room of her future home, a little disappointed, a little flattened.

'Sorry it's rather cold,' Andrew said. 'I don't think Mrs Burr's particularly strong on lighting fires. But then she doesn't usually have to do it.' He shovelled on more coal from an imposing scuttle. He had taken the morning off, with difficulty, to settle Miranda in, which he thought rather a noble thing to do. It did not occur to him to wonder what she had expected of a bachelor apartment, or how it would feel to be transported from the cosy clutter of Erasmus Road. A few of the ladies he had brought to the flat, on very short-term stays, had been, though decent enough, from very modest walks of life. To them its dignity and spaciousness had been breath-taking. It had amused him to see them daringly throw their funny little bits of lingerie over the great pompous chairs, and strew their bright bazaar-bought earrings and brooches on top of the frowning dressing-chest. He would not have been surprised if Miranda had done the same.

But she merely stood and looked, quiet. He had reckoned on the possibility of morning in bed, with perhaps a scramble to dress again and rush off to his next interview, but apparently that was not to be the case. And so, with instructions about ringing down to James for more coal, and finding a cold-lunch tray laid ready by Mrs Burr in the kitchen, he left in good time, only quickly brushing her cheek with his lips. He liked to economise on pleasures, to save them up, make them know their place. And he enjoyed anticipation almost as much as the pleasure itself.

When he had gone the flat seemed extraordinarily quiet. Through the shut windows the traffic of Marylebone Road could be heard, and, in lulls, the chiming of the church clock. The rooms were airless, since neither Andrew nor the cleaner ever troubled to open the windows. Miranda went into the bedroom, which he had not shown her. It was large and severe: a plain oak double bed, massive wardrobe, dressing-table and washstand. There were no photographs (which seemed strange indeed after Erasmus Avenue), the brushes and toilet articles laid out on the dressing-table bore no monogram, and told nothing about the owner. The room might have been in an hotel, so impersonal it was.

Miranda, if she had been honest with herself, would have been forced to admit that she longed to be back in Morden. In the office, taking tea and biscuits brought by Bertie, or typing peacefully some long involved document; gossiping with Poll, embroidering a blouse under Rachel's tuition, listening to Harold rambling on about his experiments in chemistry – anything but to be alone in this cheerless unfamiliar place. But she put the thought away. You got yourself into this, she told herself, so just make the best of it. It's very thrilling, really – alone in a man's rooms, unchaperoned, in the most deliciously scandalous circumstances. The thought reminded her of Editha: she began to compose a letter to her.

But why not write one? In a secretaire she found writing paper, and a portable typewriter on a table. As she typed, purple passages full of exclamation marks following each other like waves, she began to feel a great deal better.

But the day dragged. The lunch prepared by Mrs Burr was inadequate and unimaginative – slices of slightly tired cold ham, bread and butter which had been cut too long ago, and the means for making tea. There were plenty of books, but Miranda found them a singularly dull lot – foreign travels, military history, memoirs, politics and reference-books, exploration and archaeology, formed the bulk of them. She wondered what Andrew read for amusement. At last she settled down with a volume of murder trials, full of details so frightful that she was less aware of the clock's slow tick and the darkening of the afternoon and the lighting of street lamps.

Half-way through the book, sated with horrors, she fell asleep, and woke two hours later, stiff, cold, hungry and a little frightened to find herself in the dark in this strange room, among looming shapes of furniture. She was struggling to re-light the dead fire, striking match after match, when Andrew's key turned in the lock.

'Good Lord! What d'you think you're doing?' was his less than cordial greeting. He cut short her explanations by swiftly lighting the gas and brushing her aside to make up the fire himself. 'Could you not see it was going out? The place is as cold as charity.'

'Well, I fell asleep, you see . . . I'm sorry . . .'

'All right, all right.' He went into the kitchen, still in his overcoat, to mix himself a hot toddy. It did not occur to him to wonder how a perfect stranger to the flat, unaware where anything was kept, or of the coal-consuming habits of the grate, would have contrived to create a welcoming scene of warmth and cosiness and a prepared meal to greet him. It seemed to him that with a woman in the place a man had a right to expect such things. He surveyed the contents of the food-safe; the remains of the ham, a piece of wax-hard cheese, bread and a jar of pickle. It would have to do. He disliked preparing food and only kept the barest essentials in the flat.

Miranda had followed him in and hovered, feeling a chill in the atmosphere which was not merely the temperature of the rooms. She had expected a rapturous greeting, apologies for his lateness, comfort for her after a long lonely day, and instead was being made to feel a nuisance. Andrew glanced at her, pale, rumpled with sleep, looking as put out as he felt, and began to have serious doubts that he had done the right thing in picking her up and planting her in his life. But she was there, and he must make the best of it. The bedtime reward might well be worth the slight annoyance of his homecoming.

Women needed feeding and a bit of cosseting to put them in a good mood. He abandoned the notion of bread and cheese. 'Wash your face and comb your hair,' he said, as to a child, 'and I'll take you out for a bit of supper.'

'But you've just come in.'

'Then I can just go out again, can't I.'

The place he chose was a small restaurant, hardly more than a café, a few minutes' walk away in Baker Street. It was warm, the proprietor friendly, the food cheap and simple but more than welcome to one who had eaten almost nothing that day. Andrew, watching her, marvelled; he had forgotten what young normal appetites were like. But the colour came back to her face as she began to turn back into the girl who had captivated him. He made her laugh with a blistering account of the playwright he had been interviewing at his Hampstead home, a curmudgeonly wrong-headed old devil who had tried to lecture him instead of shutting up and answering questions. His impersonation of the old man's hideous Ulster accent was wickedly accurate. They drank rough red wine and scalding, very good coffee; excitement began to creep back into the evening. As they walked back to the flat his arm was round her waist.

Miranda had never seen a man wearing pyjamas; her grandfather had favoured the old-fashioned nightshirt. Andrew's pyjamas were rather dashing, with a Cossack collar and a side-fastened jacket. The sheets were cold, but her nightdress was fortunately of serviceable flannel, long-sleeved and cosy. Andrew eyed it questioningly, but she neither apologised for it nor offered to remove it, only lay smiling up at him. A warm, willing young mistress, well versed in love; what could be better? He climbed into the high bed and pulled her to him.

She had tried not to shriek, she had not been able to help struggling, and now she was not able to help crying a little with pain. Andrew turned up the oil-lamp on the bedside table and stared down at her, grim-faced.

'Why the hell didn't you tell me? Why the hell did you lie?'

She had been shocked and hurt, and it had not been at all what she had thought it would be, that evening in Rachel's parlour. Trying to wipe her eyes and her nose on her sleeve cuff, she said chokingly, 'Lie? what do you mean? I don't understand.'

He laughed, a short unamused laugh. 'You may be naïve, my girl, but you can't be as stupid as that. Come on, now, why did you do it?'

She sat up against the pillows. 'I truly do *not* know what you mean, Andrew. Why are you so angry?'

'You did just happen to mention,' he said icily, 'that you were experienced. Now I find you're a virgin – or you were until about five minutes ago. Do you suppose I'd ever have brought you here if I'd known that? I may be loose in the morals but I'm not a cad – I hope. So what's your explanation?'

Experienced. She had never said she was experienced. Surely he had known . . . Then the memory began to come back of something she had said the first time he kissed her; she had laughed, and thought of the ludicrous episode of Godfrey Arnold, and said something, impossible to remember what. And he had taken it as an admission that she was a Scarlet Woman, one who went about jumping lightly into the bed of any man who asked her.

'Will you listen to me,' she asked, 'and stop looking like that? I'll try to explain.'

'I shall be most interested. And try to make it convincing.' His inner conviction was that she had played a trick on him, for some purpose he could not guess – blackmail, perhaps, or to get out of an unwanted engagement. He was very angry, but he listened.

When she had finished the stumbling explanation, which sounded as silly to her own ears as it must to his, the stern look had gone from his face.

'Good Lord,' he said. He reached for his dressing-gown, put it on, and lit a cigarette. Then, sitting on the side of the bed, he contemplated Miranda.

'I think I ought to send you home tomorrow. You see – and

it's difficult to say this without appearing to insult you, but I assure you that's not my intention – the situation's very different from what I'd imagined it to be. I thought you were an experienced woman. I expected you to stay with me as long as it pleased both of us, and then move on. Now I see that's not so. And I can't take the responsibility for an innocent like you. I don't want to be anyone's substitute for a father, or an uncle, or a guardian. I've my own life to lead, and I'd expect any woman who shared it with me to lead hers, just as independently. Understand?'

'Yes,' replied Miranda, who did. Now that the initial shock was over she felt very calm and clear-headed. 'I quite see that you wouldn't want anyone to be a burden to you. But you can't exactly send me home tomorrow, can you – because I haven't got a home. I was only staying with the Porters as a paying guest. Do you think I could really go back to them, after all the fuss there was about me leaving? I don't think the firm would have me back, either; Mr Ashe wasn't a bit pleased when I gave notice. So I'm rather stuck, aren't I.'

Andrew was forced to agree. Since he had struck out for himself in life he had given little or no thought to the convenience of anyone but himself. Now, it seemed, he would actually have to consider the needs of the young person who now occupied the middle of his bed, in a state of pretty disarray, but not, he was glad to see, likely to create an embarrassing and noisy fuss. Another new experience for him was the realisation of how much he had misjudged her and her situation; as though a few posed theatrical photographs and a brace of over-emotional actors necessarily meant loose living. He should have known better, from his observation of people of all sorts, but, to do him justice, he had seen very little of the world of theatre. It was salutary, for once, to learn that he had something yet to learn.

'The point is,' Miranda said, 'how do we still feel about each other? I mean, do you still like me? Or has all this put you off me completely?'

'I might ask you the same.'

'Goodness, you *are* Scottish, aren't you. Anybody else would have been gallant about it. Well, the answer is no, it hasn't. I thought you were rather awful just now, but there were misunderstandings on both sides.'

'Aye, there were,' Andrew said gravely. 'Well, if you're prepared to take a chance, so am I, though I doubt we're both as mad as hatters. Now may I come back to my own bed?'

With a smile that warmed the chill of midnight, Miranda threw back the sheet and welcomed him in. It was very true, that bawdy song of Ophelia's, she reflected. 'By Gis and by Saint Charity, Alack, and fie for shame, Young men will do't, if they come to't, By cock, they are to blame.' But the maid who came to the young man's window to be his Valentine was just as much to blame, after all, so the game was equal. She began to speculate whether Anne Hathaway had got into that situation with her Will; and suddenly was asleep.

Andrew turned and put out the lamp, very quietly, not to wake her.

CHAPTER THIRTEEN
A Separable Spite

Life with Andrew Craigie was never easy; on the other hand it was never dull. Miranda resolved that it would not be her fault if their alliance failed. From the first she made up her mind that what Andrew wanted, within reason, he should have. He wanted passion, and of that she had plenty, appetite growing with what it fed on; in a very short time he taught her its language as interpreted by him, and she gave him her young fresh eagerness to enliven his slightly jaded tastes. He wanted admiration, having built himself up into what he admired; she listened, asked questions and remembered the answers, looked through his files – every article he had written, every case he had worked on, meticulously pasted up. One evening she said, 'Why should you have all the trouble of doing this? I could do it for you.'

He hesitated. Nobody could do anything as thoroughly as he did it himself. But, humouring her, he handed over a copy of the *Recorder* containing an article of his, and four later copies in which were printed letters commenting on it. She produced pages of clippings so neatly put together and dated that he could find no fault in them. After that he never touched the files again except for consultation.

Very meekly, she suggested that she might take on the settling of any standard payments – rent, caretaker's fees, insurance cover and the like. 'They'd look much better properly typewritten, and save your time.' He was surprised to find that she was right. Of personal correspondence he seemed to have none, other than letters from his mother, written in a small timid hand under an Edinburgh postmark.

One morning the envelope was black-bordered. He looked up from the letter, tight-lipped. 'My father's dead. I shall have to go up there.'

'Oh. I'm sorry.'

'No need to be. And no need to look shocked, either. I was about as fond of him as you were of your grandmother. Kith and kin! Thank God we can choose our friends. I wouldn't even be fashed going to the funeral, but it would grieve my mother, and there are things to see to she could never tackle. I'll be away a week, maybe. You'll be all right?'

'I'll be fine.'

It was a shade lonely at first, the rooms empty of him, reminding Miranda of her first day in the flat. But now it was no longer unfamiliar, only forbidding. She sat surveying it, the big stark bachelor rooms, the drab colours. She addressed it. 'You're a beast, a great ugly beast, and don't you deny it.' It reminded her very much of the surroundings in which she had been brought up. There had been nothing she could do with the house in Birmingham, but this was a different matter, and at her mercy. Wearing an apron from the cleaner's cupboard and armed with a short stepladder she set about the reformation of Flat 12, Kent and Sussex Mansions.

Down came the pictures, the faded monochrome beaux and belles with their improbable hair-styles and Victorian faces. Down came three sporting prints from the room Andrew used as a study, a fox-hunt with the hounds closing in on their victim and two others showing earlier stages of the chase. Miranda was fairly sure they were not reflective of Andrew's personal taste. She measured the blank spaces they left on the wall, and made a note of them. The only picture in the bedroom was a sepia print of a classical nude, poised on the edge of a sunken marble bath which she was pensively eyeing. Her figure was singularly undeveloped for such a large young woman, her expression one of half-witted chastity. 'You shan't be made to blush any more, my dear,' said Miranda.

Into the wardrobe all the pictures went, and the gloomy vases which were the flat's only ornaments, more suitable for funerary urns than for decoration. The only living thing was an aspidistra, dusty and depressed; only Mrs Burr ever watered it. Miranda carried it out to the landing for James to remove.

The actual furnishings were not so easy to dispose of. But in the bedroom she took off the counterpane of dingy brown moquette; it had never seemed an apt accessory to love. Then she went shopping.

In the picture department of an Oxford Street store she discovered a collection of coloured prints of French Impressionists. Knowing nothing else of them, she knew that they were light and lovely, the sort of paintings Rachel liked. She chose a dozen or so. A golden field of corn in the summer sun, a twisting cobbled Paris street with a church campanile floating about it, a young girl with a flower, a Pissarro all heavenly blues: it was like putting together a rainbow. She paid for them with three pounds of the money Andrew gave her for housekeeping – it seemed a great deal, but she hoped it would be worth it.

The vases she did not replace. In a curiosity shop she found two old pieces of pottery, a red and white deer running against green foliage and a flat-back group, a peasant boy and girl, arms linked, in singing blues and pinks, each bearing flowers. They were unfashionable, but she fancied them very much.

In the bedding department of the store she kept her ringless left hand gloved and bought a coverlet of heavy drab silk embroidered all over with Chinese designs of fantastic birds, formal trees and bridges, palanquins and tiny figures, all in pastel colours.

Her purchases, when they arrived by delivery cart, seemed appallingly large and numerous. The austere James, carrying them from the lift one by one, made it silently clear that whatever Madam had been up to, it would lead to no good. She ignored his disapproval, giving him the usual shilling for services. After spending so much money, what was a shilling?

When the pictures were up, hung to the accompaniment of several oaths learned from Andrew, Miranda stood back, and was wonderfully satisfied with the effect. The drab walls retreated behind luminous colours and delicate lines that brought another world into the place, a world of clear skies and warm winds and France in soft rain. On the mantelpiece the deer and the innocent rustic couple gazed amicably at each other on either side of the solemn marble clock. The large pompous leather sofa and armchair were bright with four silk tapestry cushions which had been irresistible.

The bed-cover was a field of flowers, transforming the room. As a final touch Miranda hung over the mantelpiece her *pièce de resistance*, Manet's *Olympia* reclining in all her arrogant beauty, the glorious creamy flesh clad only in a black velvet neck-ribbon, a bracelet and one tiny slipper. Miranda straightened her frame. 'There,' she said to herself, 'if that isn't an inspiration, I don't know what would be.'

But on the evening of Andrew's return she was nervous, certain that she had done the wrong thing. At the sound of his key she started guiltily and ran into the little hall to pacify him with her welcome before he saw the changes she had wrought. He kissed her warmly, the slow sweet kiss that always melted her. But Andrew was never amorous until he got his coat off and washed. As she plied him with questions about Edinburgh and his journey, still holding him so that he should not go into the room too soon, he guessed at some guilt from her unwonted chattiness.

'Do you not want me to go in there? Because I'd be glad to get out of this draught.'

'No, it's not that . . . well, yes, it is, in a way. Oh, I'll *have* to let you see. I made a few changes.'

As he stood, looking at the changes she had made, which with a journalist's eye he took in at once, she said nervously, 'I suppose I shouldn't have gone behind your back, only it was all so dull and depressing. I didn't *think* you'd like it.' She led him into the bedroom, so that he should see the worst.

He said, 'Mphm. What have you done with the old pictures?'

'I put them away.'

'Good. I thought you might have sold them, and they don't belong to me.'

'I'll get them out again,' she said miserably.

'No, don't trouble. D'you think I'm going to change that bonnie piece for whatever was there before?' He indicated Olympia. 'You're an astonishing woman, Miranda. I shouldn't wonder if you've a touch of the family genius in you after all.'

Her face was transfigured. 'You mean you like what I've done?'

'I think it's not half bad. That's great praise from a Scotsman, you know.' He sat down and pulled her on to his knees. 'I could not have told you what was on the walls or the bed, I tell you that frankly, and I tell you too that I don't much care what's around me. But maybe it's good for me to see things now and then. What do you know of the Impressionists, by the way?'

'Who?'

He nodded. 'I thought so. You've just got flair. And a lot besides.' He began to kiss her, starting with her eyelids and working downwards.

Olympia stared at them, square-jawed and implacable.

The meal that was set before Andrew was hot, plain and filling. Miranda had been aware of his displeasure at coming home on that first evening to find the place cold and foodless. It never happened again. She was not a great cook, but simple easy food pleased him, and a few comforts he had never known before; a stone bed-warmer on the coldest nights, fresh coffee which had not stood about in a jug for hours, a proper cooked breakfast when he had time for it. He was living well.

Now that she had the domestic routine organised, it was time to approach him on another matter.

'I can't just sit here all day and every day.'

'Why not? Very pleasant life.'

'Would you like it?'

'Well, of course not. But that's different, surely. Women expect to stay at home.'

'I don't. I liked working for Mr Ashe. I'm going to find myself a typewriting job.'

'There's not the slightest need. Don't I give you enough to live on?'

To be quite truthful, she would have had to answer that he did not. After her weekly wage at the solicitors' office it was disappointing to feel unable to buy anything for herself beyond the mere necessities of life, and she would not, could not ask him for more. Instinct and knowledge of him told her that he was not over-fond of spending money. The lean years when he had lived in Glasgow at poverty level had left their mark, and Fleet Street life was chancy. Now he was successful, next week he might be free-lancing again and out of favour. So Miranda said no more, but followed the advertisement columns until she found one that looked likely, for a young woman to work at agreed hours for an author living in Adelphi Terrace, close to Charing Cross Station, between the Strand

and the river.

Gabriel Proudfoot was middle-aged, badger-grey, excessively absent-minded, and the author of solid, serious novels of repute. He lived with his almost equally vague wife in pleasant eighteenth-century rooms looking on to the river. He was gratified to find someone with ears young enough to catch the low mutter of his voice, which had made dictation a struggle in the past for more than one lady secretary. Working for him also required a great deal of patience, waiting with pencil suspended for him to think up the next passage of meticulously balanced prose. Fortunately the surroundings helped – elegant old furniture, the sweeping view from the long window of the river and its traffic, the Angelica Kauffmann ceiling, a roundel of painted nymphs and cupids, goats, swans and garlands.

Thus Miranda worked and dreamed, and on Saturdays collected her wages, some of which inevitably went towards extra luxuries for Andrew. The Proudfoots exhibited not the slightest interest in her personal circumstances, nor was Gabriel the kind of employer from whom a pretty typist need expect unwelcome attentions. Miranda knew that if she suddenly disappeared, and the police called to enquire, he would be quite unable to describe her appearance.

So a year passed. In Morden the Porters marvelled that Miranda's *affaire* had lasted so long. Polly visited her occasionally for afternoon tea, approved of the staid yet homely air of the flat, and brought welcome news of the others. Rachel and Ricky were touring comfortably enough, Ricky had gone on for F.R. when F.R. had badly sprained an ankle climbing trees as Caliban, and hanging upside down from them with a fish in his mouth, Rachel had suffered from a nasty cough all winter but was better as soon as they settled in Stratford again. Edward had won an angling cup. About Harold his mother said very little; Miranda sensed a certain reserve, and knew herself to have been a severe disappointment in that direction. Always Polly's visits ended with a wistful query.

'But why doesn't he marry you, dear?'

It was easy enough to shrug off. 'There's no need – we do very well as we are. It wouldn't be his style. Don't you think ideas have changed about such things?'

Her own heart gave a different answer. The rest of life was only a dream compared with the reality of Andrew. Only twenty, but fettered to a man for life; that was her fate. Her life with him was like the tenancy he held of the flat; he was not her own. Impossible not to see the averted faces of other dwellers, when they met her in the lift or on a landing; impossible not to notice the difference between James's manner to her and his cordiality when he spoke to others. He would not like his wife and daughters to know what went on in his flats, all of a piece with these Suffragettes and this new ragtime music and gramophones and all the disasters in the papers. It was not pleasant to be classed as a disaster in connection with Andrew, whose glory she wished to be.

And he gave her no cause to hope. Sometimes he would be casually brusque, as to a servant, sometimes kind, and at night tender, wooing, seeming her slave as she was his. But under it all lay cause for fear. Miranda began to practise small superstitions, she who had thought actors slightly mad with their reliance on lucky hares' feet and unlucky words in the dressing-room. One must not step on the line between paving-stones, look at the moon through glass, pass a sweep without touching him, or a piebald horse without wishing. If only the bad influences might be propitiated, might not touch their fragile happiness . . .

The letter from Birmingham came one morning, before she had left for the Adelphi. It apologised for the lawyers' delay in giving her any information about her grandparents' estate, and thanking her profusely for her consideration in letting them know her change of address (after more than a year, gratitude indeed). The head of the firm wished her to know that, after long investigation, her grandparents had been assumed to have died intestate. However, searches had revealed that, in fact, Mr Albert Heriot held substantial investments in stocks, all prosperous and yielding steady percentages. Here followed a list of them: the total amounted to a staggering sum – not riches, but enough, as the benevolent writer suggested, to bring in a reasonable income if re-invested as profitably as had been done in the past. She would duly inherit after probate.

So they had benefited her after all, the two who had not even troubled to make a will and put her name in it. It was Bedelia

Heriot's last gesture of lovelessness towards the grand-daughter she had resented, and Miranda's pleasure in the legacy was dimmed by that knowledge; but it should not stop it working for her good. She made an appointment with Mr Ashe, confident that he would forgive his former typist's waywardness now that she was a modest heiress.

For some reason she held back from telling Andrew.

He failed to notice her contained excitement when the letter came, having preoccupations of his own.

Again and again he thought back to the morning when he had been summoned to the presence of his editor, the great, revered, dreaded Macdonnell, the Attila of Fleet Street. There was a question of policy to be discussed, the degree of provocation to be used in a new series of articles he was to write, which might be taken in some quarters to be downright attacks on the German emperor, at a time when other newspapers were trying desperately to present him as an apostle of world peace. Both enjoyed argument; it was a pleasure to them to find points of disagreement. They were interrupted by the buzzer on Macdonnell's desk.

'Yes. Ask her to come in.'

There was sufficient resemblance to Macdonnell in the woman who entered to make their relationship unmistakable. Like her father, she was tall, strong-featured, slightly sandy in complexion, but, unlike him, could have been called almost handsome. It was a merciful thing, thought Andrew, that women did not usually inherit massive intellectual heads all bone and brains.

'Aileen.' Her father rose, gesturing her to a chair. 'An unexpected pleasure.' He was not given to regarding un-heralded visits to his sanctum as pleasures; Andrew sensed a close link between father and daughter.

'I hope I'm not interrupting, papa.' Her voice was softer than her looks suggested, very faintly Scottish, a lady's voice. 'But I thought we were to meet at the Savoy.'

He looked at his watch. Andrew had never seen his Chief disconcerted before. 'I'm extremely sorry, my dear – it slipped my mind.' Suddenly he buried his face in his hands. 'My God, and it's your birthday.'

'Never mind, papa, it doesn't matter.' The disappointment

was not meant to show, but it did, a little.

'It does matter, and I deserve to be shot,' said her father. 'The trouble is I've a meeting at two sharp, so there's hardly time to give you a worth-while luncheon now. Could you not have stayed and taken it by yourself?'

'I would have felt unpleasantly conspicuous, papa.'

'Of course, of course.' His face brightened. 'I'll tell you what – Craigie here will squire you. There! Won't that be better than your old dad's company? You're free, of course, Andrew.'

Andrew knew that he was under orders not to have a previous engagement. Gallantly he replied that he would be delighted to escort Miss Macdonnell back to the Savoy. He was not unwilling; it was something to be asked to do the Chief's daughter a favour. On the way he stopped the cab and bought a bouquet of spring flowers as a birthday tribute. Ladies always liked flowers, and they required no imagination to buy. He was rewarded by a blush and a murmur of real pleasure.

Over lunch, at their window-table looking on to the Thames, he found that he was enjoying himself as well as fulfilling a duty. Aileen Macdonnell was an exceedingly well-brought-up young lady, quiet, even shy, in manner, but responding sensibly to everything he said and even giving back some shrewdly amusing comments. Andrew guessed that she was not far off thirty, but there was something oddly girlish about her which went strangely with her Macdonnell face; perhaps virginal was the word. The extraordinary thought came into Andrew's mind that she would make a splendid mother. He banished it at once, putting it down to the superb wine his expense account had bought them.

So well did they get on that he was bold enough to ask her to lunch with him again, and saw the delight in her face.

Soon he knew all there was to know about her. She was an only child, now, her brother having been drowned tragically young in a boating accident. She had been brought up in Scotland, dispatched to Switzerland to a finishing school, and now lived with her parents at their home in Surrey. (Andrew visualised it as a battlemented Gothic mansion with enormous gardens and a tennis court, which turned out to be the case.) She led a very quiet life and was just a little frightened of London. It was clear to Andrew that 'quiet' meant 'lonely', and also clear that she liked his company very much. Her shyness had put men off in the past; in his obvious admiration she blossomed.

And he did admire her. Her clear blue eyes, the fresh healthy complexion, the gentle voice that reminded him of his mother's, all these he liked, and the untouched quality of her.

When the invitation came to dine at the house near Dorking he told Miranda that the occasion was business. She, used to his absences, accepted it without question. But the next bidding was to a weekend's stay, quite in the country-house style that had been so popular in King Edward's day, and this time he lied outright, saying that he was commissioned to cover a naval occasion at Portsmouth; fortunately there was one, and he would get a full briefing from the colleague who was really covering it.

Miranda was a little, a very little, suspicious of something withdrawn in his manner. But he was not always communicative about his work, sometimes downright reticent. She was suddenly lonely when he had gone, and without warning went down to Morden. But Rachel was ill, with the bad cough and fever she suffered from sometimes, and the house was like a nursing-home. Polly was kind but abstracted, Harold a little distant, because he now regarded Miranda as out of his sphere, another's property, and Edward's manner to her was more formal than it had been. Ricky was on tour: that was the worst of it, that Rachel could not be with him. Her temperature became higher with fretting, and Miranda, cowardly, left after a night's stay.

A few days afterwards Andrew came home with a box tied with the ribbon of the most famous of Knightsbridge stores. He gave it to her almost brusquely. 'For you.'

'Me? What is it?'

'Open it and see, daftie.'

It was a doll, some two feet long, a very grown-up doll with a painted face, cupid's bow lips, blue-shaded eyelids, pink cheeks, in the costume of a Russian ballerina, eastern brightly-coloured silks and a turban: the Sultana from *Scheherazade*. It was very decadent and very expensive. Andrew was watching her face.

'Well?'

'It's beautiful. What a surprise! This isn't any special day, is it?' Certainly not her birthday, or his, and they had no anniversary to celebrate.

'Does it have to be a special day? Can't I give you a present any time?' (But he gave her very few presents; it seemed wasteful to give them to someone he lived with – presents were for winning favour with people.) 'I thought you'd like it because it's theatrical,' he said.

In fact, Miranda did not like it very much – it looked at her down its snub nose in a very superior way, and had something wicked about it. But Andrew had given it to her, and that made it welcome. She cradled in one arm and kissed him, and he gave her an embarrassed smile and a dismissive pat.

A fortnight later he came home earlier than expected, with a bright and determined air to him, and swept her away from the paper-hanging she was busy with in his study. 'Come on – we're going out to dinner.'

'But Andrew, I wanted to finish this, and I'm filthy – look at me! This paste sticks to one so.'

'Never mind that – go and get ready.'

'Can't I even wash my hair?' She pulled off the scarf wound round it and ran her fingers through its tangles.

'No.'

He took her to a restaurant she had not been to before, an elegant place run by a stately Swiss. At a secluded table with a shaded lamp they sat for an hour, eating rich food (though Andrew showed small appetite) while he talked almost unceasingly; in anyone else it would have seemed like chattering, but his talk was well-informed and witty, and ranged over world affairs like, Miranda thought, a talking newspaper.

Suddenly he pushed away his plate, the gâteau on it almost untouched.

'Miranda, I've something to tell you. I'm going to be married.'

She stared at him, speechless.

'To Aileen Macdonnell – you know, my Editor's daughter.'

'Oh.'

'I thought you should be the first to know.'

She thought she was saying, 'Very kind of you,' but no

sound came from her dry throat.

'I can see you're very upset. I'm sorry.' He put his hand over hers, and she let it lie, not feeling it, or anything but a numbing cold.

'You've made me very happy, you know.'

It was funny how dramatic things happened over meals. The time they had declared their need for each other, and sealed their bond, had been in that City chop-house. Chops and roast potatoes and delicate Swiss escalopes and soufflé and passion and heartbreak, what a strange and unfortunate mixture. For a dreadful moment Miranda thought she was going to be sick, then, with an effort, recovered and managed to speak.

'What happened to your freedom?'

'What do you mean?'

'The first time – the first time you took me out. You said, "A man in my profession shouldn't marry. I have to be free. It wouldn't be fair to my wife." I remember what you said, exactly.'

'And you said you didn't mind about being married – I remember too, you see. Well, to answer your question, there's a time for everything, including marriage, and I've reached that time.'

'And will it be fair to your wife?'

'Aileen has a family to support her if I should have to leave the country or go into a dangerous situation. I shall feel perfectly comfortable about her, in such a case. And besides . . .' He had meant to explain himself so coherently that no reasonable woman could fail to be impressed. But somehow he found a great disinclination to put it into words. And besides, they're so rich and well-connected. It will do me a lot of good to be the great Macdonnell's son-in-law, nobody will ever by able to sack me for a whim, or if they do I'll get taken on quick enough by someone else. They'll look up to me, the boy from Glasgow who fought his way to the top; maybe one day I'll inherit the mantle. Now if I'd married you I'd have married a nameless girl, with only an improbable legend for her portion. You must see that I'm doing the reasonable thing . . .

But he said none of this, faced with her stony look and her whiteness. It brought back the day he had been sent to report

178

on the victims of a mine disaster, the face of a young wife waiting for her man's body to be brought to the surface. Looking at the remains of his gâteau with hatred, he hoped the waiters were not watching and noting. Émile was well-known for his dislike of anything approaching misbehaviour or painful scenes in his restaurant.

Andrew had a last try to salvage the evening. 'It may be possible – I can't be sure, but it may – for me to keep on the flat. Aileen won't want to live in town, and I shall need something central. Or I might take a smaller place – somewhere just off Piccadilly, perhaps. Then we could see each other, at least. Would you like that?'

'I don't think I feel very well. Please may we go – back?' Impossible to say "home" any more. She had not felt very well even before the dreadful conversation had started. The remembered smell of the wallpaper paste seemed to have lingered on and mingled with the scents of expensive cookery; as she got to her feet she staggered slightly. Andrew caught her arm, now really afraid of a scene.

The telephone bell was ringing as they emerged from the lift. 'Blast,' Andrew said, fumbling with the key. Unlike the run of telephones, it continued to ring after they were inside the flat. Miranda heard him say, 'Yes, she's here. Hold on. For you!' he called.

Harold's voice spoke in her ear. 'I'm sorry to ring you so late. But I have to tell you something. Auntie died this evening.'

'*What*?'

'She got a lot better after you saw her. Then it started again and . . . it was pneumonia. The doctor said she was very frail, nobody could have done anything. Miranda? Are you there?'

'Yes. Yes. Oh, poor Rachel. I don't know what to say. Would your mother like me to come down?'

'I think so, yes. She's very upset. It's all so awful. *I'd* like you to come,' Harold's voice was wistful.

'All right, I will. Tomorrow, as soon as I can.'

This second blow gave her the excuse of spending the night in the little cupboard of a spare room, and unlatched the floodgates of tears.

The week that followed should have been for Andrew one of joyful liberty. Miranda had left for Morden early in the morning after his revelation, without seeing him. He had got all that over, he was free to see Aileen when he liked, to talk with her on the telephone and discuss wedding arrangements with her mother. Mrs Macdonnell was a stately lady of powerful personality, liking nothing better than manipulating people and organising events. Meeting her for the first time, Andrew understood Aileen's shyness and timidity. With two such parents, her own strength had no chance to show itself.

Mrs Macdonnell was working towards a knighthood for her husband. She knew every string to be pulled; the achievement of the honour was only a matter of time. So the wedding of her daughter was to be an affair of such grandeur that those concerned could only be influenced favourably by it. She set the wedding date some months ahead, for the beginning of September, to be quite sure of booking St Margaret's, Westminster, and securing as many Conservative celebrities as possible. It would all help to make up for the social obscurity of the bridegroom and his unfortunate lack of relations. She was gracious towards him, Macdonnell beamed on him now that his daughter's marriage was assured, Aileen was quietly happy.

But the fortunate bridegroom found it hard to join in their elation. He felt as though an oppressive cloud hung round his head, and a leaden weight was situated somewhere behind his third rib. It was ridiculous, since he had done nothing to Miranda beyond telling her what she had known all the time, that their association was a fleeting one and must come to an end. She had no excuse for feeling hurt or looking at him as if he were a murderer. She'd be glad, one day, to find herself free of him, free to make her own way in the world. Perhaps even now she was beginning to feel her wings, back with the people who were closest to her, who would persuade her that nothing better could have happened to her than to break with him.

If only he did not miss her so much.

Miranda took Polly's hand in both of hers. 'It's been a dreadful week, Poll. Shall I tell you something that will cheer you up – or at least make you feel different?'

Polly smiled, not quite her old beaming smile yet, but a good try. 'And joy comes well in such a needful time. What are your joyful tidings?'

'I'm going to have a baby.'

CHAPTER FOURTEEN
Now am I in Arden

The view from the parlour window was familiar, delightful in the early sunshine of the May morning. Henley Street, little shops looking across at each other across its width, leaning chimneys, red roofs, over-hanging upper storeys; and half-way up on the left, the decent three-gabled frontage of the Birthplace, awaiting the day's visitors. It had survived, poor thing, its experiences as an inn called the Swan and Maidenhead (and what would the Bard have made of *that*?) and as a butcher's shop, to become a place of pilgrimage. And, to Miranda, her ancestral home.

She called herself Mrs Forbes now. It was her father's name, and it made her more difficult to find. Her husband, she told people, was abroad, in Canada. As that was where the Stratford-upon-Avon Players, as they were now known, were touring, it seemed likely enough that the husband of somebody in Stratford might be with them. In any case, the neighbours did not ask too many questions. There had always been a gulf between town and theatre.

Miranda eased herself into the deep window-seat. Already she was beginning to find the baby slowing her up, and it certainly showed – there was every need for the wedding-ring she had bought. Curled up comfortably, watching the early shoppers, it was pleasant to think back to the time, a few weeks before, when she had broken the news to Polly.

Polly had reacted with shock. 'Oh, Miranda. My dear, how *could* you?'

'Sheer carelessness. Rachel did tell me how not to. But I don't mind – I'm glad, really.'

Very quickly the shock turned to excitement. Polly began to look more like herself than she had done since her sister's death. Neither she nor Miranda wanted to dwell on the days when Rachel had lain upstairs, ethereally beautiful and young in a bed of spring flowers, and Ricky had sat by her side until Edward, with gentle force, had made him come downstairs and sat with him while he tried to eat. They had cabled for him when Rachel's illness had begun to alarm the doctor; by a miracle the cable had reached him in a city from which he could sail directly. But he had missed Rachel, by a day. Not even Polly knew whether he truly understood that she was dead, or whether he lived in Lear's self-delusion. 'This feather stirs . . .' Stony-faced and silent, he endured until the day of the funeral, then for the last time went upstairs and shut himself in with her.

Nobody dared to go near him. But, only a few minutes before the undertaker's carriages were due, the front door was heard to bang. Edward, hurrying upstairs, found no sign of Ricky or the one piece of luggage he had brought with him. He had not been able to face the funeral. An anxious cable to the Bensonians brought the reply, ten days later, that he had rejoined the company.

And so, after such tragedy, Polly began to brighten at the thought of the new life that was coming to her Shakespeare Girl. Miranda refused to talk about Andrew, beyond saying that he was getting married, but not to her. She had only become certain of her pregnancy in Morden and the knowledge effectively banished the first shock of his betrayal. Now there was something to live for.

'I shall be perfectly all right,' she told Polly. 'I've got enough money, thanks to grandfather's investments, not to have to work. I'll change my name and buy a ring and go to live where he . . . where I shan't be found.'

'But, dear, we want to look after you.'

'I know, and it's what I knew you'd want. But not yet, Polly – not till I've made a place for myself and . . .'

'William?'

'Who knows? Possibly. Of course, I might decide to call him Hamlet if he's a he. Hamlet Forbes . . . No, it doesn't sound right.'

Harold, solemnly and earnestly, offered to marry her. He had not taken the news as happily as his mother.

'Harold dear, thank you a thousand times. But just now I

couldn't. Later, I'll think about it.'

And, oddly enough, she did. The last year had wrought changes in Harold. The puppy-fat and the spots had melted away, he was taller, tougher, a man rather than a boy. The spectacles were no longer Billy Bunterish, but gave him an air of cleverness. On the whole, he was decidedly presentable, and there would be a lot to be said for being part of his loving, caring family. But still she must say, 'Not yet.'

She would not tell them where she was going. There was a chance (it was not a hope) that Andrew would follow her, remorseful, and try to persuade her to keep a clandestine share of his life; she was not going to allow herself to be torn by that. And he should not know about the baby. Let him marry his Aileen without complications. To know any more about Miss Macdonnell, even what she looked like, would be unbearable, the sort of pain one should not have to endure.

Her return to the flat was carefully timed for a day when she knew Andrew would be out of town, yet she looked nervously over her shoulder, going from room to room, in case he should suddenly appear. The place was untidy, even dirty, the bed unmade, the remains of the sort of hurried scratch breakfast he used to have on the table. She felt a pang of pity, which made her all the more anxious to be out of that haunted place and away. Hurriedly she gathered together her possessions and crammed them into a suitcase and a carpet-bag. Soon nothing of hers was left in sight. Except the ballet-doll, sprawled in a chair.

Miranda picked it up. ' "A peevish self-willed harlotry," ' she said to its sneering painted face, then threw it into the carpet-bag. It would hurt Andrew so much to find his only real gift to her rejected, left behind when she had taken everything else.

She left the flat without a backward look, pushing her key through the letter-box. James, fortunately, was not about. Outside the Mansions her cab was waiting.

That had been weeks ago. After a few days of rest at the Shakespeare Hotel, she began to look for a small house to buy with a withdrawal from her capital. The third agent she visited had one on his books: a cottage, said to be in part sixteenth-century, at the end of Henley Street. It had a good parlour, with an ingle-nook almost, but not quite, big enough to sit in, a curious little kitchen built on to the back, a sizable bedroom with rafters and upright beams, a smaller one for Hamlet, or whoever he turned out to be, and, as was to be expected, no bathroom. The builder Miranda consulted saw no difficulty about building a small one on the ground floor, over a yard adjoining the little garden.

Buying the furniture was a joy past expression. All of it was to be second-hand except for utility articles, and old, if possible. In a barn-like shop kept by a Mrs Smith, of gypsy features and ample proportions, Miranda found a bed with half-posts and curious carvings, a stout table and ladderback chairs, a clothes-press, and a large, handsome mahogany chest of drawers, which gave her particular delight. As she pulled the drawers in and out, surprised at the smooth running of them, and stroked the smooth wood, Mrs Smith, eyeing her swelling figure, remarked, 'Nesting, that's what you're at, my dear. I bet, now, you're thinking which of them big drawers 'ud be for baby-clothes? And, likewise, you can't wait to get that ole chest home and start a-shining it up.' She lit her clay pipe, and pulled on it with enjoyment. 'All female animals is the same. With mice, it's tore-up paper, while cats goes for hat-boxes. Wonderful, is nature. They talks about these New Women and the vote and such, but, you ask me, it's nesting as matters to females. That, and loving of their men. Your man good to you, is he?'

'Very,' Miranda replied. Oh Andrew, how far from good. She tried to imagine him choosing furniture for their house, helping to make a home for their child, and failed. He never noticed his surroundings. He had only praised her choice of pictures out of politeness. He was best forgotten.

Nature had provided her with the cure for longing after him: absorption in her coming child and its home. Desire for him had left her, to her surprise. Less and less was she troubled by sudden visions of him, the poise of his fine head against lamplight, the dark copper flame of his hair, his smile, that could be so sweet. Only now and then, enraptured by some new pleasure of her cottage, she turned to share it with him, and found emptiness, and jealous pain.

In the choice of the cottage she had deliberately sought comfort from the nearness of the house in which she felt she had a secret share. Whenever the fancy took her, she visited the Birthplace. The Bard had been neglected, in what she thought of as Andrew's year. Now she turned to him again, the one she knew better than her shadowy father. The curator may have thought her a rabid Shakespearean or a harmless eccentric, but gave her a cheerful greeting every time, and ceased to escort her round.

Each room held thoughts, reflections. Did he sit with his family round this hearth? As a child, the eldest hopeful son, glad to be home from the Latin cramming and the beatings of school; as a bright youth, noting the looks and the ways of those about him, already putting them into words in his own mind; as a young man lovesick for Anne Hathaway's beauty, trembling at the thought of having to tell his parents he had deflowered her, and must marry her . . . and that he would follow the Players?

In the back room she would stand in front of what they called the Stratford portrait, and talked to it, though silently, for the town was small and people chattered of anyone too noticeably eccentric. Am I truly yours, and would you own me? Would you like me to call my child Hamnet, if it's a boy, after the son you lost? Did you find it enough, after the storms of life and dispriz'd love, to settle for Stratford and peace?

The dark eyes, in their baggy frames of ill-health or sleeplessness, looked back at her, answering only, 'Discover for yourself.'

Now, in the month of June, feeling remarkably well, energetic by day, instantly asleep at night, her cottage straight and comely, Miranda took the train to Coventry. Outside the station a line of cabs waited, the horses asleep on their feet or lunching from nosebags, their drivers seeming equally apathetic. The driver of the foremost cab glanced up from his newspaper at what looked to him an unprofitable fare, a young woman without luggage.

'I would like to go to Bedington, please,' Miranda said.

The driver scratched his head. 'Where, miss?' His gaze travelled down her figure. 'Mum.'

'Bedington. It's a village east of Coventry, on the river.'

He looked about him, as if expecting a compass to appear magically in the sky, indicating the direction of the east. 'Don't know it, mum.'

'There's an old house there, Curteis Hall.'

He shook his head, then brightened. 'Ah. You want Combe Abbey. That's real historic, that is.'

Patiently Miranda persuaded him that she did not want Combe Abbey, however historic, and suggested that Curteis Hall might not be far from it. She consulted the notes she had made from Sykes-Harker's manuscript. 'Binley – that's where Combe is, isn't it – is only two and a half miles from Coventry. Could we go in that direction and see if we can find a sign to Bedington?'

The driver, not a travelled man but prepared for mild adventure, agreed that this could do no harm. They would go out on the Stoke Road, he thought. Driving through the centre of Coventry, Miranda was charmed by the ancient streets, the mediaeval and Tudor houses which were part of what she was trying to find, however unlikely the quest seemed. The driver, who knew his own city better than its outskirts, pointed to various landmarks, the three spires, the window where Peeping Tom was supposed to have spied on Lady Godiva as she rode clad in her hair – and there his statue was, still looking out – and, through an archway, 'That's Palace Yard, that is, where a lot of royalties used to stay.' Miranda looked with interest at the glimpse of gables and leaded windows; a book in the Stratford library had named it as the lodging of the young Princess Elizabeth in 1605. Could Mary Curtis have been in her train?

They were out on a country road, rattling along past churches, a castle turned farmhouse, meeting the river as it glanced through trees and brakes. Miranda remarked that it looked very small compared with the Stratford Avon, to which the driver, with a sudden burst of memory, recollected that it was not the Avon at all but a little river running from it, called the Sowe. As Miranda was pondering on the fate which had positioned Stratford on the parent river rather than the tributary, thus saving it from becoming world-famous as Stratford-on-Sowe, she saw a sign-post pointing to Bedington.

It lay between the road and the river, which embraced the

hamlet like a glittering arm. There was a tiny church with a Saxon porch, a few cottages, a very modest small inn, the Plough, and the Hall. It stood behind a yew hedge, in an acre or so of land; what more it had possessed had long since been given over to farming. Miranda's heart sank as they neared the house, and she saw damaged windows, curtainless, broken steps, tiles missing. So nobody lived there, and it was on its way to being a ruin.

The day was hot now. Wanting all the time she could get in the place, she suggested that for a few shillings the driver might like to refresh himself and the horse at the Plough, while she explored. He was only too willing; it made a nice change from Coventry.

For all its forlorn appearance, every door to the house was locked. In the church Miranda found an old man cleaning brasses, who said that the key was kept at a cottage which he pointed out.

Here were the memorials Sykes-Harker had learned of from the obliging vicar. Rogerus Curteis, armiger. A Latin epitaph of great length, and below it, the simple rhyming epitaph of his wife, with a pathetic postscript, 'Also manie children'. Then, much later, their son Edward and his wife Joan, deceased in the 1630s. After that no more Curtises. Vaguely disappointed (the vicar might just have missed one or two), Miranda wandered, reading wall-tablets, the names of people who might have known the family, surveying things these Elizabethans would have seen, bosses, corbels, Early English windows, a stone angel holding a tablet.

She shivered; the church was cold. Outside the sunshine seemed almost tropical, after that chill.

The old woman at the cottage was sunning herself in her doorway, her aproned knees spread and a cat between them. Miranda had some difficulty in making her comprehend what she wanted, but eventually the old head nodded in understanding. She handed over a large iron ring with several keys on it.

'You don't want to go livin' there, mistress, a nasty damp old place not fit to rear a babe.'

The largest of the keys fitted the thick oaken main door, which creaked ear-piercingly as it opened. Inside was cold and dark; chill breathing from the stone walls, light filtering only thinly in through the uncleaned windows. Miranda was in what had been the great hall of the mediaeval house, the soaring roof like the upturned hull of a ship, rafters embossed with armorial bearings whose colours were all gone. At the end, under the minstrels' gallery, a Tudor screen's carvings were only shapes under a thick layer of dust.

The room leading from the hall was panelled, with a high ceiling of elaborate plaster-work whose pendants were in all stages of disrepair, some merely heaps of dust on the floor. Another, lower-ceilinged room had walls of plaster bearing faint traces of paintings. A fine oak staircase, with a carved heraldic beast every foot or so along its baluster, led to a maze of first-floor rooms, all handsome in their time, abandoned now, with the ominous scent of wood-rot in them. Here and there were pieces of furniture, chairs and chests, joint-stools and a bread-table, looking ancient enough to have belonged to the house in its beginnings.

Stepping carefully, Miranda climbed a smaller staircase to a gallery running most of the length of the building, lit by transomed windows at either end. A bird frightened her as it rushed shrieking across and out through a broken pane.

Slowly she came downstairs again, looking into room after room for what had once happened in them. In this, the great bedroom, so many children had been born and died, Ursula Curteis's, Joan Curtis's, Mary herself. And Joanna, the child of shame, perhaps not here, but in some smaller room, and there would be no rejoicings, no decking of the cradle or specially-baked almond cake. There must have been a christening, for the lack of one would have condemned the child to Limbo, and Christian folk would surely not do that . . .

Suddenly tired with stair-climbing, Miranda went back into the painted room, where a substantial oak stool stood against a wall – like a wallflower at a dance, poor thing. It seemed sound enough, punctured by plenty of worm-holes, but from the number she had seen while furniture-buying she judged the worms to be extinct, since no dust appeared. A longing came over to take it out of the sad house, it and other forgotten small pieces, to her own warm cottage, where it could be burnished and cared for. She sat down on it, leaning her head back against the wall, feeling slightly mazy and remote. Perhaps the stairs had been too much for the growing heaviness of her body. The dim paintings swam before her eyes, the figure of a youth, perhaps a page, a gauntleted hand bearing a hawk, a woman's face with high shaved forehead and pointed hat, vivid, then faint again.

Time ceased, and thought, and identity. There was utter silence, but for the buzzing of a fly. And the voices.

The woman's said, 'You should not have come. They will be so angry.'

The man's voice was light, a little hesitant. 'Could I leave you forlorn?'

'It was far for you to ride, and bitter cold.'

'I shall do very well. My cloak is fur-lined.'

A little laugh – or was it a sob? – and an incoherent murmur. Then the woman. '. . . .but I am glad . . . sir. Only go now before they find you.'

'Do you think I would hide myself from them, Mall? I hope I am as good a man as Sir Roger, even though I bear no arms.'

'But that is all the matter! Shall I bring shame on you as well as myself, and you so famed and respected? Who will hurt me here, in my home? They will be long-faced and preach at me for a time, then all will be forgotten.'

'And the child – will she be forgotten?'

A pause. 'She is sent away. They put her out to nurse the day after she was born, so that I scarcely held her. What else should they do?'

The man, very low-spoken. 'I have a grandchild, young Bessy. But this babe is the last I shall get. Would you have her cast away, like my Perdita? Poor thing, condemned to loss . . . Leontes' doom for our daughter.'

A burst of weeping, that faded and swelled like a sound in a high wind. Then the man, gentle, a wealth of tenderness in his voice, which was more of London than of Arden, as was the girl's. 'Thou art weak from childbed, my dear. No more weeping now. Trust to me and all shall yet be well. Can you ride your horse? Then make ready, and we'll go find our Joan . . .'

A cry that was full of tears and joy, and the clear girlish voice passionate with thanks; but the words seemed to blow away, or die on the air.

Miranda stirred. Her foot tingled when she moved it, as though she had sat absolutely still for a long time. The sunshine through the grimy window seemed to have shifted across the floor; how long had passed? She got up stiffly, slightly dizzy as she had been before . . . whatever had happened? Be careful of the floorboards, remember the way out, lock the door. The old cottager did not answer to her knock, and she hung the key-ring on the back door of the cottage.

At the Plough the cab-driver was sitting on a bench with a pint pot beside him, his handkerchief spread over his face. His horse had been taken out of the shafts, and was grazing contentedly on the green. His master roused with a start and stared up at the church clock.

''Alf-past three – must 'a been asleep. You finished with that hold 'ouse, mum?'

'Yes, thank you. Can we go back now?'

From the box he turned to ask her, 'See anyone up there?'

'No,' she said. 'I saw no one at all.'

The cottage in Henley Street was warm and welcoming. The girl who came in to help had lit a fire; soft shadows lay in the corner of the parlour, the plaster and beams were made sharply black and white by the leaping of the flames. Miranda took off her coat and hat and stretched out in the comfortable armchair, her feet on a cushioned stool. Perhaps it had been a dream, imagination producing vividly real impressions as it often did on the edge of sleep. She had been thinking of Mary Curtis; the thoughts had been transmuted into imagined voices.

But if she had indeed heard them? One theory of ghosts was that they were images left on the air by intensely felt experiences. If the scene she had overheard had happened, Mary must have felt such joy and relief at the rescue of herself and her child by her eminent lover that the impression had remained in that old room over the centuries, disturbed neither by human life nor the glare of artificial light, which was said to banish ghosts. If it were true – always if – then there was an explanation for Mary's disappearance from the family memorials. He had taken her and her babe away, he who had lost his only son in childhood and had written out the sorrow of it in his plays. Joanna should not be another Lost One. But where had he taken them? Not to New Place, certainly. Even had Anne Shakespeare been the most tolerant of wives, the scandal would have been all over Stratford in five minutes. To a safe home in a village nearby but not too near, perhaps: Welford, Bidford – Bidford, which he visited often – had he been to see them that night he caught his fatal cold? 1616 – Joan would have been two and a half . . .

Miranda slept. The baby kicked violently. She laid her hand over its restless feet, smiling because it, too, was safe.

CHAPTER FIFTEEN
Love goes from Love

When Andrew had returned home and discovered Miranda's flight his reaction had been one of fury. He might have been relieved that she had so conveniently tidied herself out of his life and saved him the pain of a parting scene; he had, after all, more or less told her to go her own way. But he was angry, strangely and unjustifiably disappointed.

There was no need to panic and go to the river police; all her luggage had gone, and suicides seldom bother to remove their possessions before removing themselves. Instead he went to Morden, arriving at the hour of tea. Edward answered the door.

'Mr Porter?'

'That's right.'

'Andrew Craigie. Of course, we've met.' Unlike him to forget a face. 'Have you got Miss Heriot here?'

Edward shook his head and looked blank. He had been told to say nothing if Craigie came enquiring, but he was not at all sure how to deal with questions. Feeling vaguely that he was not supposed to let the man in, he assumed a rocklike stance on the doormat, amiable of aspect as ever, hoping one of his family would come to his rescue. The door behind him opened. Andrew just recognised the squarely-built young man as the fat schoolboy he had met on his second visit to the house. Harold glared at him.

'What do you want?'

'I'm looking for Miranda Heriot.'

'Look away. Shut the door, pa.'

It was not in Edward's nature to shut doors in people's faces. While he was nerving himself to it Andrew said in his loudest, most authoritative voice, 'Let me in, will you. The girl's disappeared and I want to find her. Come on, let me in – we can't talk on the doorstep.'

Harold put a hand on his father's arm, drawing him back, and said, 'If you must.'

Polly was at the dining-table. She pushed aside her last cup of tea, and said, unsmiling, 'We've been expecting you, Mr Craigie.'

'Mrs Porter. I know Miranda's been staying with you . . .'

'You've taken a long time to come looking for her.'

'Well. I knew you'd had a bereavement, and it seemed better to leave things . . . So where is she?'

'Not here.'

'Then where?' He felt a complete fool, facing these ordinary, unimportant people, all hostile to him.

'I shouldn't think you'd want to know,' said Harold, 'after the way you treated her. Or do you usually chuck young ladies aside after you've ruined them, and then go looking for the pieces?'

His mother flashed him a warning glance. He went on, 'Do you think we're going to hand her over to *you*, you cheating, lying swine?'

Edward breathed, 'Now, son,' but Harold went on, 'Young ladies need protecting against men like you. You can search the house, if you don't believe us, and then I'll have the great pleasure of kicking you out.'

Andrew had never been so discomposed in his life, and he had been in some difficult situations. He said carefully, 'I'm not aware of having lied or cheated, in Miss Heriot's case. I wonder what she told you.'

Polly said, 'All right, Harold. Miranda told us you'd broken off your association with her because you were going to marry someone else. Is that true?'

'Well – yes.'

'So why do you want to find her?'

And he did not know. He simply did not know. He of the razor-sharp brain stood there looking foolishly at them all, six blue eyes staring impassively. He took in the woman's black dress, the crape bands on the arms of the men, and increasingly wished he had not come in person. It would have been so much easier to write.

'I want to know where she is,' he said, 'that she's all right. I thought she was with you – but when I got back to my flat today all her things had gone.' Suddenly his behaviour seemed to him unutterably silly, and his look was so mortified that Polly said more kindly, 'Miranda told us particularly that she didn't want you to follow her. She wants a completely clean break with you, and we're not surprised. She hasn't even given us her address, though in time she will, of course, so that you can't possibly trace her through us.'

'But you must have some idea, surely. I mean, she looks on you as her family.'

'We haven't.' Polly's face was stony, both father and son were leagued with her, against him. He began to retreat.

'But you will let me know, later, when you know yourselves?'

'Certainly not. We don't at all approve of you, Mr Craigie, and we think it's a pity our girl ever took up with you. And now perhaps you'll go. We're not ready to receive visitors at the moment.'

He bent his head and backed into the narrow hall. Only Harold followed him. 'If it wasn't for upsetting my parents,' he said, low and grim, 'I'd knock you down and black your eyes, and enjoy it, you filthy cad. Get out of the house, and when you've gone I'll put some disinfectant down.' The door slammed behind Andrew with a thunderous bang.

So that lad's in love with her, he thought, walking towards the tube station. Enough to hate me like poison. I'd have thought he'd be glad for her to be set free. What a tale she must have told them; though that was not like her. He passed the office where she had worked. A light still burned there, and he thought of calling in to ask if they knew, though it had been so long since she left. But she would not have told them.

Next day he went to see Gabriel Proudfoot, and was received courteously but blankly. The author had known nothing of Miranda's circumstances, had never heard of Andrew himself (and that was just a little unwelcome to his vanity). 'I had a very nice letter from her, saying that for family reasons she was obliged to discontinue her work for me. I shall miss her very much, very much indeed.' He sighed. 'It's not easy, you know, my calling. Sometimes I think I'll try to get the hang of these typewriters myself. But with such an output –

a book a year, if you can imagine that. Perhaps you read my last?' Before leaving Andrew had to inspect Mr Proudfoot's collection of his own works, in all their editions, and endure the author's rambling commentary. At the door he managed to ask, 'Where did Miss Heriot's letter come from?'

'Where . . .? Oh, I see. From somewhere in South London. Now where could it have been? Catford? Balham? Tooting? Curious, I always believed she lived in town, though I don't know why I should have that impression . . .'

Andrew extricated himself. There was no one else who would be able to tell him.

He wrote a curt note to Mrs Burr telling her to clean the flat thoroughly and put anything she might find of Miss Heriot's to one side, in case it should be sent for later. That lady, reading it, smiled cynically; she had an observant eye, and she dealt with the laundry. It would be interesting to think Mr Craigie had done the young lady in and disposed of the body somewhere, but Mrs Burr doubted it.

Andrew was due to spend Sunday at the Macdonnells' stately home. It was an ambience he enjoyed; opulent surroundings, rich entertainment, acceptance of himself as one who had arrived socially. And Aileen's pleasure in his company was so charming. This Sunday, for the first time, she irritated him, watching him with soft eyes, smiling whenever she caught his glance. Miranda's devotion had been like a light, in which he could bask or not, as he pleased. Aileen's was like an enveloping garment, stifling and immobilising him. As he thought these thoughts he disliked himself for doing so.

He stood at the French window of the library, where sherry was served before luncheon, and stared out at the steady rain falling on the gardens. Usually he liked the view, allowing himself to speculate on his chances of owning a similar one in the future; Macdonnell would never tolerate the transplanting of his daughter to surroundings that were a come-down. Today it looked just as dreary as any other view would, in such miserable weather.

Aileen came to his side and put her arm through his. 'Penny for them, dear.'

'Not worth it. Just thinking about the bloody English weather.'

'I seem to remember some quite bloody Scottish weather.'

'That's true.'

'Have some more sherry.' She refilled his glass without waiting for him to accept. He disliked it, excellent though it was of its kind – a dour, liverish, morose drink. Macdonnell would have offered him whisky if he had asked for it, his matchless old single malt. Now he could hardly hand the glass back to Aileen and say he'd changed his mind – though why not, for God's sake? Presumably when they were married she'd let him please himself occasionally.

'You *are* low in your spirits – I knew it,' she said. 'What is it? Tell.'

'It's absolutely nothing. I got up feeling a bit rough this morning, that's all.'

'We'll go for a long walk this afternoon,' she said brightly. 'That ought to cure you.'

But it did not, the monotonous trail along suburban roads, varied by a suburbanised common with seats by the path and men walking their dogs in defiance of the rain. Andrew wished he were far away, in a glen he knew where the Highlands began, with rough country to conquer, great distances to scan, mountain upon mountain rising before him as he climbed. There a man could think, work out things in his mind, discover his soul – if he had one.

Aileen sensed his continuing depression, and was tactfully quiet. She would have to learn her man's moods and go along with them. At tea her mother talked weddings.

'Did I tell you I've got a marvellous organist? Gerald Greystone. Not their usual man, but they didn't mind at all when I said we wanted only the best. Oh, and the Kirkbys are coming, after all. Dora was afraid they'd still be in Deauville, but they've decided to come back early – isn't that nice. Andrew, you're not eating, and I ordered *patum peperium* specially for you. Has Aileen tired you out, dragging you over half Surrey?'

'No, I'm fine, thank you.' He took another of the delicate sandwiches. Aileen was smiling at him (but when was she not?). He noticed that the fresh rainy air had given her a beautiful colour, and that her hair had gone into tiny curls at the front. She looked as wholesome as a scone; he was pleased to experience a surge of warmth towards her. She was not to blame for his black mood.

But though it lifted, it came back like a fog that will not clear, hanging about him greyly. He noticed it least when he was working hard, and so threw himself into every assignment with something near to violence. Those he interviewed found him unrelenting in his questioning, unsparing of their feelings – one such victim wrote an indignant letter to Macdonnell complaining of the brutality of his employee. A difficult story, an investigation involving physical risk or formidable problems, was something he delighted in because it used up his energies and concentration. The times he hated were the arrival back at his flat after work, and the waking to find himself alone in the austere bedroom. (He had taken down the pictures Miranda had hung and stored them away.) It was a sort of retrogression, a return to what he had been before her coming, a creature driven only by ambition, not knowing affection or human companionship.

It would have helped to have a companion now, someone with whom he could reason out what he felt. But there was nobody. The associates he met in bars and in the corridors of the *Recorder* would not have known what he was talking about. So he tackled his unease alone, reasoning as positively as he could. What troubled him, he told himself, was no more than the remains of a Presbyterian conscience, possibly an unwanted legacy from his father, and it was quite unjustified. He had not seduced Miranda; she had been perfectly willing. Her emotion at his announcement of the engagement was natural, but she had shown very good sense in removing herself entirely from his life. Doubtless by now she was over it all, involved with some other man. It was for the best that he should not know where she was, or he might have been tempted . . .

To brood over his imagined sense of guilt was unfair to himself, to his paper, and most of all to Aileen. He determined to put every effort into behaving well to her. The other thing would fade in time. To assist its passing, he invited her to the flat, chaperoned by her mother; surely her presence would exorcise the other one. They both thought the place gloomy, impersonal. Mrs Macdonnell said that it reminded her of a men's club, and a very stuffy one at that. 'Certainly you must have a place in town, Andrew, but something a good deal brighter than this. Smaller, too. I'm sure we can find just the right place. A nice little *pied-à-terre,* where you can stay the night, Aileen, after a late function or a theatre. You won't always want to travel back to Surrey.'

'Oh, we're going to live in Surrey, are we?' Andrew asked. His future mother-in-law noticed no sarcasm in his tone.

'Well, where you like, of course – but Aileen's father and I would like her near us, naturally, and there are some really charming houses always to be had. Reigate, now . . .'

They left, and blankness remained behind them. No trace of Aileen left on the air, only her mother's voice, still talking on.

He began to show more amorousness towards Aileen, holding her hand, kissing her more lingeringly, venturing on small intimacies. He felt her stiffen, almost back away, the first time he touched her so, then force herself to relax, even learn to respond with shy pleasure. She seemed to take up a lot of room in his arms; he did not quite know what to do with such amplitude. He had always favoured slender women, much shorter than himself, and he preferred darker hair. But he was perfectly willing to extend his experience and acquire new skills.

Nothing, even the thought of a warm and willing Aileen in his bed, could lessen his dread of the wedding itself. The arrangements for it seemed to him on the scale appropriate for a coronation; he could only be thankful that Mrs Macdonnell had not insisted on Westminster Abbey. He went into St Margaret's in a quiet hour, trying to familiarise himself with it, so that he would not feel too arrant a fool, standing there in morning dress, with top hat, beside his best man (who? he had no friends) waiting for a blushing lace-shrouded Aileen to come up the aisle on her father's arm, between serried ranks of faces which appeared almost daily in the Society columns.

He noticed that he was drinking more. Macdonnell's single malt took the edge off a dull dinner-party, taken quickly, two or three measures of the precious stuff, and followed up by excellent wine which the ladies hardly touched, so that the men had more than their proper share. And at home his one nightcap of spirits turned into two or three. He looked in the mirror for signs of bloating, but there were none as yet. He hoped he was not turning into a Fleet Street soak.

Late spring moved into summer, a summer of glorious weather; London sweltered, while Londoners dreamed of golden sand and blue sea. But within the great newspaper offices there was no thought of holiday, for the news they were turning out was as black as the print. Civil war threatened in Ireland, the gunmen were out, the old bitter hatred of England flaring up to meet the Ulster Volunteers, raised to resist Home Rule. Death was in the air; the young Archduke Franz Ferdinand and his wife were murdered by a fanatic in Yugoslavia; the German Emperor put on his spiked helmet, declared war against Russia and France and invaded Belgium.

Britain, pledged to support Belgian neutrality, was in honour bound to defend the little country. And, on 4 August, found herself at war with Germany.

Andrew faced his future. At the same moment that he reached his decision – and it had not been hard to reach – Macdonnell sent for him.

'Sit down, Andrew. I don't have to tell you what this is about.'

'No, sir.'

'I want you to go to France, as soon as you can. This war may not be a long one, but I'll need you to cover it. Nobody could do it better.'

'I flatter myself they couldn't. Thank you, sir.'

'It's what you wanted yourself?'

'Of course.'

Macdonnell's fingers drummed rhythmically on his desk. 'I'm sacrificing Aileen's happiness in asking you to do this, and it's not easy for me. But it's got to be done. There'll be no wedding in St Margaret's; even my wife accepts that. What do you want to do about it?'

'I had given it thought, sir. If Aileen wants to marry me in the circumstances – knowing the risks a correspondent faces in the war zone – it will have to be a special licence and a registry office.' He smiled. 'I'd prefer that, in fact.'

'It hadn't escaped me. So would I. But women, you know, women! Still, Aileen's a sensible girl, I don't think she'll make a fuss about bridesmaids and all that. Better talk to her yourself about it, though. Go as soon as you can. But first we'll get down to details. I want you to join the next consignment of troops . . .'

From the trivial they proceeded to the important.

Andrew laid the situation before Aileen as kindly as he could.

'I'm extremely sorry, of course. But it would be unthinkable for us to have the kind of wedding we'd planned, with the country at war, and in any case, I can't delay for a month.'

'I know, Andrew. I knew as soon as the news broke. It would be dreadfully unpatriotic.'

'With a special licence we could be married almost at once. It wouldn't be the same, I know, but we could have a religious ceremony later, if you want that.'

'I don't mind at all. It's Mamma who would be disappointed.'

'Well, then, that's settled. What a sensible girl you are.'

'Everybody says I'm sensible,' Aileen said quaintly. 'I wish they'd think of another adjective – like fascinating.'

Andrew sought for the right gallant remark, failed to find it, and said, 'Of course there won't be time for a honeymoon. So I'll take you for the best slap-up luncheon a bride ever had. After that I'm afraid I'll have to join a troop train at once.'

She was saying so little about this momentous thing, gazing at him with a look he could not interpret.

'What's the matter? Are you worried about the danger? Because . . .'

Aileen shook her head. 'No. I know war correspondents have to face danger, and you wouldn't want to be let off more lightly than our soldiers. No, Andrew. I'm not going to marry you in a registry office, because I'm not going to marry you at all. Don't say anything. You see, dear, I know you don't love me in the way you should. I think you're quite fond of me, and I think, if you don't mind me saying so, that you like the idea of being Papa's son-in-law.'

'Aileen!'

'Please don't try telling me lies, Andrew. You think I'm such an inexperienced mouse that I don't know how a man behaves when a woman attracts him – really, really attracts him, I mean. And I don't attract you, do I, in that way. I can tell, from the way you touch me and kiss me. It's funny, isn't it, because nobody else ever has – kissed me, I mean, unless you count Postman's Knock. I even think I know that you're in love with somebody else, or still thinking about her, at least. Now look me in the eye and tell me it's not true.'

Miserable, Andrew met her clear gaze, wise and sweet and not angry, as she had every right to be. And said, 'God forgive me, it's true.'

'There, I knew it. And there *is* somebody else?'

He nodded.

'Where?'

'Lost.'

'Go and find her, Andrew, when you get back from France. You'll make her as happy as you'd never have made me. Oh, it's such a relief to have told you. I've wanted to, more and more, but I was too much of a coward to face Mamma about it. And then Papa said that war was coming, and I knew it was the answer. Rather a nasty way to have one's problems solved . . . Now hadn't you better go back and tell Papa what's happened, and get on with your preparations. Telephone him, if you like.' She stood up and offered her hand. 'Goodbye.'

'Goodbye, Aileen. I didn't deserve you. You're a wonderful girl.'

She laughed. 'That's better than "sensible".'

After he had left she went, very calmly, upstairs and shut herself in her bedroom. When she faced her mother she would be quite composed again.

On a bitter winter night when frost-bright stars looked down on the Avon and the huddled roofs of a sleeping Stratford, Miranda gave birth, after a long and cruel labour, to a healthy, active, furiously angry son. As the midwife wiped her face and prepared to change her sheets and nightgown she said, 'You settle down, now, and we'll have a nice cup of tea. Pity your husband couldn't be with you.'

'Yes,' said the patient, and sniffed very loudly so as not to cry, which would be ridiculous after what she had just been through.

In London, as the iron grip of night-frost stilled the air, people behind darkened windows listened to the far booming of the guns in Flanders.

CHAPTER SIXTEEN
Full fathom five

The baby was christened neither Hamlet nor Hamnet, nor any of the other fanciful names with which Miranda had amused herself. He became, at the font of Holy Trinity, Valentine Francis; the second name in double compliment to her father and Benson, the first because she liked it. 'Why not Proteus?' Polly suggested tartly. 'If you want to be reminded of your son's father, that is. He was the faithless Gent of Verona – Valentine was the good one.'

Miranda did not want to be reminded of her son's father. With the beginning of her new life in Stratford she shut the old one out from everything but her dreams, into which it filtered. In the first months she had furtively looked at the 'Marriages' columns of national papers, for a Craigie-Macdonnell notice. When none appeared up to the beginning of November she made herself stop it. The wedding had been postponed because of the war, or perhaps it had been celebrated in Scotland and not mentioned in the English papers – though that seemed unlikely. The *Recorder* was not even glanced at, after that; only the local paper with its comfortable domestic items among the war news.

Valentine rapidly grew out of his early prune-like appearance into a strong, long-limbed, violently active child with the face of a mischievous cupid and thick curling brown hair with a glint of chestnut in it. Miranda, who had had nothing to do with small children, rapidly established a close relationship with him. They understood each other perfectly before he could speak, driving each other into tempests of laughter, subsiding into a blissful peace which came upon them at night or rest-times, the baby only waking her with crying out of necessity. Everything ordinary babies were supposed to do according to the *Book of Child Care*, Valentine did earlier –

and, of course, better. At eight months he had reached the stage when a carpenter had to be called in to construct a gate at the top of the stairs, against the time when he should learn to crawl, and all sharp instruments and fragile ornaments were kept out of his reach.

Miranda adored him. But her will, like his, was strong, and any danger of his becoming spoiled was checked by Daisy, the young girl who had been Miranda's household help and was now nurse-maid as well. Daisy came from a large, poor family, the eldest girl who had helped to bring up her mother's brood. She had a loud voice and a firm hand, and though her language was sometimes not of the sort *Child Care* advocated ('remember that your baby's ears are delicate, and that his little mind may be storing more than you imagine') it was clear that Valentine looked on her as a worthy opponent and a person on whom to practise wickednesses he would not inflict on his mother.

As he was promenaded in the streets of Stratford in his bassinet, looking in kingly fashion from side to side, some quality in him drew stares of admiration. But not, unfortunately, only stares. A child so conspicuous attracted attention which might have overlooked a somnolent pudding in ribbons and laces. Impossible not to notice women who talked, their heads close together, broke off to study mother and child inquisitively, gazed after them, and talked again. The first person to challenge Miranda openly was the sweet-shop keeper, Mrs Greene, a sharp-eyed lady who lived alone and was nourished by gossip.

'Husband not able to get home yet, Mrs Forbes?'

'Not yet.'

'Pity. I always think it's a pity when they miss baby's early days. Expecting him soon?'

Miranda fastened a button on Valentine's coat. 'I'm afraid I don't know.'

'Oh?' Funny, her tone indicated. She studied the new-looking ring on Miranda's finger, no scratches on it such as wedding-rings acquire with wear, and thought of the absence of letters from abroad for Mrs Forbes which her close friend the postmistress had noted. It was an irresistible temptation to mention these things to a customer who came in for a quarter of striped humbugs and remained to gossip. In due course the customer passed on the speculations of Mrs Greene to her sister in Great William Street, from whom it got back to sundry people who were familiar with the sight of the young woman and the handsome baby. And so to Daisy's hard-worked mother, past scandal herself, good-natured enough, but concerned that this particular spicy tale affected her daughter.

Daisy burst into the cottage without knocking. Her face was very red, her hair tousled, for she had left home without bothering to put herself to rights.

'Mrs F! you know what they're saying hereabouts? My mum just told me and I fairly let fly at her, I did, saying such things. The very idea!'

'Well, what, Daisy?' Miranda had had a bad night with the teething Valentine and was in no mood for one of Daisy's storms of protest. Still less for the subject of it.

'They're saying you're not properly wed. An unmarried mother, was what that ole cat called you – not my mum, the woman next door. Said it wasn't a fit house for me to work in, and mum ought to stop it.'

'Oh dear.' Miranda felt like putting her aching head in her hands. It had been inevitable that such talk would get about; she had simply not allowed herself to think about it. As Daisy ranted on about the small-mindedness and spite of her mum's neighbours and Stratford people in general, she thought intently of what might be done to stop the rumour. The absent Mr Forbes could obviously not be produced, and the mechanics of writing letters to herself with foreign stamps on baffled the imagination. Mr Forbes could be killed off, of course. But some superstitious qualm forbade that. Whatever was done would have to be done soon, for Valentine's sake more than her own; he must not grow up to be pointed at.

'I'm ever so sorry for you, Mrs F,' Daisy said. 'Bloody ole cats! Wouldn't surprise me see 'em all fly off up Borden Hill on their broomsticks, devil's kin they are and no mistake.'

Daisy was sorry for her. That was the line to take – give people something to pity. Heavy-eyed and tired as she was, it was not difficult to sound melancholy.

'I'd better tell you the truth, Daisy. Mr Forbes and I are separated. He . . . found someone else, just after I knew

Valentine was on the way. That's why I came here – I didn't want to stay where it had all happened. I have no parents, you see – no relatives of any kind – so I thought it would be best to come and live among complete strangers. I never thought of them saying things like this.'

Daisy's eyes were widened to their full extent. 'Oh, Mrs F! Oh, I *am* sorry. Aren't men rotten? I wish I'd the hanging of 'em, that I do. Why, just fancy, the heartlessness of it –'

'Daisy, please. I've told you now, and I don't want to talk about it any more, if you don't mind. But if you could just say a word to your mother, perhaps she could mention it to someone who'd put people right. Would you do that for me?'

It was done, that morning, by an impatient and vehement Daisy. And so the pointing fingers dropped and the whispering voices were silenced; even though there were some who shook their heads, muttering that there was no smoke without fire.

And it had only been the truth, after all; with one detail left out.

Up in the tiny loft one day, searching for a box stowed away up there at the time of the removal, Miranda came upon the Scheherazade doll. It reminded her sharply of the time she longed to forget. She dropped it back into the suitcase where it had lain.

'You're not coming downstairs – no, you're not. You've got an evil face. I suppose I ought to sell you, but I wouldn't care to pass you on to anybody.' She shut down the lid on the painted pout and bright silks.

From this incident came the germ of an idea which grew into a pleasant and profitable occupation. A women's journal was running a series instructing its readers in the making of simple objects at home, for sale or use. The series was suddenly axed when complaints were received about the need for comforts for the troops, and the frivolity of spending time on anything else; but not before Miranda had read an article on making soft toys for small children. She decided to try her hand at an elephant, a beguiling creature in the drawing, using a piece of grey plush, and a quantity of beads, sewn on to a scrap of scarlet cloth for the saddle (if elephants could be said to wear saddles) with two sparkling beads for the eyes.

The effect was spendid, but the elephant refused to stand up.

The stuffing used for his legs was loose and lumpy, causing them to change shape somewhat ludicrously. At last Miranda, infuriated, unpicked the feet and gave the legs a central 'bone' of wire, binding the stuffing to it with cotton twine. Valentine received the elephant graciously, put it in his mouth, violently bent the legs in all directions, and settled down to pull off the beads, one by one.

Miranda sighed. At least it was keeping him quiet, but what a waste, after all that thought and work. If only babies were not little savages. Pretty toys should be appreciated and treasured. Idly she began to manipulate the length of wire left over, producing, without really intending it, a small skeleton shape – spine, neck, arms and legs. Then it seemed only logical to cover the thing in wool padding, like the body of the elephant, and add a head. A miniature person lay on the table, begging to be clothed and given features.

Over the next few days, when permitted by Valentine, she worked on the figure. It became feminine, with a small high bosom and tiny waist. The head, neck and forearms took on humanity with the application of modelling clay, the kind that set hard; they were surprisingly easy to form, for one with small fingers and a delicate touch. Scraps came out of the linen bag, others from the dressmaker who lived over the fish-monger's. At last the little creature was finished; she stood alone, a girl from the sixteenth century, in a wide farthingale of green velvet, leg o' mutton sleeves slashed with black, a wisp of gold thread for the embroidery of her bodice, and a tiny lace coif on hair made from rug-wool. The face, only roughly shaped, was neatly painted, dots for eyes and a rosebud mouth, in oil paints which would not smudge or fade.

Daisy was awestruck. 'You never made it all yourself, Mrs F? Well, I'll be damned, that I will. Didn't know you was an artist. What you going to do with it – not give it to that Val? Look what he done to the elephant.'

'No, I'm going to sell it – try to, anyway.' It was a great temptation to keep the doll, but even more so to earn a bit of extra money, when one lived on interest.

The owner of the 'fancy shop' in Bridge Street showed little enthusiasm, pointing out the crudity of the face-modelling and the sewing that was cobbled here and there. It never did to praise such objects too much. He was, therefore, able to beat Miranda down to a price he himself thought ludicrous, but it surprised and pleased her that he was willing to pay anything at all.

'I could do some more for you,' she offered. 'I can make them better than this.'

'Well, mind they are. Don't want goods coming to pieces when customers get them home.'

Leaving the shop, she looked back wistfully. The doll had been like a piece of herself, formed from nothing but ingenuity and imagination, another Shakespeare Girl of wool and wire. Greensleeves was all my joy, Greensleeves was my delight . . .

Now one was made, the others were easy. Six nameless, faceless creatures, varying in size, soon turned into characters from the plays. A tall Prospero wore a sweeping cloak sewn with cabalistic characters and moons and stars, a long-legged Romeo in a flame doublet and blue tights partnered a Juliet in white net, with a wreath of tiny artificial flowers in her hair, a Henry the Fifth had plate-armour stiffened with glue (very difficult) and painted gold, a Titania wearing the huge butterfly wings Constance Benson had worn, a Rosalind in brown forester's dress. Over the faces Miranda took immense pains, sculpting the features with tools from her sewing-basket, and painting them from drawings she had already made.

The fancy shop bought them all, at a realistic price. They stood in the window, fetchingly arranged against a velvet drape. Miranda passed and re-passed, watching one after another disappear. She began to take longer over each one of their successors, making every one more perfect. For the first time she knew the satisfaction of creativeness, and the blissful forgetting of worries. As though the small people had brought her luck, the worries themselves began to fade. Nobody now looked at her speculatively in the street. She found a friend, Jenny Churcher, a young woman with a husband in France, who was not unlike Editha – Editha, now in London, caught up in social gaieties – someone to talk to, laugh with, exchange baby notes with, for Jenny had a daughter three months older than Valentine.

And old friends reappeared. Pushing the bassinet down Chapel Street, Miranda saw a familiar figure striding rapidly up the slope towards her, coat flying open, grey hair streaming in the breeze, the far-off intent look not taking her in until they almost collided. He stopped abruptly.

'Miss Er . . . wait, I've got it, Heriot. The illustrious Shakespeare Girl herself. Well met, my lady! Well, well. But no, you can't be.' Valentine bounced up and down, shaking the silver bells on his harness and beaming an angelic smile upon the tall gentleman who was eyeing him.

'No, I'm Mrs Forbes now, and this is Valentine. I'm very pleased to see you again . . .' It seemed presumptuous to address him as Pa or F.R., now that she did not belong to the company. She decided on 'Mr Benson.'

'I'm delighted. It's been a long time since we saw you. Come, come and sit down and tell me all about yourself.' With his own peculiar force he almost propelled her and the baby-carriage through the narrow gate into New Place Gardens, the elegant pleasaunce that had once been the Bard's own, and now belonged to the public. They sat down on a bench, bright beds of flowers to each side of them, before them the wide lawn where one old man was feebly pushing a mower beneath the mulberry tree which people said was descended from the one chopped down by a Georgian vicar furious at the interest shown in his house by Shakespeare pilgrims. He had pulled down the house, too, earning himself eternal obloquy. But the old garden had peace in it still, the peace it must have brought to the ageing playwright weary of London.

F.R. talked, freely and cheerfully, of many things. Of his own efforts to join up, as so many of his friends had done, actors now replaced in the company by girls and women. 'But the idiots wouldn't have me. So back to Stratford for a month's season. And then – who knows what? The war will be over, please God, and we can begin to plan again.'

He was not only rehearsing as hard as ever, but doing what war-work he could – driving wounded soldiers about, lavishing on them the best seats at the theatre, reciting the 'God for Harry!' speech in public, to encourage the idlers to enlist. Miranda would not have been surprised to learn that in any spare time he had he was making bandages or knitting comforters. Yes, Constance was with him, ready to give the public her Titania once again.

'But,' he said, fixing Miranda with a gaze of noble reproach, 'You must have known we had returned. Why did you not seek us out?'

'I thought you'd all be too busy. And there would be so few people I remember. You wouldn't want me about.'

'Want you? Dear child, of course we want you. With our boys away we need every woman-Jill we can get. When can you come? Have you a nursemaid, nanny, anything to look after this fine fellow?'

Miranda replied that she had not exactly a nursemaid or nanny, but an obliging girl. With the doll-money, and perhaps a little from the theatre, she could afford to pay Daisy extra for evening work.

'Good, good. Tomorrow, then, ten sharp, a run-through for *Henry*. Oh, and if your obliging girl can't oblige, bring the little lad with you. He can walk on.'

'Well, not exactly *walk* on, yet . . .'

'No matter, he can be carried. Yes.' He surveyed Valentine. 'He could be the infant Queen Elizabeth; even the hair's right, a touch of red. And we could black him up for the Indian child. Full of possibilities.' The Gild Chapel clock clanged out the hour, and F.R. recollected with a start that he ought to be somewhere else. Waving a brisk farewell, he cantered towards the gate, where he turned, flung up his arms, and cried with all the strength of his lungs, 'God for Harry, England and SAINT GEORGE!' Several old ladies quivered with shock, but Valentine laughed. He liked loud voices. There were a lot of things he was going to like, from the moment he entered the theatre.

The month that followed was all delight to Miranda, a return to her first days in Stratford, but without the nervous anxieties of those days. Everybody was friendly, the few people from the past glad to see her, charmed by Valentine, who spent almost as much time in the theatre as at home. Nobody asked any questions about his origins. He soon became used to the dimensions of the stage and the bright lights, seeming, indeed, to be fascinated by them. He responded happily to the admiration of the ladies in the company, allowing himself to be nursed by them, travelling from one pair of willing arms to the next. Miranda felt a spear of jealousy as she saw him so independent of her; but it was for the best. He was weaned now, a separate person of strong character, learning from voices and faces and sights. Every day he seemed to grow in intelligence, making sounds that were attempts at words, crawling and trying to stand. 'Sharp, isn't he,' people said. Only nine months? More like eighteen, I'd have thought.' And F.R. pronouced 'An Old Soul, I believe. A pilgrim who has trodden the way of Shakespeare before.'

Miranda shivered. For the first time she carried Valentine into the Birthplace and held him up before the portrait. He pointed to it, then looked enquiringly up at her.

'Yes. That's your great-great . . . I don't know many greats. Your ancestor, anyway. He's all the family we have, baby.' To the portrait she said, 'Please look after him, if you can. For your Hamnet's sake. I suppose I shouldn't be praying to you, but F.R. wouldn't think it was wrong. Saint William of Stratford. And if you'd anything to do with my coming back to the company, thank you. I've never been so happy, you know.'

The impassive face looked back at her. It was not easily readable. 'Others abide our question. Thou art free. We ask and ask: thou smilest and art still, Out-topping knowledge'.

After a first night it was irresistible to find out what the local critic had said. Miranda bought the paper and began to read the notice in the shop. 'Mr Benson's old fire has not deserted him . . .'

Smiling, she folded the paper. Glancing along the others lying on the counter, a bold black headline caught her eye. 'Our Special Correspondent lost in the Dardanelles. Andrew Craigie goes down with the torpedoed battleship Eagle.'

The story was a long one, for those days when bad news came in so thickly that space was rationed. Andrew's brilliant coverage of the war from its beginnings was recounted in detail, his qualities as a versatile journalist, his expertise and bravery as a war correspondent, the esteem in which he was held in Fleet Street. He was compared with great ones of the past: Russell of *The Times*, O'Donovan of the *Daily News*, men much senior to him in age yet surely no more able in their field. 'Had he lived, Craigie must certainly have received the highest decoration His Majesty can award.'

Miranda found herself sitting on someone's window-sill, the

paper still in her hand. Her knees were trembling too much to carry her further. She read the story again, making little sense of it. In her imagination Andrew had been still in London all this time. When reports of the terrible fighting overseas had come in, they had been about him, and she had never guessed it. That was almost as hard to take in as the fact of his death. When she had bitterly imagined him living in comfort in some Surrey villa, he had been in the trenches, at sea, behind the front line, among flying shells and men dying horribly, getting his dispatches back to his paper whatever the difficulty or risk. And she had not given him one thought, one prayer.

The story made no mention of his wife. Surely it was usual to say what family a dead person had left?

She could not weep for Andrew; the shock was too great. That night she went to the theatre as usual, leaving Valentine behind, and walked on as a page. Nobody guessed from her manner that anything unusual had happened.

Next morning she went to a telephone box in a quiet spot and rang the offices of the *Recorder*. Impatient voices answered, passing her from one to another, until a woman came on the line who understood her question.

'Mr Craigie's wife? I don't follow you, madam.'

'I wondered . . . where one could get in touch . . .' It was not true, but some excuse had to be given.

'I think you must be mistaken. Mr Craigie wasn't married.'

So everything had been different. No suburban home, no complacent Aileen, no half-brother or half-sister to Valentine on the way, as she had sometimes conjectured.

And now he was gone.

CHAPTER SEVENTEEN
Remembrance of Things Past

The sound of the knocker reverberated through the cottage in the stillness of Sunday afternoon. Valentine stirred in his sleep, making a noise between a whimper and a mew. He was beginning to acquire the actor's habit of sleeping long and heavily in his spare time, and he had had a strenuous time the evening before as part of several crowds in *Julius Caesar*. Miranda, too, had slept heavily on her bed, in a light dressing-gown, trying to escape from the heavy August heat. She trailed downstairs, hoping that whoever was at the door would not object to her informal dress.

The dumpy little woman in black beamed at the sight of her astonished face. 'There! You're in, and I thought you might not be. But I've disturbed you, I can see.'

'Polly! Good heavens, what are you . . . come in, come in. Where have you come from? Why didn't you write? Oh, how marvellous to see you.'

Polly was taking off her coat, skewering up her bun with hair-pins, and looking appreciatively round the sitting-room. 'How very nice you've made this – I haven't seen it since Valentine's christening, have I. Such nice bits of old stuff, no modern rubbish. Well, I didn't write because I didn't know I was coming until yesterday. Suddenly it all got too much for me – this awful heat, you've no idea what it's like in London – and London itself, so depressing, everything blacked out at night since the Zeppelins came, and bad news all the time. So I thought I'd give myself a holiday and come up here to Tibby's. She was delighted, dear old thing. And besides, I wanted to see you, very much. But I can see I chose a bad time.'

'Not a bit. I was sunk in swinish slumber, that's all, and it was quite time I got up. Oh, listen to that.'

Valentine had discovered a pleasing alternative to crying

when he wanted attention. He would rock his considerable weight in his cot, producing a steady bumping sound on the ancient floorboards. This was now heard, insistently demanding. Miranda went up and brought him down, to be received ecstatically by the visitor.

'Oh, you splendid creature, aren't you handsome! Don't remember me, do you. How on earth has he got to be this size, in a few months?'

'I've no idea, unless it's with going to work at an early age.'

Polly listened, entranced, to the tale of Valentine's stage career, and Miranda's own. Over tea they talked as only friends can talk who have not met for half a year. Polly heard news of the company and F.R.'s enthusiastic war-work, and gave Miranda her own news of Edward, patiently tramping the streets as a Special Constable, and Harold, fuming in the Army Pay Corps because his eyesight had debarred him from active service. 'Not that he was all that keen about fighting, but he wanted to do something scientific to help the war effort, like inventing a better gas than the Germans have got, or something that could be dropped from aeroplanes and send the whole country into a coma, like *The Poison Belt*. Germany, I mean, not us.' Polly herself was organising bazaars and sewing parties and doing part-time library work to take the place of a man who had joined up.

She talked so vivaciously and without pause that Miranda, knowing her, felt that something serious lay behind it all, and hoped they were not to talk of Andrew. But Polly said at last, 'I brought you something. But first I'm afraid you'll have to read this.'

The cutting was from an American theatrical paper, among news items from an eastern state.

DEATH OF NOTED BRITISH ACTOR. Richard Savage, well-known for his striking performances in Mr Frank Benson's Stratford-upon-Avon Players, who visited our city last year, was on Thursday found dead in his lodgings. On the return of the Benson company to England he had joined another tour, which had taken him to many areas of the United States and Canada. It is not known why he was resident here at the time of his death, which was apparently from poison. He will be remembered for such roles as John of Gaunt, Jacques, Claudius, Parolles . . .

Miranda said, 'Oh, no. It must be a mistake.'

'Far otherwise. In fact, though I was shocked, of course, I wasn't really, truly surprised. We always knew he couldn't live long without Rachel. I rather thought it might have happened just after she died.'

'Had you – had you heard from him?'

'Not a single word. It was F.R. who told us he'd rejoined them. Or rather not F.R. but somebody else, who didn't know him well and forgot to say how he was.'

'But why didn't they tell me – at the theatre?'

'My dear, actors don't remember things long, however sad. And, well, you know F.R., a mind elsewhere – it would never occur to him. It's awful, still.' Her voice shook. 'I know you never liked him much, and he did have a lowering visage, to the world at large. But we were all very, very fond of him; he made Rachel so happy. I could only think of him as a dear brother-in-law. Do you know – you may find this hard to believe – but I think I knew, when it happened. We were sitting by the fire one night, Ted and I, and Timon asleep on the rug. Quite suddenly Timon woke with a start, the way cats do, and got up and asked to be let out. A bit later I went out to make the cocoa and saw the front parlour door was open, which it shouldn't have been, because of lights showing. So I went in – and Timon was in Ricky's chair, dead.'

'Oh, Polly!'

'He'd been perfectly all right, just his usual self – hadn't even had a fight lately. But he was dead, and I think that was when Ricky . . . he cared for him more than he did for Rachel. Perhaps they were two of a kind . . .'

After a struggle, Polly composed herself. 'I said I'd brought you something, besides this dreadful news. When they investigated his death they found our name and address in his room – *not*, thank God, his wife's – and cabled to us. Then there was a lot of telegraphing – we wanted to go over there but it was expensive enough as it was, and what good would it have done Ricky? In the end they just sent over his personal things. This was among them – it was in his hand when they found him.'

The scrawl on a scrap of paper said, 'Juliet, I come; this do I drink to thee.'

In the silence that fell between them the bells of Holy Trinity began to ring their summons to Evensong.

Miranda said, 'Isn't love an extraordinary thing. Rachel said to me, when I told her I was going away with Andrew, that I was looking for love and didn't care where I got it. And that Andrew didn't mind a lot about it. She was quite right, of course. I thought it was all bed and kisses and . . . that sort of thing, and one had to be young, or it was ridiculous. But they, Rachel and Ricky, weren't young, and they were the truest lovers that could ever be.'

'Antony and Cleopatra weren't young, either, if you remember. You're learning, child.'

'Did you know that Andrew had been killed?'

'Yes.'

'I didn't even know he was in the war.'

'And is your heart broken?' Polly asked softly.

'No. Because it all seems quite unreal. I can't realise it, even yet. I think I'm almost as much angry as sad, because I haven't the right to grieve for him. He wasn't married, after all. So I could have been still with him, and written to him and sent him things, and – it's all been such a stupid waste. Except for Valentine. Don't let's talk about it any more.'

Polly scrabbled in the large folk-weave bag she carried everywhere, and produced an envelope. 'I feel like a conjurer pulling rabbit after rabbit out of the hat. This is what really concerns you, and I want you to read it after I've gone, because if I don't go now I shall be late for Tibby's supper, and I know she's looking forward to a long back-hair chat.'

But Miranda was already unfolding the letter. The much-battered envelope was addressed to Richard Savage, Esq., care of an English accommodation address, and was dated two years previously. The handwriting was big and uneducated, and had many flourishes.

Dear Old Man [it began], Ta muchly for yours of last month, which reached me kindness of Doris where I used to hang out, though as you see I am no longer there, as my chest is too bad now for me to tread the boards, and I was lucky to get took by this place where they look after such as us that are past it. What price this Lloyd George then? Up the Liberals, don't I wish I had got one of these pensions.

I trust you and yours are very well though you don't say much. Last time we was together I know Carrie was giving you trouble. As to your asking about Frank Forbes, yes indeed I do remember him, a nice young chap quite a cut above me and the other buskers in our little party. Pity he went so soon but some couldn't stand the life. I would be very pleased to see you old man if you could find the time. Hope you're working and keeping fit. Do you remember . . .

Miranda skipped the pathetic summonings-up of past good times. The signature was bold. 'Yours aye, Jimmy.' The letter heading was St Ethelburga's Home, Coburg Road, Southend.

'Jimmy Pleasants, of course,' Polly said. 'He and Ricky used to be great pals when they were young, perhaps because Jimmy was such an optimist and Ricky was inclined to look on the dark side, even then. I don't know where they knew each other, but Ricky's often mentioned him as a case of virtue not being its own reward. Apparently he was a first-class comedian who was never appreciated, or badly treated, or something. Of course you'll go and see him.'

'Of course. If he's still alive. The letter sounds as though he isn't well, and it's two years since he wrote it. *Why* didn't Ricky pass it on to you sooner, Polly?'

Polly shrugged. 'How do I know, dear? He wasn't very good at things like correspondence, and perhaps Rachel never saw it, or she'd have known it was important to you. Gracious, I've just remembered Thursday's Tibby's night for serving Patriotic Stew. Do you think we'll ever eat and drink properly again?' It would have surprised Polly to realise that she had almost dropped her old habit of incessant quotation. Things like war and tragedy had their own way of taking the poetry out of life.

Leaving Valentine in Daisy's care, Miranda made the journey to Southend-on-Sea. It was an ugly little town, made no less ugly by shore defences. Its sands, its pier, it boarding-houses, all had the look of things deserted; what had been a Cockney playground, only a year before, in the bright sunshine of 1914, was a sepulchre now, waiting for the Zeppelins to come back to the east coast and drop their futile bombs in accordance with the Kaiser's policy of "frightfulness". After all, when he won the war he was not going to live in Southend. Buckingham Palace would be all right, the cynics said.

Coburg Road lay on the outskirts of the town, away from the sea – and from anything else. There were no shops in its dreary length, or any sign of activity beyond an undertaker's establishment, situated conveniently within sight of the windows of St Ethelburga's Home, a late Victorian house of brick and yellow stone, ornamented (if that was the word) with wooden pinnacles, its woodwork painted an institutional shade of green. Miranda thought it looked very unlike anybody's home.

The elderly maid who answered the door said that she would report Miranda's arrival to the Superintendent, whose approval was required for all visitors. He proved to be equally elderly, a mild-faced man with pince-nez. He explained to Miranda that his charges sometimes received visits from those who disturbed them.

'Theatrical people are sometimes inclined to be, ah, emotional, excitable. We feel it our duty to protect them from undue upset.'

'I promise not to upset Mr Pleasants. Is he very ill?'

'An asthmatic. Chronic, I'm afraid, an illness of many years standing. Very lucky that he was recommended to us in time; he became quite incapable of working about ten years ago, and but for being taken in here . . . well, I doubt if he'd be alive today.' Miranda learned that the Home had been founded by an actress who had married into the aristocracy and assigned some of her considerable wealth to the care of broken-down members of her old profession.

A nurse appeared to say that Mr Pleasants was ready for his visitor. She led Miranda up a flight of stairs to what had been a master bedroom, in the house's early days, and was now part of a ward. It contained twelve beds, each discreetly surrounded by curtain-rails.

Jimmy Pleasants was sitting up in bed. His sparse grey hair had been hastily brushed into slickness, and he had persuaded the nurse to change his pyjama jacket for his best one, with bright blue stripes. It was a very long time since he had had any visitors. A red spot burned in each of his yellowed cheeks, and he smiled brightly. As Miranda approached his bed the nurse swished the side-curtains close; they were virtually alone.

'I don't think I've had the pleasure,' he said, making it sound like the first line in a comedy sketch.

'Miranda Forbes. I'm sorry I didn't have time to write and say I was coming. You won't know me – I'm a friend of a friend of yours.'

'Ah. And who – of the many – might that be?' He cocked his head engagingly on one side. He looked very ill, Miranda thought, as though he might break into pieces if the wind blew particularly hard.

'Ricky Savage.'

'Ricky Savage! Well, God save the pigs. Haven't heard of Ricky for – oh, must be best part of twenty years. Wait, though. He wrote me a letter. That's right, a letter. Before I left Doris's, that would be, or was it afterwards? Memory's not what it was, dear. Day in's much the same as day out in this place, not but what I'm grateful. Hold on, it's coming back to me. Old Ricky wrote me, and I answered back, and that was the last time I heard from him. How is he, the old b – sport?'

Something whispered to Miranda that it would be wiser not to mention Ricky's death at this point; perhaps not at all. She said, 'He was in America, last time I heard of him.'

'America! Fancy. High-flier, Ricky. Always good class stuff. D'you know, dear, he almost got me a break into legit., once. Friend of his, one of the clever, er, customers that likes to change everything round, thought old Bill Shakespeare's funny men ought to be the real thing, low comics, you know, a chance for 'em to do a bit of straight stuff as well. So Ricky got me this part, rum sort of name – Gobble, would it be?'

'Gobbo?'

'That's right, now it comes back to me. I had to say, "Certainly my conscience will . . ." ' He struggled silently, mouthing. ' "The Jew my master . . ." No, it's no good.Only remember it started with that, because I was scared enough to . . . I was scared. So I took a drop to get my spunk up, and the fact is, when it came to the curtain I was lushy. No other

220

word for it, lushy. So I lost that crib, and I believe it started my luck turning the wrong way.' He began to cough alarmingly, with a choking sound. Miranda put her head out of the curtains and summoned the nurse, who hurried in with a glass of water.

'Beg pardon,' said Jimmy, recovering. 'Didn't mean to go off like that, only it brought things back. Blow me, if I'm not blatherin' on about the dead and gone, when there's a pretty young lady come to see me. Beg pardon again, my dear.' He threw her a smile of such ruined charm that she had an impulse to jump out of her chair and embrace him. But she said, 'Please don't think about it – it's very interesting, and I'm sorry you were so unlucky. But what I wanted to ask you was, do you remember someone called Frank Forbes? I think you may have been pierrots together.'

For a moment she thought his memory had failed, as blankness came over his face. Then he shook his head, like on shaking away a cloud of flies. 'Frank Forbes. Good God! That takes me back.' He mused. 'Funny, the older you get the clearer the old times get. Must have been I dunno how many years. A handome, fair-faced lad was Frank. Came of a good family, but had this fancy for music, the stage, all that. Joined up with an outfit I was with, J.G. Wastell's Minstrels, playin' the banjo, singin' sentimental songs. He was the pretty one, we was the comics and heavies. I remember them songs. *Rose of the Morn*, that was one. And then there was *Genevieve*. "O Genevieve, sweet Genevieve, the days may come, the days may go, But still the voice of mem'ry sings . . .", no, that's wrong. Anyway, Wastell was a mean 'un when it came to handing out the dibs, so Frank and me and a chap called Algy Gibbs, we lit out on our own. Algy played the piano, and we got hold of one on wheels. First place we went to was . . . No, it's gone. Somewhere south coast, one of the only ones with a sandy beach. We didn't have a proper pitch, because we couldn't afford the Council's rent, so we went up and down the prom, bottling.'

'Bottling?'

'One of us went round with the bottle, pet, collecting the pennies. We didn't do bad, so next place we got some proper pierrot costumes and whitened-up. Whited our faces with zinc and lard, love, I can see it was before your time. Well, another chap joined and we started working the north, Morecambe, Blackpool, the Welsh places. We got a proper pitch in one of 'em – paid rent for it. A good life, it was, unless the rain came down which it mostly did; then we'd put out the notice "If wet under the pier." What was I talking about?'

'Frank Forbes.'

'Oh yes. Well, after Frank got married . . . What's the matter, dear? Yes, he married this kid that used to come and make eyes at him – where was it? Somewhere up there. He used to mash all the ladies, young Frank, but this time it was the real thing. Lovely girl, dark, serious-looking.' He became lost in memories.

Miranda asked shakily, 'What was her name?'

'Don't remember, dear, it's so long since. Only it was something that seemed to suit her. Got it! Grace, that's what it was. You're not well, dear, I can see that, and I ought to know. Nurse! Any chance of a drop of tea for this young lady and me?'

'I'm all right, Mr Pleasants,' Miranda said, 'really. Please, please go on.'

'What came next? Well, first she travelled with us, this Grace. Couldn't sing, but she learned to do a sort of little dance to Algy's tunes, and took the bottle round so pretty she did better than we had out of the fellers, though the females didn't care for her. But you know how it is, baby coming along, Frank quit and got rooms in London. He wasn't well then; too much If Wet under the Pier. Coughed terrible – not like I do, but the other sort. Next thing I heard, year or so later, they was both gone, her with something she took bad with after the baby, him with the consumption.'

'Mr Pleasants, are you quite, quite sure they were married?'

He frowned. ' 'Course I'm sure! What sort do you think we were? What's more, I was there. Little church at . . . let me think. Place in Yorkshire. Never mind, it'll come to me. I can tell you where they're buried, though. Cemetery round back of Camden Town. St Chad's, that was it. Forget who told me.'

The nurse arrived with a tray of tea. 'Mr Pleasants, you're talking too much, I can hear you all over the ward. Now you know what happens when you do that. I'm sorry, Miss Er, but if you wouldn't mind I think Mr Pleasants ought to rest now. Do drink your tea first, though.'

Miranda caught the train back to London in a sort of dream. It mattered very little that her parents had, after all, been married. Yet, in a strange way, it did matter; just as it mattered that Valentine had no father. And the sting was gone out of her grandmother's senseless spite, that had made her write that lying entry in the Bible, and pass on the lie.

The churchyard of St Chad's was small and shabby. No fresh flowers decorated its graves, tramps were slumped on its benches, black sparrows pecked about the grass. Some of the headstones were so old as to be illegible; Miranda searched every one that might have been put up within the past twenty-five years.

At last she found it, small, grey and modest. 'Grace, most dearly loved wife of Frank Forbes. Sweet Flower.' And underneath Frank's name, and a date eight months later than that of Grace's death.

Miranda had bought the roses only in the hope that she would find what she was seeking. Now she took them from the florist's elaborate wrapping, and covered the humble mound with them, so that in all that drab garden of death it was the only patch of exultant colour, pink and white and crimson making a scented coverlet. 'Sweet flower, with flowers thy bridal bed I strew.' That was what her father had meant: Paris's mourning for Juliet in the tomb. So he had known, to choose that for her epitaph, about the family Bible, and the other entry in it, and the blood that flowed in Grace's veins, and her daughter's. Now they were one in their knowledge, the three of them, two dead and one living, but a family still.

Before catching the train back to Stratford she ordered from a famous store a parcel of foodstuffs such as a bedridden invalid might enjoy, the best of everything, and wrote a card for them to enclose. 'With love and thanks from Miranda Forbes.' It would puzzle Jimmy, but he would enjoy the treats.

Polly heard the story out, and cried heartily. It was like a play, she said, and of course one shouldn't cry, but one so often did at happy endings, which this was in a way.

Then for the first time, with Valentine on her knee, asleep for once, Miranda told Polly of her experience at Curteis Hall, the voices, and what they had said.

'No, I don't find it hard to believe,' Polly said firmly. 'I find it extremely easy. I won't say "There are more things" because it's been said too often. What I want to know most is, what did he sound like?'

'It's hard to say. I've never heard anything exactly like it. A bit Cockney, and yet sometimes a word sounding countrified, and some very strange vowel-sounds – rather like F.R. at his oddest. I couldn't possibly imitate it.'

'And his voice?'

'Light. A sort of light baritone. One could tell he was able to use it like an actor's, and yet it was soft. Gentle. I shall never forget it.'

'And I,' said Polly, 'shall never stop envying you, not as long as I live.'

CHAPTER EIGHTEEN
Journeys end . . .

The war ground on its terrible way, eating up lives, ships, homes, villages, towns, cities. After the tragic retreat from Gallipoli the Military Service Act called for the compulsory enlistment of all single men between eighteen and forty-one; later it would apply to married men of the same age. The streets of Stratford, in that spring of 1916, saw only boys, old men, walking wounded or those whose button-holes carried the blue badge with the gold crown that proclaimed them On War Service.

Only one piece of light relief cheered that gloomy spring. It was the Tercentenary of Shakespeare's birth, and in celebration of it King George the Fifth had knighted F.R. Benson, in the Royal Box of Drury Lane Theatre, still costumed as Julius Caesar, half-wig, bloody toga, dust instead of grease-paint marking the expression-lines of his face. When he came back to Stratford the townsfolk harnessed themselves to his open landau, in which he and Constance sat laden with flowers, a chaplet of bays crowning the new knight's head. Noble dames of the London stage came to perform scenes from his tableau *Homage to Shakespeare*.

But Sir Frank would not stay in Stratford. His country called, he said, and he and Lady Benson would devote themselves to war work. The Old Vic Company took over the summer festival, under the direction of Ben Greet. Miranda applied to keep her walk-ons and tiny speaking parts, and was surprised to be accepted. The men available were scarce, and any female who could make herself into a convincing youth was welcome. Long ago Constance had shown Miranda how one might create a convincingly boyish figure by winding a towel round and round the waist; it worked perfectly.

Valentine, now coming up to two, had become so active and

vocal that it was no longer safe to allow him on a stage. He was very tall for his age, his hair redder than it had been, growing in waves and curls that produced an effect far from girlish, and when clipped, curled all the more. His memory was such that Daisy's language had to be watched keenly, and even she realised it, substituting strange and meaningless words for the oaths which had peppered her speech. She adored Val, as he called himself; Miranda thought he was partly the reason why she had not become engaged to one of the attractive young men in hospital blue whose injuries invited the pity which is akin to love.

Now, in late summer, the end of the season was approaching. After it the theatre would close, and who could tell when it would open again, and in what circumstances? The Kaiser admired Shakespeare and had celebrated the Tercentenary in Germany; in the dreadful case of his winning the war, perhaps the plays would be presented in German translations for the benefit of the occupying troops, and performances would conclude with *Deutschland über Alles* or *Die Wacht am Rhein*. All the kings would wear spiked helmets and tom-cat moustaches, and the queens long blonde pigtails. The company joked about it: one had to joke.

One hot August night after the last performance of *Richard III*, Miranda thankfully removed the surcoat of woollen chainmail and the helmet in which she had been clashing her sword against those of other ladies at Bosworth Field. It was a relief to come out of the stage door into the air, even though the river smelt dank and the night was moonless. Somebody stepped forward from the shadows, saying, 'Hello.'

'Harold!'

'No less.'

'Well, how nice. Were you in front?'

'Yes. I spotted you in all those changes. Jolly good battle.'

'Wasn't it? But so infernally hot. I don't know why Richard didn't just die of heatstroke instead of having to be killed.'

'A case of "My kingdom for an ice-cream".'

'Don't – I could just eat one.'

Harold fell into step with her. It was like living backwards, to be walking home from the theatre with him. He seemed even taller than last time she had seen him, and looked, even in the half-light, straight and slim in khaki. She commented on the becomingness of uniform; Harold snorted. 'If it weren't for my blasted giglamps I'd be wearing it to some purpose. You've no idea how infuriating it is to be stuck with the money-bags when other chaps are out there dying like flies. That's what you get for being bright at maths.'

'I'd rather you didn't die like a fly just yet, Harold.'

'Would you? Good.' He linked his arm in hers, and she let it stay. It was curiously comforting and agreeable to have a man's company again. As they walked towards Henley Street – for she assumed without asking that he expected to escort her home, and would want to see it – they talked of all that had happened, except for one thing. He had a week's leave, he said, and was spending it between Morden and Stratford. Polly was at home, too involved in hospital work to be with him. Mrs Tibbs was well, but sad about the prospect of all theatre life vanishing from the town. 'She's felt like an actress herself, you know, all these years. Doesn't think anyone's going to take her rooms now, poor old thing.'

Daisy had put the kettle on ready for Miranda's homecoming. She stared to see Harold, and Miranda could sense some embarrassingly frank remark about to spring to her lips. Hastily she said, 'This is an old friend, Mrs Porter's son, Daisy. We've got enough for supper, haven't we?'

'Well, there's a nice bit of streaky bacon – had to queue half an hour for it – and that Miss Tombs round the corner what's so struck on Val give him two eggs when we was out.'

'That's lovely. You'll stay for supper, of course, Harold?'

Of course he would. He had been nervous before she appeared from the stage door, afraid she would not be pleased to see him, fob him off with a curt greeting – be accompanied by some chap, perhaps, though just what chap, these days, was conjectural. He was utterly happy, for the first time since war had broken out, watching her move about her cottage, beautiful, now, instead of merely pretty, with the maturity of motherhood on her, and the grace gained through stage movement. He had thought of her constantly since the day she had left his mother's house. Through the boredom and frustration of his army life she had been something to cling to, the ideal of his boyhood, lovely as a Stratford April morning.

And she was here, not a shadow, but herself, bettering his dreams.

Harold loved his mother and felt strong kinship with her, but his home life had not been a complete one. She was not a woman to express her emotion, nor did she care very much about her home, academic at heart as she was. Harold knew, had always known, that his gentle vague father could have been a great deal happier than he was, with a wife who petted and tended him, and made his surroundings comfortable. Harold had never said anything critical about his mother, but at heart he had always been sorry about his father's lonely fishing expeditions, neglected den, and single bed in a room apart from his wife's. And throughout his own boyhood it had been Mattie who mended his clothes, noticed when he needed new school equipment, made up lotions for his adolescent spots, old Mattie, childless herself yet more of a mother to him than his natural one.

Which had resulted in his determination to settle down himself as early as possible in the sort of home he had never had, with a wife who would be everything his mother had not been.

And yet she loved him and cared about his happiness. That was why he was here tonight: because she had told him that the man who had treated his girl so foully had been put out of the way for good. (God bless the Kaiser, Harold thought. It might be the only time he would say it, but he meant it heartily.) Give her time, Polly had said – give her a year to get over him. And before the year was up she had written to him urgently, with many underlinings, urging him to go to Miranda and try his luck, *now*. So he was trying it.

Miranda enjoyed Harold's company. He was good-natured, mildly funny, refreshing to talk to, warmly appreciative of the least thing she did to entertain him, if it was only making a cup of tea. Towards Valentine he was benevolently courteous; having no notion how to behave to small children, he talked to him as man to man, which Valentine enjoyed, calling him Hal and fascinatedly taking off his spectacles and putting them on again at an angle, climbing on to his knees and generally haunting his company until Miranda had to apologise for him and shoo him away.

'I don't mind,' Harold said. 'I've never known any kids. They're rather fun, if they're like him. And I like being called Hal. It sounds rather Shakespearean, don't you think? Why don't you call me Hal? Hal and Val, a double act.'

'I might get used to it in time. But I'm quite fond of Harold, you know.'

'Are you?' At his intent tone and gaze she blushed.

'I mean I think it's got a certain nobility – a sort of Saxon strength.'

'Good Lord, you sound like Ma.'

He knew when the perfect time came. They had walked, after the performance, up to Trinity and over the mill-stream bridge into the meadows, and slowly back along the river-side by the path that ended at the Swan's Nest. Traffic had ceased on Clopton Bridge. They stood and looked at the theatre, a dark turreted shape, soon to be empty and idle. Not a swan floated beneath them, all gone to their island by the mill, but the sharp high voices of bats were all about them.

Harold said, without turning his head, 'Miranda, will you marry me?'

She had known it would come. But, spoken at last, she felt her knees tremble and her mouth go dry. It would be so easy to say yes. Yes to companionship after loneliness, to a kindly surrogate father for her boy, to a family of her own, dear familiar Polly and Edward to take the place of a speechless, impassive old portrait, and the memory of a London grave. Yes, to a husband who could be relied on not to become a war casualty. And yet something held her back. When Harold took her hand and drew her against his shoulder she was utterly comfortable and content; but there would be more, in marriage, and the face of it was hidden from her yet.

To Harold the silence was endless. He seemed to have been standing on that spot since the beginning of time, with just this scene before him; he thought it would be found engraved on his heart, like Calais on Queen Mary's.

At last she said, 'I'd like to say yes, Harold, here and now.'

'Oh, my dear . . .'

'No, hush. I need time to think. There's so much . . . It's such a huge thing to have to decide – for you, and me, and Val. I'm so very fond of you and I've been so happy since you came.

And we've known each other so long; you know the worst about me, and I suppose I know the worst about you, though I can't think what it is. There's nobody I'd rather marry than you, Harold. Only – here and now – it would be wrong to say yes.'

He hid his disappointment. He had thought to have his fate decided by now, and instead he was back in the limbo of hope and fear. 'That's all right – of course I understand,' he said cheerfully. 'Take all the time you want. Wait till after I've gone back, if you like, and see how it feels without me. Whatever you want, that's what I want too.'

'You're so sweet, so good.' He put his arm round her waist, and close together they walked back to the waiting cottage, where he left her with a brother's kiss, and looked back longingly at the closed door and the curtained window.

The man in the London hotel room pushed away the cup of cold, bitter coffee. The grey light, thickened by autumn fog, showed him his drab impersonal surroundings: things used by countless other travellers before him. The ancient chambermaid had brought him a newspaper; he scanned the front page. A great trench advance on the Somme from Barleux to Chaulnes, the outskirts of Ginchy in British hands, a Russian victory and four thousand prisoners. So it went on, so it would go on, perhaps for ever, until they were all killed, Allies, Germans, Russians and Greeks and Bulgarians, all rotting corpses in stinking mud, and there was no life left anywhere, no green fields or houses or gardens. A great sickness of soul filled him. He looked down from the window at the grey London street. It would be so easy to push up the sash and let himself fall. That would make an end of everything. No more nightmares.

But he would probably merely break all his bones, and face life again, a useless cripple. That would be just his luck. Wearily, slowly, he put on his coat and went down the red-carpeted stairs, out into the foggy air. There was only one thing that offered even a glimmer of hope.

Daisy paused in the middle of pegging out one of Val's best shirts. It escaped its gyves and fell into a flower-bed, causing her to utter an oath even Miranda had never heard. She picked it up and shook it.

'Bleedin' tramps!' she said to herself. 'Always round bothering, collections for this, that and the other. Tramps, no better, that's what they are. All right, all right, keep yer hair on.' Muttering, she stumped through the cottage to answer the door.

Miranda, upstairs, winced at Daisy's shout, which the person at the door must certainly have heard too. 'Somebody wants yer. Don't know who 'tis, after money, most likely.'

Valentine looked over the banister and said, 'Man's poorly.'

'Oh dear. Well, I'll see about it. Don't you dare open that gate, Val.'

'Yes?' The person at the door certainly looked poorly at first glance, haggard and stooped, holding the side of the door-frame as though it kept him from falling. Then she met his eyes, and a shock-wave went through her like the impact of a bursting shell.

The man tried to smile and speak, and crumpled at her feet.

An hour later the little house was calm again. Andrew lay on the sofa, under a blanket and a small rug which Val had insisted on bringing down from his own cot, a glass beside him half-full of the brandy a bewildered Daisy had fetched from the public-house.

'I'm ashamed,' he said, managing now to smile. 'I thought it was delicate females who swooned, not great strong men.'

'I never saw anything less like a great strong man than you,' replied Miranda, 'though you don't look quite as dreadful as you did. As for fainting, I only did that once, at school during prayers. Do you feel like telling me where you've been, and why you had to give me the worst shock of my life? No, I think you'd better just rest.'

'It amazes me, how calm women are. Who's that?' Val was sitting on the floor, nursing his favourite wooden horse, very quiet. His true actor's instinct told him that it was a time for listening and taking in impressions, not for talking.

'That's your son,' Miranda said, and then wished she had not, since all the colour the brandy had brought to Andrew's face had fled from it again. He shook his head slowly, trying to shake the daze out of it. Val, watching him, thought he was really a very nice man, though not at all like Hal, and so very old, grey hair that curled like his own, with lots of red in it. He wondered why his mother was holding the man's hand in both of hers; she had never held Hal's like that. Andrew opened his eyes and met his son's, and Miranda let the hand go, so that it could reach out to Val.

'Hello,' said Val. 'Would you like a frog? I know where there is one.'

'Thank you – if it isn't too much trouble.' When Val had gone he said, 'Good God, why didn't you tell me? If I'd known . . . I had no idea . . . I can't believe it. How did it happen?'

'The usual way, I suppose, and I didn't tell you because you had other things on your mind, and I could manage perfectly well. Now don't worry about anything. Valentine's here, and I'm here, and we're so glad to see you, and I'm very happy.' At which she began to cry, kneeling at his side and clasping him so tightly that his racked body protested, but he said nothing, holding her to him.

By instalments, ceasing when he tired, the story unfolded. When his ship went down after the torpedo attack in the Sea of Marmora he had been rescued by a naval boat, with two or three others. They had been lucky at first; then their luck turned, and they were captured by the Turks. His companions died; he would never tell Miranda how. Through the laxness of a drunken guard he escaped, and began an overland trek which had reduced him to the level of a beast trying to outwit its hunters; in strange country, and with winter coming on. How many weeks he had travelled so he could not remember, only that he had gone northwards and found himself in Rumania, not yet at war with Germany.

There a long and serious illness put him out of action for a month. He was taken in by a farmer and his family, in the foothills of the Transylvanian Alps, who nursed and generally befriended him. It would have been easier and cheaper for them to have killed him and fed him to the animals, but they were kindness itself to the penniless stranger, giving him money, when he was well enough to travel, until, by means of working as a labourer and begging lifts in carriers' carts, he struggled into France in the spring: in time for the battle of Verdun. When he eventually reached the British lines he was almost beyond communication with his own countrymen. 'They thought I was either a spy or mad, and I don't blame them.' And at last he was able to telegraph to the *Recorder*, and begin again to send home reports.

'When was this?' Miranda asked.

'March – I think.'

'And they were pleased, of course, to have you back? They made a story of it?'

'Yes. Well, of course they would.'

'I see. So people knew you were alive.' Polly knew, Polly who read all the papers; Polly who had let Harold come to Stratford unbriefed with the news, for he would never have concealed it. Polly had deliberately kept it from her.

'Yes, they knew. Not that they were getting much out of it – other chaps had done the job perfectly well while I was skulking about in foreign parts. Then I capped my uselessness by getting trench fever. They sent me back to Blighty, but I don't remember anything about it. When I came round I was in a military hospital somewhere in Sussex. I . . . Miranda, it was worse getting better than being ill. When I finally got to London I was in such a state of hopelessness I wanted to die. I wished I *had* died, with all those chances of doing it. There seemed nothing, nothing at all in the world; it was the dark night of the soul, whoever said that. Then I thought of you. I thought you might just be alive – God, a Zepp could have got you for all I knew! I couldn't hope you'd want to see me, but I felt I had to see you, or I really should go round the corner into melancholy madness.'

'So you found where I was from Polly Porter,' Miranda said thoughtfully.

'Yes – how do you know?'

'It was the only way you could. Go on.'

'Well – she wasn't keen to tell me. In fact she said some fairly harsh things, which I fully deserved. But her husband came home, and was very good and reasonable about it, and in the end she told me – largely, I believe, because she thought she'd have a dying man on her hands if she didn't. And here I am, and . . . and it was only yesterday I felt like that, Miranda.'

She moved so that his head lay against her shoulder, his cheek against her breast. You shall never feel like that again, my darling, you shall feel better and better until you are quite well. Life has taken the pride of your youth and crushed your spirit, your looks have gone and your strength, and I love you more than I ever did. *"I am your wife, if you will marry me; if not I'll die your maid."* It won't be easy – you will hurt me and I you, again and again, but we have no choice. Farewell, dear Harold, thank you for loving me.

Val appeared, a furious small creature cradled in his hands. 'I found my frog. Would you like him?'

Andrew touched the frog's cold head. 'He's bonnie. Let him go free, laddie, and then come back to me.'